"When writers as ... lene Fowler, and Jerrily ... gue as convincingly as ... take notice." ... ne

Murder of a ... Covered Cherry

"Denise Swanson neatly seasons the cleverly crafted plot . . . with a generous dash of romance as Skye's relationship with Scumble River's police chief, Wally Boyd, continues to simmer neatly along." —*Chicago Tribune*

"The Scumble River mysteries are great fun. . . . Denise Swanson makes humorous writing appear effortless."
—*Mystery News*

"Top-notch storytelling with truly unique and wonderful characters." —*Crimespree Magazine*

"[A] hilarious mystery." —*The Pilot* (North Carolina)

Murder of a Botoxed Blonde

"With its endearing hero, terrific cast of realistically quirky secondary characters, and generous soupçon of humor, *Murder of a Botoxed Blonde* . . . is a delight."
—*Chicago Tribune*

"Tight plotting and plenty of surprises keep this series on my must-read list." —*Crimespree Magazine*

"This fast-paced cozy has it all." —*Romantic Times*

Murder of a Real Bad Boy

"Swanson is a born storyteller." —*Crimespree Magazine*

"Another knee-slapping adventure in Scumble River."
—*The Amplifier* (KY)

continued . . .

"It's no mystery why the first Scumble River novel was nominated for the prestigious Agatha Award. Denise Swanson knows small-town America, and she writes as if she might have been hiding behind a tree when some of the bodies were being buried. A delightful new series."
—Margaret Maron

Murder of a Smart Cookie

"[Swanson] smartly spins on a solid plot and likable characters."
—South Florida Sun-Sentinel

"[A] hilarious amateur sleuth mystery. . . . [Swanson] has a lot of surprises in store for the reader."
—Midwest Book Review

Murder of a Pink Elephant

"The must-read book of the summer."
—Butler County Post (KY)

"One of my favorite series. I look forward to all my visits to Scumble River."
—Crimespree Magazine

Murder of a Barbie and Ken

"Swanson continues her lively, light, and quite insightful look at small-town life . . . a solid plot [and] likable characters who never slide into caricature."
—The Hartford Courant

"Another sidesplitting visit to Scumble River . . . filled with some of the quirkiest and most eccentric characters we ever have met, with a sharp, witty protagonist."
—Butler County Post (KY)

Murder of a Snake in the Grass

"An endearing and realistic character . . . a fast-paced, enjoyable read."
—The Herald News

"This book is delightful. . . . The characters are human and generous and worth following through the series."
—Mysterious Women

Other Scumble River Mysteries

Murder of a Royal Pain

A Scumble River Mystery

DENISE SWANSON

AN OBSIDIAN MYSTERY

OBSIDIAN
Published by New American Library, a division of
Penguin Group (USA) Inc., 375 Hudson Street,
New York, New York 10014, USA
Penguin Group (Canada), 90 Eglinton Avenue East, Suite 700, Toronto,
Ontario M4P 2Y3, Canada (a division of Pearson Penguin Canada Inc.)
Penguin Books Ltd., 80 Strand, London WC2R 0RL, England
Penguin Ireland, 25 St. Stephen's Green, Dublin 2,
Ireland (a division of Penguin Books Ltd.)
Penguin Group (Australia), 250 Camberwell Road, Camberwell, Victoria 3124,
Australia (a division of Pearson Australia Group Pty. Ltd.)
Penguin Books India Pvt. Ltd., 11 Community Centre, Panchsheel Park,
New Delhi - 110 017, India
Penguin Group (NZ), 67 Apollo Drive, Rosedale, North Shore 0632,
New Zealand (a division of Pearson New Zealand Ltd.)
Penguin Books (South Africa) (Pty.) Ltd., 24 Sturdee Avenue,
Rosebank, Johannesburg 2196, South Africa

Penguin Books Ltd., Registered Offices:
80 Strand, London WC2R 0RL, England

First published by Obsidian, an imprint of New American Library,
a division of Penguin Group (USA) Inc.

First Printing, April 2009
10 9 8 7 6 5 4 3 2

PUBLISHER'S NOTE
This is a work of fiction. Names, characters, places, and incidents either are the prod-
uct of the author's imagination or are used fictitiously, and any resemblance to actual
persons, living or dead, business establishments, events, or locales is entirely coinci-
dental.
    The publisher does not have any control over and does not assume any responsibil-
ity for author or third-party Web sites or their content.

*In memory of Caroline Babcock—
an inspiration to us all.*

Acknowledgments

Thank you to Paula Washow for the dentist idea—sorry I couldn't use your great title suggestion—and to Lois Hirt, who has been encouraging me to use a dentist office scene for years. Which brings me to my own dentist, Dr. Dan Streitz, who is nothing like Dr. Paine—except, of course, for the good characteristics. Mandy Korst—thanks for sharing your crazy prom adventure with me. And a special thanks to Luci Hansson Zahray, aka the Poison Lady. Hugs to my new niece, Rachel Dosier.

Author's Note

In July of 2000, when the first book, *Murder of a Small-Town Honey,* was published in my Scumble River series, it was written in "real time." It was the year 2000 in Skye's life as well as mine, but after several books in a series, time becomes a problem. It takes me from seven months to a year to write a book, and then it is usually another year from the time I turn that book in to my editor until the reader sees it on a bookstore shelf. This can make the time line confusing. Different authors handle this matter in different ways. After a great deal of deliberation, I decided that Skye and her friends and family will age more slowly than those of us who don't live in Scumble River. While I made this decision as I wrote the fourth book in the series, *Murder of a Snake in the Grass,* I didn't realize until recently that I needed to share this information with my readers. So, to catch everyone up, the following is when the books take place.

Murder of a Small-Town Honey—August 2000
Murder of a Sweet Old Lady—March 2001
Murder of a Sleeping Beauty—April 2002
Murder of a Snake in the Grass—August 2002
Murder of a Barbie and Ken—November 2002
Murder of a Pink Elephant—February 2003
Murder of a Smart Cookie—June 2003
Murder of a Real Bad Boy—September 2003
Murder of a Botoxed Blonde—November 2003
Murder of a Chocolate-Covered Cherry—April 2004
Murder of a Royal Pain—October 2004

The Scumble River short story and novella take place:
"Not a Monster of a Chance" June 2001
"Dead Blondes Tell No Tales" March 2003

Scumble River is not a real town. The characters and events portrayed in these pages are entirely fictional, and any resemblance to living persons is pure coincidence.

CHAPTER 1

Let the Good Times Roll

On Mondays, school psychologist Skye Denison liked to play a game called Name That Disaster as she made the ten-minute drive to work. It entailed guessing which calamity, catastrophe, or cataclysm would be waiting for her when she arrived.

Skye's assignment included the elementary, junior high, and high schools in Scumble River, Illinois. This meant the crises could vary from a little boy who misunderstood his mother's instructions to stick it out, to a thirteen-year-old methamphetamine user who thought he was Superman trying to fly from the roof of the junior high, to a cheerleader holding her own private sex party for the winning basketball team . . . or any little messes in between.

It was assumed Skye would automatically take on any duty that even bordered the realm of special education. In addition, her job description was vague enough to allow the principals to assign her any task they didn't wish to perform— up to and including picking up their dry cleaning, although, to be fair, none of them had tried that yet.

One of the chores Homer Knapik, the high school principal, had recently handed over to Skye was to be faculty liaison to the Promfest committee. Promfest was an event designed to discourage the junior and senior classes and their dates from getting drunk, crashing their cars, and making babies after the prom.

Homer had assured Skye that it was an easy assignment: Just attend a few meetings and help put up some crepe paper. But as she approached the high school cafeteria, where the first gathering of the Promfest committee was being held, she could hear the raised voices through the closed doors, and she knew the principal had lied to her—again.

Skye crept into the cavernous space, willing herself to become invisible, which was a stretch, considering her generous curves, long, curly chestnut hair, and dramatic emerald green eyes. Her back against the rear wall, she surveyed the crowd.

The room was filled almost entirely with women in their late thirties and early forties. An occasional male also occupied the picnic-style tables arranged in rows facing the stainless-steel serving counter, but the men gave the impression they were ready to make a run for freedom at any moment.

Skye noticed one guy sitting by himself, and took a seat at his table. He was the only man in the room who didn't look as if he wished he were somewhere else. Instead, his expression veered between amusement and disbelief as he scribbled furiously in a small notebook.

Skye smiled at him and asked, "Who are they?" gesturing to the front of the room, where two attractive women stood nose-to-nose yelling at each other.

"The one with the black hair is Annette Paine, and the blonde is Evie Harrison. They both think they're this year's Promfest chairwoman."

"And they want to be?" Skye couldn't imagine why anyone would actively seek that position. "Why?"

"Lots of power and a good way to strengthen their daughters' chances of being elected prom queen." He gave Skye a sidelong glance. "Both of them are former queens themselves—Evie in 1983, and Annette in 1982."

"Oh. I heard they were campaigning for their daughters, but didn't realize Promfest was a part of the battle." Skye cringed. "This is going to get ugly."

"Already has."

Abruptly the shouting increased in volume, and Skye's attention was drawn back to the front of the room. Several women had left their seats. About half were crowded behind Annette, and the remaining faction stood behind Evie. It was beginning to look a lot like a scene from *West Side Story*. Skye wondered which were Sharks and which were Jets.

"I don't know where you got the impression that you were chairing this committee." Annette poked Evie in the shoulder with a perfectly manicured fingernail.

"I got the *impression* from the election last year." Evie bristled. "You remember the election, don't you?"

Annette smoothed a strand of hair back into her chignon. "That vote was invalid. We didn't have a quorum. The legitimate election took place the next week." Her icy blue gaze lasered into the brown eyes of her rival. "As I recall, you claimed you couldn't make it because you *had* to visit your parents in Florida."

"You deliberately held that meeting while I was gone." Evie stamped her Etienne Aigner–shod foot on the worn gray linoleum. "A meeting you had no right to call."

"As the assistant chair of the prior year's committee, I was certainly within my rights to call a meeting." Annette flicked a piece of lint from her Yves Saint Laurent cashmere cardigan.

"That committee had already been disbanded." Evie's voice climbed into that high, squeaky pitch that only other women and dogs can hear. "You had no authority whatsoever."

"You're questioning my authority?" Annette seemed to be struggling for breath, and one of her lackeys handed her an inhaler. Impatiently she took a quick puff, then said to Evie, "I wouldn't go down that road if I were you." When Evie's silence lengthened, Annette prodded: "What? Are you lost in thought?" She arched a flawlessly plucked brow and mocked, "I imagine that's pretty unfamiliar territory for you."

Evie lunged at her rival, hands wrapping around Annette's throat. Annette grabbed two handfuls of Evie's hair and pulled. Before Skye could react, the two women's supporters had dragged them apart.

Both groups stood panting and glaring at one another until a voice from one of the tables rang out: "Let's just take another vote and get on with it. Some of us have lives."

The women who were still seated clearly didn't care who the chair was and murmured their agreement, but the ones standing protested.

Skye looked at her watch and blew out an impatient breath. Much as she hated to get involved, she would have to become an active participant and hurry the committee along. If she didn't get out of here by the end of first hour, her whole morning's schedule would be messed up. She was supposed to be starting Brady Russell's three-year reevaluation.

Students who received special education services were required by law to be tested by the school psychologist triennially. These reevals made up the bulk of her duties, and if she fell behind, she would have to cut her counseling and consultation hours—the part of her job she most enjoyed.

She required at least ninety minutes without interruption to give Brady the intelligence test. She would have to find another couple of hours to administer the academic and processing assessments on another day, not to mention time to do the classroom observation, teacher interviews, write the report, and attend the multidisciplinary meeting. Some school districts had gone to abbreviated reevals, but not Scumble River.

With the clock ticking away precious minutes, Skye stood, ready to make an impassioned plea along the lines of "Can't we all just get along?" when Annette leaned toward Evie and whispered furiously in the blonde's ear. Evie narrowed her eyes, jerked her chin for Annette to follow her, and moved away from the others.

Skye moved closer to the man next to her and lowered her voice. "Aside from Evie and Annette wanting their daughters elected prom queen, I can't imagine why being in charge of putting up a few streamers, hiring a deejay, and setting out some chips and punch is such a big deal."

"Where have you been? From what I've heard this morning, maybe that was true when Promfest was originally conceived, but each year the parents try to outdo what was done before. Nowadays they take over half the school, set up inflatable adult-size ball pits and crawling tubes, hire magicians and hypnotists, and give away door prizes that range from dorm-size refrigerators to flat-screen TVs."

"You're kidding!" *Shoot!* She had heard rumblings from the students that Promfest had become more elaborate, but she hadn't taken too much notice, since most of the kids she worked with had more serious problems than what to do after the prom—not that many of them even attended the dance.

"Not at all." He leaned back in his chair and crossed his legs. "There're also the party favors, which last year consisted of a full-size wheeled suitcase filled with DVDs, popcorn, chocolates, et cetera."

"Holy smokes." Skye was stunned. *Note to self: Pay more attention to what's going on in the whole school, not just the part concerning the kids I work with.*

"Think a teenage Chuck E. Cheese party on steroids," he added.

While Skye was attempting to come to terms with that image, a loud gasp drew her gaze to where Annette and Evie stood off to the side.

As Skye watched, the blonde shot Annette a look of pure loathing, walked back to the center of the room, and announced, "For the good of the Promfest and the sake of our children's special night, I concede the chair to Annette Paine."

Skye sat back down and stared speculatively at Evie, then raised an eyebrow at the man next to her. "What in the world could Annette have said to make her give up a position that was obviously important to her?"

"Got me." He tapped his pen on his notebook. "But I'm going to find out."

"Oh?" It wasn't often that Skye met someone who was even nosier than she was. "Why?"

"It's my job."

"Really?" Skye studied him for a moment. He was in his mid-thirties and devilishly handsome. "What do you do?"

"I'm the new reporter for the *Scumble River Star.*" He held out a tanned hand to Skye. "My name's Kurt Michaels. I'm also starting a column called 'Talk of the Town.'"

"Gossip?"

"I like to call it vital information." He shrugged. "After all, it's the lifeblood of any small town."

"True, but considering you're an outsider, will people give you the real scoop?"

"I guess we'll see. My first column is in this week's paper. But ask yourself this. You're a native Scumble Riverite, correct?"

Skye nodded.

"And which of us knew about the feud between Annette and Evie for Promfest chair? Not to mention the rivalry between their daughters Linnea and Cheyenne for prom queen." He got up and headed for the door. "I'm out of here." Over his shoulder he added, "Nothing else interesting is going to happen."

Skye watched him as he left, his powerful, well-muscled body moving with an easy grace. On second thought, considering his sexy smile, hot body, and oodles of charm, the ladies of Scumble River would almost certainly be willing to tell him all their secrets, not to mention those of their neighbors and friends. Heck, if he took off his shirt and gave them a look at his six-pack abs, they'd probably be willing to make up a scandal or two.

Kurt was right: The rest of the meeting was a snooze. It started with Annette explaining that the main mission of the Promfest committee was to solicit donations and raise money, and eventually led to her announcement, "The first fund-raiser of the year is our A Ghoul's Night Out haunted house. We need volunteers to sell tickets, construct the set, and act as the monsters. I'm sending around a sign-up sheet, and I expect to see not only your name, but those of your spouse and teenager, as well."

There was a murmur from the crowd, and several hands shot into the air.

Annette ignored them, passing the clipboard and a pen to those at the table closest to her. "Remember, in order for your student to fully enjoy Promfest, he or she will need a bank account full of Prom Bucks to spend on food, games, and activities. And you can earn these PBs with every hour you volunteer, prize you solicit, and donation you make. Just for attending today's meeting you've earned your teen five thousand PBs."

Skye watched in amazement as the parents vied to sign away their free time; then she quietly got up and slipped out of the room before the volunteer list reached her table. Not that she would have volunteered for any activity, but she particularly hated haunted houses.

She hadn't been in one since she was six years old, when her brother, Vince, who was ten at the time, abandoned her to go play with his friends. She had wandered around lost and crying until some adult finally noticed her and led her to an exit.

Skye shuddered at the memory, quickened her steps, and nearly ran toward the safety of her own office. A few weeks later, when she stood over the dead body of someone who had been vibrant and alive just a few minutes before, she thought back to this instant and realized how silly her fears had been. Because no make-believe monster could possibly inspire the terror she felt in that moment, knowing that a real murderer was somewhere very near.

CHAPTER 2

From This Moment On

As Skye slid into her desk chair, panting, she noticed the phone's message light flashing. The bell would ring in five minutes. Three minutes later, Brady Russell would show up at her door expecting to be tested. Did she have time to listen to her voice mail and get set up for him as well?

Cradling the receiver between her neck and shoulder, Skye punched in her password—she knew she couldn't concentrate with that little red light blinking. While she waited for her code to be approved, she grabbed Brady's file and reread the note his mother had written her.

> *Dear Ms. Denison,*
> *Brady did not fail English last year. He is just passing impaired. Please find out why and fix him.*
> *Sincerely,*
> *Dodie Russell*

Skye vowed to try her darnedest to comply with Mrs. Russell's request, and started to fill out the identifying data on the IQ protocol. She was figuring out his exact age—the current date minus his birthday—when the mechanical voice said, "You have three messages."

Shoot. She'd been hoping for hang-ups, but nothing was ever quick and easy in this job.

"Message number one, left Monday, September thirteenth, at eight fifteen."

There was a slight pause; then Homer's voice boomed from the receiver: "Where in blue blazes are you? Come to my office immediately."

The next one, left at eight twenty-five was also from the principal, but the volume of his voice had risen considerably. "Opal said you signed in at seven thirty. Are you ignoring me?"

By the time the last message was recorded, ten minutes ago, his irritated baritone blasted in her ear: "Get your butt down here ASAP. I don't have all day to babysit this woman."

Apparently the first crisis of the day had materialized. Skye reluctantly locked Brady's file in her drawer, taped a note to the door telling him to go back to class, and hurried to the principal's office.

Behind the counter, Opal Hill, the school secretary, said, "Thank goodness you're here. Mr. Knapik has been looking all over for you."

"Why didn't he have you call me over the PA system?" Skye asked.

"It's broken, as is the furnace, again." Opal's watery brown eyes made her look as if she were about to burst into tears.

"So I take it Homer is in a foul mood."

"Oh, my, yes." Opal's pink nose twitched. "You'd better go right in."

Skye took a few steps down a dark, narrow hall, knocked on the principal's closed door, then opened it a crack. "You wanted to see me?"

A gruff voice yelled from behind a massive desk, "It's

about time. Why are you standing in the hall? Get your rear end in here."

Skye took a calming breath. Homer was Homer, and she couldn't change him at this stage in his life, which, metaphorically speaking, was about five minutes before he signed his retirement papers. Putting a pleasant expression on her face, she entered the office. A plump woman in her thirties with long reddish brown hair was seated on one of the visitors' chairs.

Homer waved toward the woman and said, "This is our new social worker, Jacqueline Jennings. She completed her internship a year ago, and before that taught for eight years in New York. Due to an illness in her family last fall, this is her first job as a school social worker, but she has very impressive letters of recommendation."

Skye's first thought was, *Wow! She sounds almost too good to be true.* Her second was, *Why didn't anyone tell me that the district finally hired a social worker? Bad enough that none of the principals mentioned it to me, but for crying out loud, my own godfather is the president of the school board.*

Realizing her silence could be taken as rudeness, Skye smiled at the woman and held out her hand. "Nice to meet you, Jacqueline. I'm Skye Denison, the psychologist."

"Call me Jackie." The woman's grip was firm and dry. "Mr. Knapik has been telling me all about you."

"Not all bad, I hope." Skye glanced at Homer.

"No, of course not." The woman chuckled. "In fact, he was quite complimentary. He made it sound like the school couldn't run without you."

"Really?" Skye was shocked. She thought Homer was oblivious to all the work she did. "I'm flattered."

"Yeah, yeah, yeah." Homer lumbered up from his desk, reminding Skye of a dancing bear. Not because of his shambling movements or his rotund shape, but because of the hair that enveloped him like a fur coat. His eyebrows looked as if two furry worms were mating on his forehead, wiry antennalike strands protruded from his ears, and a thick pelt covered his arms and hands. Tufts even poked out between the buttons of his shirt. "So you do your job. You want a medal?"

"Yes, please," Skye teased, a little giddy from Homer's praise.

He grunted, then said, "Jackie, as I told you while we were waiting for Her Highness to show up, Skye will introduce you around and go over your duties with you."

"Wonderful." Jackie stood and shook hands with him. "It's an honor to work for you and with all your wonderful instructors."

"Right." Homer snorted. "You might as well know right now that's not how it is here."

"How what is?" Jackie's tone was puzzled.

"Think of it this way. In some schools, teachers have affairs with their students. In Scumble River High, it's a lot more likely they'd have contracts out on them."

"I see." Jackie's laugh was forced. "Well, remember, I'm here to do anything you need me to do."

Skye kept her expression bland. *Anything he needs? Boy, is she opening herself up for trouble.* Out loud she asked Homer, "Where's Jackie's office?"

"Same as yours." He smirked. "You two have to share."

Dang. Skye had been begging the district to employ a social worker for the past four years, and they had always claimed that they couldn't find anyone who would take the job. She hadn't realized that hiring someone would mean sharing her office. Skye had wrested it away from the coach/guidance counselor only two years ago.

Oops. She was being rude again, thinking instead of speaking. She hurriedly said, "Great. Well, then, I guess that's it. Should I show Jackie around the elementary and junior high, too?"

"Got me." Homer put a hand on each of their backs and propelled them toward the door. "Ask Caroline and Neva."

Once they were out of the office area, Jackie said, "I take it Caroline and Neva are the other two principals?"

"Yes. Didn't you get to meet them at your interview?"

"No." Jackie chuckled. "I really didn't have much of an interview. I faxed my résumé to the district last Tuesday, Dr. Wraige called me on Wednesday, I came in on Thursday, and he and Mr. Patukas offered me the job on the spot. They seemed a little surprised when I accepted."

"Wow. I guess they've been telling me the truth all these years. They really were trying to hire a social worker. Any idea why no one else wanted the job?"

"Nope." Jackie shrugged. "It was exactly what I was looking for."

"Oh?"

"I needed to be closer to my mother. She lives in Clay Center. I moved to New York right after high school and have lived there ever since, but my father passed away recently and I'm an only child. So . . . " She trailed off, gesturing her lack of choice with her hands.

"I'm so sorry for your loss. Is your mother ill?" Skye asked as she guided Jackie down the hall.

"No, just elderly and alone."

"Well, we can sure use you." Skye motioned around her. "This wing holds the classrooms for all our fine and practical arts. The other two wings hold math and science, and English and history, respectively. And, of course, the special-ed rooms are all in the back."

"Why's that?"

"You know." Skye made a sardonic face. "It just seems that principals like to keep those kids as far from the office as possible. Of course, our job is to make sure that although they might be out of sight, they aren't out of mind."

"The special-ed students aren't integrated into regular classes?"

"Most of the day they are, but nearly all the kids have at least one or two periods in the special-ed room," Skye explained. "And the ones with more severe challenges are there most of the day."

"I see."

After they had finished touring the school, Skye ushered Jackie into their office. She flicked on the light switch, illuminating a ten-by-ten room painted an unusual shade of yellow. Skye's beat-up desk, a trapezoidal table, a few chairs, and a half dozen file cabinets occupied the meager space. There were no windows, and the overhead fluorescents cast a greenish light.

Skye plopped down into her old leather chair and pushed aside the piles of papers and folders that were stacked a foot high on the desktop. She pointed to one of the two folding chairs facing her and said, "Welcome to your palatial office suite at Scumble River High. We'll have to get the custodian to find a desk for you."

Jackie remained standing, her gaze slowly sweeping the small, crowded area. "Where would we put it?"

"Maybe we can get some of these file cabinets moved. All but one is filled with guidance records that date back at least ten years, which means they should have been destroyed long ago." Skye could read the other woman's disappointment, and was a bit confused by it. She would expect a seasoned educator to be used to appalling conditions. Lack of space was a problem in most schools.

Jackie nodded, a frown on her round face. "Where are the social work records?"

Skye shrugged. "It's been so long since we've had a social worker, there aren't any separate records. I've been doing the histories and all the counseling, so everything is in one file."

Jackie finally sat down, her expression determined. "Well, now that I'm here, that will all change."

"Uh, right." This was what Skye had wanted. She had been asking for help, and would be happy if she never had to take another social history, but something about this woman bothered her. Skye couldn't put her finger on it, but

Jackie seemed . . . familiar. "By the way, have we met before?"

"I doubt it." She shook her head. "I've been back in the area for only a few weeks, and I've spent most of that time with my mother."

Hmm. Skye was puzzled. Maybe Jackie seemed familiar because Skye and Jackie looked a lot alike. They were close in age and physical appearance—similar hair, eye color, and build. Although Skye would bet her next home-improvement loan payment that Jackie was wearing colored contacts and her hair wasn't naturally that shade.

Still, they had a lot in common. Both of them had had to move back to small towns, and both worked in a helping profession. So what was troubling her? Skye bit her lip. Could it be that she felt displaced? First she had to share her office; now she was being told Jackie was taking over her duties. But they were tasks she didn't want, so why did she care?

Skye resolutely pushed the negative thoughts away. She was happy Jackie had been hired, and she would do everything in her power to make her welcome.

Jackie interrupted Skye's thoughts by asking, "How are we going to work this shared office deal?"

"Since we're both responsible for the entire school district, we'll set up a schedule that puts us at different schools most of the time," Skye suggested. "I'm guessing we'll be sharing offices in all the buildings."

"Yes, that might work. But won't there be times when we both have to be in the same school?"

"On those days, such as when the Pupil Personal Services teams meet, we'll have to share the room. I guess we'll have to think of it as having a college roommate. Someone to talk over our frustrations with. Let's face it: The confidential nature of our jobs makes it kind of tough to socialize in the teachers' lounge."

Jackie nodded slowly.

"Why don't you tell me a little about yourself, roomy?" Skye asked, hoping to help the other woman relax.

"There's not much to tell." Jackie shrugged. "I'm single, looking for Mr. Right, but usually end up with Mr. Right Now. No children. How about you?"

"About the same. Though I'm finally dating a very nice guy, Wally Boyd. He's the police chief in town. I live in a big old money pit of a house that I inherited, I have a black cat named Bingo, and I'm related to most of the people in town. Are you living in Clay Center with your mom?"

"Uh, well, no." Jackie pleated the material of her skirt. "She lives in that new senior housing and there's no room for me, so I'm staying at the Up A Lazy River Motor Court while I look for an apartment."

"That's my uncle Charlie's place."

"Your uncle is the school board president?"

"Actually, he's my godfather," Skye corrected.

"You said you owned a large house. Are you interested in renting out a room?"

"Sorry." Skye shook her head. "I like my privacy too much."

"No problem."

Feeling a little guilty, Skye joked, "At least at the motor court you don't have to clean, since you get maid service."

"No, I'd rather do it myself. I don't like anyone messing with my things. I just pick up fresh towels at the motel office." Jackie stood. "Shouldn't we get over to the other schools?"

"Sure. Why don't you tell Opal where we're going while I rearrange a few appointments? I'll meet you outside. Where are you parked?"

"I managed to snag a spot in the front row."

Skye grimaced. "Was it, by any chance, the space right next to the handicapped slots?"

"Yes. Why?"

"Uh-oh. That's Homer's spot. In most cases his bark is worse than his bite, but not on the issue of parking. Let me fill you in on the facts of life at Scumble River High. Number one—don't park in the front row. Ever. Those slots are unofficially reserved for administration and department heads. The chair of the English department will eat you alive if you're in her place.

"Number two—be nice to Opal, the office secretary. She may look like a mouse, but she's the real power at this school.

"Number three—the transportation department rules above all. Never mess with anything having to do with the buses."

"How do I get on Opal's good side?"

"Food. For a little thing, she has the appetite of a line-backer."

"Interesting." Jackie paused on her way out the door and gave Skye an enigmatic smile. "It looks like a lot of things around here aren't what they seem."

CHAPTER 3

Carried Away

Skye normally loved Fridays, but this one wasn't starting out very well. She had slept through her alarm, stepped on Bingo's tail, and broken the zipper on her new pants. All of which contributed to her running late. Now she couldn't get into her office.

She checked to make sure she had the correct key, then attempted to reinsert it into the lock, but it wouldn't go in. *Great.* Skye kicked the door, but it didn't magically pop open. Too bad the master key she'd managed to acquire a couple of years ago had broken last spring.

Shoot! She didn't have time for this. In fifteen minutes she was supposed to meet with Mrs. Idell, one of the district's most difficult parents, regarding her son, Travis, one of Scumble River High's most recalcitrant students.

Skye jiggled the doorknob and tried the key again, but it still refused to fit. She blew a curl out of her eyes. There was only one solution: Find the custodian and have him open the door. Of course, this meant Skye would be late for the meeting, which was a serious problem. Mrs. Idell's Jekyll-and-Hyde personality was always tricky to deal with, and having to wait made her even more fiendish.

She'd have to have the janitor paged. Thank goodness the

PA system had been repaired. A few more days without it and Skye would have been tempted to start breeding carrier pigeons.

Naturally, the school secretary was already swamped with three other emergencies. She tapped her foot until Opal hung up the phone, handed a frantic teacher a stack of photocopies, and ushered a limping girl into the nurse's office. Then Skye said, "Can you call the custodian down here? There's something wrong with my key and I can't get into my office."

Opal tensed as if expecting to be hit. "I tried all the keys myself before I gave them out. Are you sure you put it in the right way?"

"Yes," Skye snapped. Had Opal slipped over the edge? Skye knew the secretary was strung tighter than a tennis racket, but she usually managed to avoid getting caught in the net. "Why would I suddenly not know how to use a key I've had for the past four years?"

"Well, there's your problem." Opal's expression relaxed. "You need to use the new key. Remember, the lock has been changed."

"When? Why?"

"Jackie said too many people had keys and her files were extremely sensitive, so she wanted to limit access to her office."

"*Her* office!" Skye screeched, feeling the last of her patience evaporate. "It's my office, too. She hasn't even been here two weeks and suddenly it's *her* office? Why wasn't I consulted?"

Opal flinched. "I'm sure I don't know. Do you want to speak to Mr. Knapik about it?"

"Yes. No. I mean, I don't have time right now. Just give me the new key."

"We only made three. One to keep here in the main office, one for Jackie, and one for you. The custodians will use their master keys when they clean."

"Fine." Skye forced herself to take a deep breath. "Give me the one you had made for me."

"Jackie took it. She said she'd give it to you." Opal smiled fondly. "She's so sweet. She said she'd save me the trouble, since she knew how busy I am."

"Yeah, it takes a lot of time to hand me a freaking key," Skye muttered under her breath, then said aloud, "Well, Jackie hasn't given it to me yet, and now I'm late for a meeting with Travis's mother."

"Oh, my." Opal's pale complexion grew pastier. Everyone on staff knew Mrs. Idell's reputation. The secretary hastily opened a flat gray metal box attached to the wall beside her desk and revealed row after row of keys. After selecting one in the middle, she handed it to Skye. "Be sure to bring it back when you're through with it."

Wordlessly, Skye snatched the tiny metal ring from Opal's fingers, turned on her heels, and ran back toward her office. The new key fit perfectly and she slammed the door open, flicking on the light as she rushed inside.

A few steps into the room she came to an abrupt halt. Had there been a break-in? But why would a thief rearrange the furniture?

Skye had last been at the high school on Tuesday afternoon. Now, only three days later, her desk had been pushed against the side wall and piles and piles of manila folders were stacked on and around it. Her cherished leather chair was behind Jackie's desk, which had been moved over by the door where Skye's had previously been, and the trapezoidal table that had been perfect for giving IQ and achievement tests had been replaced by a round one that would make their administration more awkward.

Skye's mouth hung open as she worked out what had happened. Obviously Hurricane Jackie had struck and this was the aftermath of the storm.

The old guidance file cabinets were lined up just inside the door, and taped to them were handwritten signs saying,

Please remove, which meant the folders on Skye's desk must be from those cabinets.

Jackie would have had to take out the contents of the huge four-drawer monstrosities in order to move them—they would have been too heavy to budge when they were full. Skye wondered when, or if, the other woman was planning to put back the files.

Skye glanced at the wall clock. Ten past eight. There wasn't much she could do now, but she did take a few seconds to reclaim her leather chair. Then, after locating the file she needed, she hurried toward the conference room, wondering what other unpleasant surprises were in store for her.

"You're late, Ms. Denison," Zinnia Idell announced when Skye had seated herself at the table. "I bill my time at two hundred and fifty dollars an hour. You have wasted sixty dollars and fifty cents."

Skye's fingers itched to write the woman a check. Instead she gripped the edge of the table and said, "I'm terribly sorry." If it were any other parent, she would have explained her delay. However, knowing there were no acceptable excuses where Mrs. Idell was concerned, Skye opened the folder and asked, "Shall we get started?"

"I'm not the one holding up the proceedings." Mrs. Idell picked up her BlackBerry. "I'm making a note to telephone the superintendent when we get through here."

"I'm sure he'll be happy to hear from you." Considering that the Idells had Dr. Wraige on speed dial, he wouldn't be surprised by the call.

"Are you being sarcastic?" Color crept up Mrs. Idell's neck, making her look like a thermometer. "Travis's education is a serious matter."

"Yes, it is. Which is why I asked you to come in." Skye attempted to take back control of the meeting. She had been dealing with this particular parent since her first day on the job. Back then, Travis had been an eighth grader, and it had come to the school's attention that he had hosted several sex parties during the previous summer while his parents were at work.

Several of the girls he had persuaded to participate had spilled the beans, which had resulted in their fathers, brothers, and the occasional cousin pounding the crap out of Travis. These beatings had caused his parents, a wealthy couple who commuted to Chicago for their high-power jobs, to demand that he be taught at home until they were convinced it was safe for him to come back to school.

The principal and superintendant had been glad to acquiesce and wait for the furor over the sex parties to die down. A few months later, Travis had been able to return and finish out the year without further incident. But upon entering high school, he had taken up his old ways.

Skye had sat in on or chaired at least a dozen detention, suspension, and other types of disciplinary meetings concerning Travis. Mr. and Mrs. Idell had consistently refused offers of counseling and/or psychological assessment, and not once had they ever conceded that their son was at fault.

Now, as Mrs. Idell finished reading the discipline referral Skye had given her, she said, "This is ridiculous. My son did not plagiarize his English paper."

Skye handed her the original essay, which the teacher had found on the Internet. "This is what he copied it from."

Mrs. Idell threw the paper back at Skye, refusing to look at it. "It's easy to manufacture evidence of this sort. You have it in for him. You've been trying to pin something on him ever since that nonsense in eighth grade. Anytime Travis has been accused of misconduct, you're right there egging everyone on. What is he? Your job security? No doubt you're afraid they'll eliminate your position if there aren't enough kids getting into trouble."

"I'm sorry you feel that way." Skye was shocked at Mrs. Idell's vicious attack. "Yes, I am the one you see when your son gets into trouble, but the only one responsible for Travis's behavior is Travis."

"That's ridiculous."

Skye paused, considering whether she should continue, and decided that despite the unpleasant consequences, she was Travis's advocate, and it was past time to talk to his mother about her parenting skills. In previous meetings with the Idells, Homer had forbidden Skye from bringing up the subject, but he was out sick today, and his message had said that she should handle the conference on her own. This was her chance to say something she should have said several years ago.

"You know, Mrs. Idell, you're right." Skye made eye contact with the woman.

"Of course I am."

"There are two other people who have a huge impact on Travis's behavior."

"Those two awful boys he hangs out with." Mrs. Idell nodded.

"No. You and your husband."

"How dare you?" Mrs. Idell's face turned scarlet and she leapt from her chair, sending it banging into the wall.

"Please sit down, Mrs. Idell." Skye felt a spark of fear. It was never good when parents started jumping around the meeting room like angry orangutans. Embarrassed by the slight tremor in her voice, Skye stated, "I'll have to end this meeting right now if you don't immediately return to your seat."

Mrs. Idell drew in a deep breath and looked around. She seemed surprised to find herself standing and sank back into her chair. Her brows met in a petulant frown. "I always knew you thought we were bad parents."

Skye ignored the woman's accusation. What could she say? She could hardly admit Mrs. Idell was right. "Uh." Skye cleared her throat. "By never admitting that Travis has done anything wrong and protecting him from the consequences of his behavior, you've shown him that he can get away with anything."

"We've had to defend him from people like you who are determined to make him a scapegoat for whatever happens in this school. Look at this spurious accusation. You can't prove he cheated."

"We feel we can and we have." Skye braced herself and added, "Thus we are suspending him for two weeks."

"You can't suspend him. He has a learning disability."

"What?" Skye knew he had never been tested for special-education services. She'd offered, thinking he might have a behavior disorder, but the Idells had always refused.

"We had him privately assessed this past summer, and the psychiatrist said that's why he acts out. He's frustrated by his disability."

"We'll need to see those records, and you can pick up a referral from the office on the way out." Skye kept her face expressionless. This parent had more surprises up her sleeve than Penn and Teller. "Meanwhile, I'll review his file and schedule a meeting of the pupil personnel services team as soon as I receive your completed form and the doctor's report."

"I'll drop both off this afternoon when I come back for the Promfest meeting." Mrs. Idell stood. "I expect the matter of his suspension to be dismissed."

"I'll have to consult with the principal. We can't make any decision until we evaluate all the information."

"Now that we know he's disabled," Mrs. Idell said, ignoring Skye's previous statement, "I want his entire disciplinary record expunged."

"I'll bring that to the principal's attention."

"You do that." Mrs. Idell moved toward the door. "And remember, unfortunate things happen to despicable people. I'm guessing fate is about to pay you a visit."

"Then he'd better bring chocolate," Skye muttered under her breath as she escorted Mrs. Idell to the front office.

After making sure the woman received the correct paperwork, and watching as she exited the building, Skye left Homer a message. The principal would have a conniption fit when he heard about Mrs. Idell's demands, but he needed to know ASAP. Mrs. Idell was probably already on the phone to the superintendent.

Skye asked Opal to make sure Homer got her note, then returned to her office. *Shoot.* What was Jackie doing there? They had agreed to a usage schedule, and the social worker was supposed to be at the junior high on Fridays.

Dang. Skye hadn't had a chance to think how to tell Jackie that she was unhappy with her behavior without sounding like she was blowing the whole matter out of proportion. But the fact that Jackie had once again moved Skye's chair behind her own desk and was sitting in it made Skye wonder if churlish wasn't the way to go.

Skye counted to ten, then said as pleasantly as she could manage, "We need to talk."

"Can it wait? I'm kind of busy right now." Jackie didn't look up from her computer screen—she had provided her own laptop, stating that she couldn't work without it.

"No. Sorry, it can't." Skye moved closer to the other woman's desk. "First of all, I'd like my chair back."

"This is your chair?" Jackie's brow puckered.

"Yes. That's why it was behind *my* desk." Skye folded her arms. "May I have it back, please?"

"Of course. I'm so sorry." Jackie leapt up and halfheartedly shoved the chair in Skye's direction. "I had no idea it was your personal property. It's just that I've been having some back pain, and the folding chairs seem to make it worse."

Skye opened her mouth to say that Jackie could keep the chair, but reconsidered. She didn't quite buy the innocent act. Wheeling the chair back behind her desk, Skye said, "Thank you. Perhaps you could ask the custodian if there's a more comfortable one in the storeroom. He's got a lot of furniture back there."

"That's a great idea." Jackie beamed. "But I'll ask Gloria. She's been such a sweetie."

"I didn't realize you'd met the night custodian."

"I often work late. Mr. Knapik seems very pleased about that."

"Oh." Skye filed away that bit of knowledge. "I also wanted to ask you not to make changes without consulting me."

"I don't understand." Jackie puckered her brow again. "What changes?"

"The new lock—which, by the way, you never gave me the key for—as well as rearranging the furniture, changing the table."

"Gee. I'm so sorry." Jackie reached into her pants pocket. "Here's the key. I meant to give it to you yesterday at the grade school's PPS meeting. Guess I forgot."

Skye plucked the key from Jackie's fingers. "It's not only this. You had the locks changed without telling me."

"I'm really putting my foot in it, aren't I?" Jackie's voice was husky. "I'll rearrange the room back like it was and exchange the table."

"Thank you." Skye felt herself weakening. Maybe she was being too rigid. "I don't mind change. I just want to have some input."

"No, you're right. I guess it's because I've never shared an office before, and I didn't think."

"I understand." Skye offered a smile. "Sharing isn't one of my stronger traits either."

Jackie hugged Skye. "I really want us to be friends."

There was an awkward silence; then Skye said reluctantly, "Me, too."

"Great." Jackie hugged her again. "I knew the minute I met you that we'd be BFFs."

"Oh." Skye wasn't sure she wanted to be Jackie's best friend forever. In fact, she wasn't even sure she wanted to be her best friend temporarily. Uncomfortable, she looked away, spotting the files piled on and around her desk. Should she mention the clutter? No. Just this once she'd take care of it. Next time Jackie could clean up her own mess.

Skye was moving the last pile of folders from her desktop onto the floor when Justin Boward stepped through the open door. Justin was one of Skye's favorite students and the editor of the school newspaper, which Skye cosponsored with her best friend, Trixie Frayne, the high school librarian. He'd been a little down for the last few weeks since his girlfriend, Frannie Ryan, had gone off to college.

"Hi, Justin." Skye took a tissue from her desk and blotted the perspiration from her face—the repairperson had fixed the furnace so well that the temperature was now hovering in the mid-nineties—and smiled at the young man. "What's up?"

"Uh, well, nothing. I actually came to talk to Ms. Jennings."

"Oh." Skye had seen Justin for counseling from eighth grade until the end of his sophomore year, when she had decided he no longer required the service. If he needed to talk to someone, why was he seeking out the new social worker instead of her?

"What can I do for you?" Jackie gestured for Justin to sit down.

"Well, I'll step out so you two can have some privacy." It pained Skye to say those words, but she got them out without showing her distress.

"That's okay, Ms. D." Justin looked puzzled. "I just want to talk about the computer class. You can stay."

"The one the school newspaper staff is funding with their prize money?"

"Yeah. Ms. Jennings is going to teach it." Justin grinned. "Remember how we couldn't find anyone for what we could pay?"

Skye nodded.

"Well, Ms. Jennings is doing it for free."

"Wow. That's terrific." Skye smiled at Jackie. "That's really nice of you."

"It's no big deal." Jackie shrugged. "Everyone talks about how much extra you do for the school. I wanted to do my share."

"I probably should take the class," Skye mused. "When will it be?"

"After school on Wednesdays next quarter."

"Darn. I'm signed up for water aerobics then." Skye pursed her lips. "Maybe I can get my money back."

"No. Don't." Jackie shook her head. "I mean, the class is full. All the computers are taken."

Skye was silent while she swallowed her disappointment, then said, "Okay, water aerobics it is." If the class was full, the class was full. So why did she feel left out?

Jackie finished her conversation with Justin, and as she was leaving for the junior high, she said, "I wanted to mention that you forgot to lock the office door. It was open when I arrived."

"I don't usually lock it if I'm not leaving the building."

"Oh, well." Jackie wrinkled her brow. "I really would like it locked anytime you're not in the room. Confidentiality and all."

"Usually I just make sure all the files are locked in my drawer or the cabinet," Skye explained. "But I'll try to remember." It would be a hard habit to break.

Once Jackie was gone, although she was still agitated, Skye finished testing a student and wrote up the report on another. Her office was no longer a haven. Jackie hadn't rearranged the room the way it had been, or gotten the old table back, and Skye hadn't wanted to nag her about it. But now she wished she had insisted. Everything felt wrong.

Maybe she was still upset by the scene with Mrs. Idell. Being attacked by a parent was always unsettling, and the woman's final words had almost been a threat. Skye tried to shrug off her sense of dejection, but it prevailed, and the minutes ticked by as she stared into space.

An hour had passed the next time she checked her watch. Skye sighed and slid open her bottom drawer. The contents glistened like crystal in the fluorescent lights. She reached for the treasure, but drew her hand back empty. She shouldn't. She kept it strictly for emergencies. She ran her finger over the smooth wrapper. Well, depression was an emergency.

She lifted the package of Double Stuf Oreo cookies onto her desktop. Yep, she really should eat them. The chocolate would raise her serotonin levels, and, besides, the freshness date indicated they would expire soon. She'd only eat one— okay, one row.

Several minutes later, as she licked the crumbs from her fingers, she eyed the remaining cookies. No. She had to stop. Resolutely she taped the packet shut and put it back in the drawer. Pushing herself away from the desk, she got up, grabbed her purse, and headed toward the parking lot.

Being alone would only worsen her blue funk, and since Wally was working the three-to-eleven shift at the police department, Trixie was going to a Farm Bureau dinner with her husband, and Vince was on a date, Skye was forced to take drastic action: visit her parents.

CHAPTER 4

Come What May

As Skye approached her aqua 1957 Bel Air convertible, she saw that the front passenger-side tire was flatter than a glass of day-old soda pop. *Great!* The perfect ending to a perfectly awful day.

When Skye threw her tote bag inside the car, she noticed a piece of paper under her wipers. Snatching it off the windshield, she read: *Karma's a bitch, just like you.*

Shit! Was this from Mrs. Idell? Was she responsible for the flat tire? She had said something very similar at the end of their meeting. Just what Skye needed, a crazy parent with a grudge against her. She'd show the note to Wally, but there was probably nothing he could do about it.

She walked around to the back. Her spare was full-size, since her father would never permit her to ride around on a doughnut, and heavier than it looked. She had her head inside the trunk and was struggling to lift the tire out when she was startled by a sexy male voice near her ear.

"Need some help?"

Jerking upright, Skye dropped the wheel, conked her head on the trunk lid, and stumbled backward.

A warm masculine hand steadied her. "Sorry, I didn't mean to scare you."

Skye yanked her arm free and spun around. Standing within kissing distance was the new reporter for the *Scumble River Star*, Kurt Michaels. She scowled, rubbing her head, and he backed away, holding his hands up.

"Where did you come from?" She gestured to the parking lot, which was empty except for her car. "I thought I was alone."

"I live in the apartments on the next street over. I use the high school's track to jog."

It showed. He wore nylon running shorts that revealed his thigh and calf muscles, and a tank top that exhibited his well-developed shoulders and arms. Skye almost drooled, then remembered she had a hunky boyfriend of her own, and forced herself to look away.

Kurt pointed to her flat. "Would you like me to fix that for you?"

"Thank you, but I can do it myself," Skye reluctantly admitted. "My dad wouldn't let me get my license until I could change a tire."

"But you'll get your pretty shirt all dirty, not to mention ruin your manicure."

"True." Skye smiled to herself, thinking that not many men would be aware of stuff like that.

He seemed to read her mind. "I have five sisters. You learn to notice or you don't survive. Besides, I'm a reporter, a trained observer."

"I hate playing the helpless female, but this *is* a new blouse. . . . "

"And I'm already dirty."

"Right. But I don't like being in anyone's debt."

"Well, I hate jogging alone; maybe you could run with me tomorrow afternoon."

"Sorry." A vision of looking pathetic as she tried to keep up with him popped into her mind, and she shook her head. "I have to exercise in the morning, before my brain figures out what I'm doing."

"Very funny." He moved her gently away from the trunk. "Then tell me something I can use in my column."

As she pondered what little she could share, since most of her work at school was confidential, he lifted the spare onto the asphalt and fished out the jack.

She couldn't tell him about Mrs. Idell's threat, or Jackie having her locked out of her own office, or bingeing on Oreos, which pretty much covered her whole day. *Hmm.* She couldn't think of a thing.

He had finished changing her tire when he commented, "This is a cool car."

"Thanks. My father and godfather restored it for me."

"Sounds like your family really takes care of you."

Skye nodded.

He put the flat in the Bel Air's trunk. "All done."

"Thanks. But I still haven't thought of any gossip for you."

"That's okay." He shut the lid, turned toward her, and leaned back on his elbows, the muscles in his arms glistening with sweat. "My column for this week is already done, so how about we say you owe me a piece of news?"

Skye stuck out her hand. "Deal."

Instead of shaking, he leaned forward, planted a soft kiss on her cheek, then walked away, saying over his shoulder, "I'll look forward to collecting the rest of my payment."

A fluttery feeling danced in the pit of her stomach, and Skye realized she was smiling. By no means blind to his attractiveness, she recognized that he aroused both her curiosity and her vanity.

Her expression thoughtful, Skye got into the car and headed toward her parents' house. In the past six months she had decreased her twice-weekly visits to twice monthly. Due to her parents' insistence that she should move into her old room and live with them until she got married—an event that couldn't come soon enough, according to Skye's mother, May. That was, as long as the groom wasn't Wally.

May had made her feelings about the police chief clear—he was too old, too divorced, and too not-Catholic.

Tonight Skye was lonely, and it had been close to three weeks since her last visit, so she steered the newly repaired Chevy out of town.

This time of year, the usually quiet countryside surrounding Scumble River was alive with combines in the fields and grain trucks lumbering along the blacktop, hauling golden hills of corn and soybeans to the silver silos that dotted the landscape.

Skye slowed as a tractor emerged from a dirt lane, then waved to the driver as she passed. She knew it was one of her parents' westerly neighbors, but wasn't sure which of the Pickett men was at the wheel. All four of the brothers were tall, thin, and prematurely wrinkled from the sun.

A few minutes later Skye slowed again to make the turn into her parents' driveway. As her tires crunched over the white pea gravel, she spotted her father, Jed, on his riding mower, almost finished cutting the acre of grass surrounding the redbrick ranch-style house. When he noticed Skye he took off his blue-and-white polka-dotted cap and waved it in the air, revealing a steel-gray crew cut, faded brown eyes, and a leathery face.

Returning her father's wave, she parked behind his old blue pickup and strolled over to the patio. A concrete goose wearing a black dress, a conical hat, and with a miniature broom fastened to its wing guarded the back door. Skye sighed in relief. The goose was a good barometer for her mother's moods. With Halloween five weeks away, a witch's costume meant all was well. . . .

Skye pushed open the screen door, entered the utility room, and paused to take off her shoes. May had replaced her old rust-colored carpeting with cream last month, and woe to anyone who left a footprint.

After tossing her tote bag on the dryer, Skye pushed open the swinging doors and strode into the large kitchen. Her stocking feet made no sound on the new beige-tiled floor.

May had been on a redecorating tear during the summer. The far wall was now painted in grass green-and-white stripes, marble countertops adorned the peninsula, and a new glass and rattan table and chairs graced the dinette.

Skye's mother stood at the sink, scrubbing potatoes with a vegetable brush. Despite her fifty-nine years and short stature, May's athletic build reminded Skye of the cheerleader her mother once was. Today she wore denim capris and a pink long-sleeved Cubs T-shirt.

Without looking up from her task, she said, "Supper's almost ready." In May's house no one was invited to eat; it was assumed that if you were around at mealtime you'd pull up a chair and dig in.

Skye noted the time on the square white wall clock—also a new addition. It was five thirty. "Isn't it a little late for you guys to be eating dinner?" They usually ate at five on the dot.

"We had a lot to do today. Dad's been in the fields since six. I walked my three miles with Aunt Kitty, Hester, and Maggie, then worked the seven-to-three shift at the station." May was a dispatcher for the Scumble River police, fire, and emergency departments, which made her disapproval of Wally even more awkward, since as the police chief he was one of her bosses. "When I got home from the PD, I had to clean up the house and do the trim on the lawn." May frowned. "Besides, you knew we were eating at six tonight."

Huh? Why did her mom think she knew that? Skye opened her mouth, then decided it was better not to prolong this conversation. If she responded, her mom would want to know what tasks Skye had accomplished that day. Merely doing her job at school would not be counted as enough of an achievement.

Hastily changing the subject, Skye asked, "What are we having?"

"Roast beef, green bean casserole, Grandma Denison's Parker House rolls, mashed potatoes, and Waldorf salad."

Yum. She had picked a good night to stop by. The menu

sounded more like Sunday dinner than Friday supper. "Grandma shouldn't still be making rolls from scratch at eighty-five," Skye said. "It's too much for her. I thought she was going to stop."

May dried her hands and gave Skye a pointed look. "Hard work is good for you."

Skye was saved from responding when her father walked into the utility room. She turned to greet him. "Hi, Dad. Finished with the grass?" A silly question, since he wouldn't have quit until he was through, but a good way to change the subject.

"Yep." Jed hitched up his jeans, which hung low to accommodate his belly. "Supper ready, Ma?"

"In half an hour." May stopped stirring the gravy, and ordered, "You'd better get showered and changed. We've got company tonight."

Jed's navy T-shirt was sweat-soaked and torn, evidence of his hard work. "Skye's not company," he protested.

Not wanting to get involved with her parents' squabble, Skye looked for something to do. She moved the salt and pepper shakers and the napkin holder from the counter to the table, then opened the cupboard to the left of the sink. Although the plates, glasses, and flatware were where they'd been for as long as she could remember, they were all new, the old ones having been sold in the summer garage sale during May's recent redecoration binge.

Skye had taken three dishes from the shelf and started to move toward the table when May said, "Aren't you staying for supper?"

"Huh?"

"You only have three plates." May held up four fingers. "There are four of us."

"Four? I thought Vince had a date."

"No. It's just you, me, Dad, and Jackie." May rolled her eyes. "Don't you remember?"

"What?" *Crap!* Jackie was just the person Skye didn't

want to see. "How could I remember something I didn't know?"

"But then, why are you here?"

"I stopped by to visit. You and Dad are leaving for Las Vegas in a couple of weeks, and I wanted to make sure I saw you before you left."

"But I told Jackie to tell you about supper tonight." May wrinkled her brow. "Didn't you see her today?"

"Yes, but, uh . . ." Skye didn't want to tell her mother about the argument she'd had with her colleague, so she hedged. "We had a lot to talk about; then she had to leave for another school. She must have forgotten to tell me."

"Well, you're here." May nodded, appearing satisfied with Skye's explanation. "No harm, no foul."

"Right." Skye frowned. Except she was now forced to spend an evening with someone she preferred to avoid. "So, how did you meet Jackie?"

"In the grocery store yesterday. She asked me to help her find something and we got to talking." May turned back to the stove—gravy needed constant stirring or it became lumpy. "She was so sweet. She hung on my every word; then she mentioned that you and she were friends, so I thought it would be nice to have her for a home-cooked meal."

Why had Jackie been in the grocery store? If she was living at the motor court, she didn't have a kitchen. She must have been picking up some snacks and soda. The vending machines at Charlie's would get expensive fast.

"She should be here soon." May's voice interrupted Skye's thoughts. "Go ahead and set the table for four." May lowered the flame on the burner, then added, "Make sure you put out the real butter for Dad. He won't touch that Country Crock Light I use for my cholesterol." May paused and gave Skye another sharp look. "But you'd better use the fake stuff. It looks like you're gaining weight again."

Was she? Skye looked down. She couldn't tell. She refused to weigh herself constantly and worry about every pound, but she hadn't been swimming every day as she

should, and she had stuffed herself with those cookies a few
hours ago at school. She guessed it was time to get back into
the pool.

"You should have seen it. Mom did everything but spoon-
feed Jackie, and Dad actually talked. She got him to tell stories from the four years he spent in the navy right after high
school. He even made a joke. He said he had a commanding
officer whose baler had run out of twine."

It was late Saturday afternoon, and Skye was on the telephone with her brother. Vince had just closed up the hair
salon he owned. "Well, isn't that what a social worker is
trained to do, get people to talk?" Vince asked. "And Mom
feeds everyone."

"Yes, she cooks and puts the food in front of you, but she
doesn't fork it into your mouth."

"She did that?"

"Well . . . not exactly, but almost," Skye admitted. "She
put the cream and sugar in her coffee for her, though."

"You sound jealous." Vince chuckled. "Aren't you happy
to have someone to divert Mom's attention from you for a
while?"

"Yeah, but . . ." But what? Maybe she was overreacting.
Time to change the subject. "So what are you and Loretta
doing tonight?" Vince was dating Skye's sorority sister,
Loretta Steiner.

"Nothing." His tone was unhappy. "She said she was
going to District Days this weekend. You were an Alpha
Sigma Alpha, too. Why aren't you going?"

"It must have something to do with the alumni group
Loretta belongs to in Naperville. There isn't one close
enough for me to join."

"Oh." Vince paused. "But you've heard of this weekend
thing?"

"I probably read about it in the sorority magazine, but I
don't remember. Do you want me to check the back
copies?"

"No." He sighed. "I guess not, but it seems like she's awfully busy lately."

"Now who's jealous?" Skye teased.

"Hey. You know I'm not the jealous type." Vince's voice held a forced casualness. "I'm only saying she should have asked you to go with her."

"I'll have to talk to her about that." Skye was glad Vince couldn't see her grin. It looked as if her big brother might finally be serious about a woman. Maybe May would hear wedding bells soon after all. Skye's smile widened. And if Vince got married, maybe her mother would get off her back. "I've got to go. Wally's picking me up at six. We're going to Joliet to see *The Forgotten* at the Cinemark, then eating at Merichka's."

"I can taste their poor-boys now." Vince smacked his lips. "I love how the garlic butter runs down your hands when you bite into one."

"I love their double-baked potatoes. I think they're the best I ever tasted."

"Mmm."

They both were silent a moment; then Skye said, "Well, I really do have to go. I haven't even showered yet."

"You could wait and invite Wally to join you."

"Men. You all think alike." Skye giggled and hung up the phone.

Her conversation with Vince had cheered Skye up, and she found herself singing while she got ready. She loved this time of year. Fall clothes were the best. The restaurant they were going to wasn't dressy, so she put on brown jeans, a leopard-print blouse, and a gold suede jacket.

She was zipping up brown leather ankle boots when the doorbell rang. After taking one last look in the mirror, she added a pair of dangly citrine earrings and ran down the stairs.

When she opened the door, Wally stepped inside, swung her into his arms, and kissed her until she was breathless. As they moved farther into the foyer, Skye froze. "Did you hear that?"

"What?" He lifted his head from her neck.

"I thought I heard the back door. It has an annoying squeak I keep meaning to oil."

"I didn't hear anything. Isn't it locked?"

"Yes." Skye moved out of his arms and headed toward the kitchen. "I thought so, but I'd better check."

"Wait a minute." He caught up with her and put a hand on her shoulder to stop her. "Let me go first." He reached down and pulled the gun from his ankle holster.

Skye frowned, then shrugged and stepped out of his way. His urge to protect her was a cop instinct, not a chauvinistic impulse.

When they got to the back door, it was closed. The thumb lock was engaged, but not the dead bolt. It was Wally's turn to frown. He turned the key that was in the dead bolt and handed it to her. "You need to keep both of these locked and the key somewhere else."

"I do. I mean, I keep them locked." Skye chewed her lip. "I don't go out this door very often—it's easier to go out the front to get to the garage. I'm sure I locked it the last time I went out this way."

"Well, it's locked now." Wally bent and petted the black cat rubbing against his shins. "Does Bingo have a secret life outdoors?"

"Right. I can just see him as the leader of a gang of cat burglars. What would they steal? Cans of Fancy Feast and pots of catnip?" Skye snickered. "Maybe it's the ghost trying to keep us apart again." She and Wally had just about given up trying to spend any time at Skye's house—although Wally wouldn't admit it had anything to do with the supernatural. His excuse was that his place was more comfortable.

But whether he believed Skye's house was possessed or not, it seemed that whenever they started to get intimate, some weird occurrence would interrupt them. Secretly—Skye had never shared this thought with anyone—she suspected the ghost of the previous owner, from whom Skye had inherited the house, was behind the mischief.

Skye had met Alma Griggs a little over a year ago. A widow who had lost her only child in a car accident, Mrs. Griggs had convinced herself that Skye was the reincarnation of her daughter. And Skye was pretty sure that Mrs. Griggs didn't want Wally around.

Whether the deceased owner was trying to keep all men away from Skye or only Wally was unclear, since Skye had broken up with her previous boyfriend, Simon, before taking ownership of Mrs. Griggs's eerie home.

Wally broke into her thoughts. "You don't really believe in ghosts, do you?"

"Maybe." She shrugged, not sure what she thought. "Bizarre stuff does seem to happen to us a lot here."

"Hey, I just thought of something. It was probably your mom. She likes to drop by and clean, right?"

"Yeah, but I don't think she's been here lately, at least not that I noticed." Skye looked around the kitchen. "Although I guess she could have been here. She does tend to clean things that already look fine to me."

"That's it. I'll bet it was May, and she opened the door to shake some rugs or something and didn't reengage the dead bolt when she came back in."

"You could be right." Skye followed him back to the foyer. Unless it was Mrs. Griggs's ghost, May was a reasonable guess. Besides, who else could it be?

CHAPTER 5

Time after Time

As usual, I-55 was under construction, causing random lane closures and unexpected braking. Skye sneaked a peek at Wally's profile, and noted that he was fully focused on the highway. Normally she would keep quiet, not wanting to distract him from the hazardous conditions, but this might be the perfect moment to tell him about her flat.

That morning when she had gotten her tire fixed, the repair shop had confirmed that it had been slashed. If she told Wally now, while he was concentrating on the traffic, he was less apt to fuss about her safety and Kurt's role in helping her.

Wally was usually easygoing, but every once in a while a teeny streak of jealousy surfaced, and Skye had a feeling that Kurt Michaels might bring it out. Or maybe she felt a tad guilty for enjoying Kurt's attentions.

It was possible Wally hadn't met Kurt yet, and didn't know how handsome and charming he was, but the likelihood of that in a town as small as Scumble River was practically nil.

How could she bring up the flat without setting off any alarms? She needed a good segue. Turning slightly so she could watch Wally's body language, Skye said casually, "How have things been at the PD lately?"

"Pretty quiet."

"That's good."

"How about school?" he asked without taking his gaze from the road.

"The usual."

"How's the new social worker working out?" Wally concentrated on passing a semi, then added, "What did you say her name was?"

"Jackie Jennings. Haven't you met her yet?"

"Not yet."

"Then you're the only one." Skye tried to keep the rancor out of her voice.

"Is there a problem with her?"

"She seems really eager to fit in and do a good job." Skye clenched her teeth. "She's even teaching the computer class the student newspaper is funding."

"I bet Justin is pleased."

"Yes. They seem to be getting along very well." Skye pulled her seat belt away from her neck. It felt as if it were choking her.

"That's great. It's nice to see him doing better with adults."

"Yeah. It's great."

Wally glanced at Skye. "You okay?"

"I guess." She sighed. "I need to adjust to her being there. I was basically doing her job as well as mine for the past four years."

"I'm sure it feels weird to have someone doing the stuff that you're used to doing." He reached over and squeezed her hand. "In a month or so you'll be thrilled to have the help."

"Probably." Skye stared out the windshield, then said as nonchalantly as she could manage, "Oh, I almost forgot to tell you—I had a flat yesterday after school."

"Why didn't you call me? I could have come over and fixed it for you. Did you forget your cell phone again?"

"I had my cell, but I didn't want to bother you while you were on duty." Skye wrinkled her nose at him. "Besides, I know how to change a tire."

"Did it take you very long?"

"Well, no." Skye worded her answer carefully, "As it happens, a jogger did it for me." She went on quickly, "Anyway—"

Wally interrupted her. "Who was the jogger? Did you know him?"

"The new reporter for the *Star*. We'd met once before at a meeting."

"Kurt Michaels?"

"Yes. I think that's his name," Skye hedged. "Have you met him?"

"Yes, and there's something about him I don't trust. I think he's up to something."

"What makes you say that?"

"I'm not sure, but my gut says he's not what he appears to be."

"Well, he seems harmless to me. And he was nice enough to fix my flat."

"Any decent guy would change a tire for a woman."

"Then you're saying he's a decent guy?" Skye raised an eyebrow. When Wally didn't respond, she went on, "As I was saying, I brought the tire in to be repaired this morning and the guy at the shop said it had been slashed."

Wally shot her a sharp look. "You think one of the high school kids did it?"

"Could be. There are some troublemakers this year, and I do sit in on most of the more serious disciplinary hearings."

"Anyone else you can think of who might want a little instant revenge?"

"One of the parents was pretty mad at me that morning." Skye pursed her mouth, tapping her bottom lip with a fingernail. "And there was a note under my wipers that sort of sounded like something she said."

"She a hothead?"

"Oh, yeah."

"I don't suppose you'll tell me her name?"

"Can't." Skye's tone was matter-of-fact. "Confidentiality. But I can give you the note when you take me home. It wasn't signed or anything, though."

"Yeah, let me have it. It won't do us much good now, but I'll start a file just in case anything else happens." Wally blew out an irritated breath. "Another possibility is that that Michaels guy did it so he could come along, play Good Samaritan, and get into your good graces."

"Why would he want to do that?" Skye asked, trying to maintain an innocent expression as she remembered Kurt's last words: *I'll look forward to collecting the rest of my payment.*

"You're pretty, smart, single, and extremely well connected in town," Wally said.

"I'm glad you think so, but I'm hardly the type men fight duels over. If he's after anything, it's the well-connected part." Skye shifted in her seat. "Though I don't believe for a minute he'd go as far as slashing my tire to get in good with me."

"You underestimate yourself."

"Well, thank you." Skye sat back. "Anyway, my money's on the angry parent."

They were silent until Wally parked the car at the theater. As he opened the door for her he said, "Let's forget all about Scumble River and have a good time tonight."

"Good idea." She took his hand, enjoying its warmth as they walked across the parking lot and inside the building.

After a quick stop for popcorn and sodas, they made their way into the darkened theater. The only seats left were in the front row, and Skye frowned as they settled in. She hated sitting that close to the screen, and was sure it would ruin the show for her, but kept silent, not wanting Wally to think he had disappointed her.

Two hours later, when the film ended, Skye was glad she hadn't complained. The movie had been terrific. Still caught up in the story, she absentmindedly followed Wally up the aisle toward the exit. When he paused to let someone step in front of him, she stumbled a little, and her gaze fastened on a couple sitting a few seats to her right. She blinked. What was Jackie doing with Simon Reid, Skye's ex-boyfriend?

Skye opened her mouth to point them out to Wally, but snapped it closed without speaking. The one person whom Wally was definitely jealous of was Simon. Besides, Skye had no desire to interact with Jackie. As Wally had said in the parking lot, this was their evening to forget Scumble River.

She and Wally made it to the car without encountering her ex or the social worker, and Skye let out a sigh of relief as Wally turned east onto Route 30. The restaurant was in Crest Hill, a town of about twenty thousand adjacent to Joliet.

Merichka's, which meant Mary's in Slovenian, had been around since 1933. Skye's grandparents had brought her parents there as children, and Jed and May had followed the tradition, bringing Skye and Vince there when they were little.

Skye smiled as she spotted the restaurant's sign, a huge boomerang with a martini glass painted on it. The first time her parents took her to Merichka's, she had asked the waitress if it was an Australian restaurant, and the woman had said no, the boomerang was a symbol that they wanted their diners to keep coming back.

Clearly the customers did return. The parking lot was packed. The only open slot was at the far end, and Wally carefully backed in his sports car. The savory smell of garlic and butter welcomed Skye as she walked through the door.

She waited at the podium as Wally gave their names to the hostess. The woman found their reservation, picked up a couple of menus, and led them up some steps, through the main dining area, and to a smaller room with windows overlooking Theodore Street.

As Wally read his menu, Skye, knowing she would have the poor-boy and double-baked potatoes, put hers aside and examined the room. There were only a half dozen tables, and most were filled with older couples or families. The exception was two teenagers who seemed to be out on their first date.

Once Wally and Skye had ordered, she gestured to the young pair and said, "Aren't they sweet? It's so nice to see kids on a real date. I know I'm showing my age, but the herd dating that's popular now seems wrong to me. I can see a group as a safety net when you're first going out, but if you never break away from the crowd, how can you get to know each other on a deeper level?"

"Maybe that's what they're afraid of." Wally took her hand. "Opening yourself up to someone is scary."

"That's true. But if you don't learn how to share yourself when you're young, it's even more terrifying when you're older."

"I agree. As you age, you have more and more in your past, which means you have more to hide." His gaze was as soft as a caress. "Or the more you think you have to hide."

Her heart raced. "Maybe people feel they have to conceal aspects about themselves because they can't stand to face them." Was Wally trying to say that she was hiding something—or, worse yet, that he was?

They were interrupted by the waitress serving their meal, and Skye found herself studying Wally as they ate. He was a handsome man by anyone's standards. Tall and powerfully built, he stood out in a crowd. When he was dressed in his police uniform, the crisp navy twill showed off his wide shoulders and muscular thighs. Tonight, clad in black jeans and a silk turtleneck, his slim waist and broad chest were emphasized.

Wally caught her staring and cocked an eyebrow. She blushed and ate the last bite of her sandwich. The cube steak was tender and perfectly seasoned, and the French bread roll was crispy on the outside and soft on the inside—delicious.

But abruptly Skye was hungry for something else. She glanced over at Wally and found that now he was staring.

He reached over, stroking her inner arm from wrist to elbow. "Are you finished?" His dark brown eyes held both desire and tenderness.

She nodded. Little jolts of electricity raced through her from his touch.

"Shall we go home?"

She tried to say yes, but ended up nodding, her throat too dry to speak. His question had been a passionate challenge— hard to resist.

He signaled their server and paid the bill, leaving a generous tip.

Skye's knees buckled as she stood, and she steadied herself by taking Wally's hand. He led her through the labyrinth of tables, the noise drowning out the thudding of her heart. They had been together for nearly a year, and his magnetism still captivated her.

They were almost through the main dining area when a whoop of laughter caught Skye's attention. She turned toward the sound and stiffened. Sitting in a dark corner at a table for two were Simon and Jackie. Skye couldn't see Simon's face, which was in a shadow, but Jackie's was animated and glowing with happiness.

Skye jerked her gaze away, taking a hasty step forward and silently urging Wally to speed up, and he quickened his steps.

As they drove back to Scumble River, Skye convinced herself that what she felt wasn't jealousy, just astonishment. She had rushed Wally out of Merichka's because she was eager to be in his arms, not because she didn't want to see Simon with another woman.

Still, how had Jackie managed to meet Simon, and wasn't it strange that Simon and Jackie had picked the same movie and restaurant that Skye and Wally had chosen? What were the odds of that happening? In a small town like Scumble River—population thirty-three hundred—it could be a coincidence, but not here in the much larger city of Crest Hill. Was Simon following her?

The next week melted away like a snowman in a sauna. It wasn't merely that Skye was busy, although she was, but that she also seemed to lose chunks of time staring into space and feeling discontented. She couldn't pinpoint what was bothering her, but plainly something was. At first she had blamed it on PMS, but her moodiness had lasted too long to be caused by monthly hormone fluctuations.

Driving to school on Monday morning, Skye vowed to be more focused and optimistic. She had a great life, and she'd better stop moping around before she messed it up. She needed to quit allowing things she couldn't control to upset her, and to seek out her friends more, rather than locking herself away in her office or house.

Unfortunately, her resolution didn't last much past the high school's front door, where Homer was waiting for her. He pounced on her like a crocodile on a lion cub, chomping through her pledge to be upbeat with a single bite.

Taking her arm, he commanded, "We need to resolve this Travis Idell mess. His mother is camped out at the superintendant's office, and Dr. Wraige is not happy."

"The intake conference is set up for Thursday." A meeting Skye was dreading.

She had read the reports that Mrs. Idell had brought her, and, as Travis's mother had claimed, the private psychiatrist who had examined the teen had diagnosed him with a learning disability. But the doctor hadn't provided the results of his assessments, and Skye couldn't determine if he had even done any psychological evaluations—psychiatrists often didn't. He also hadn't returned Skye's phone calls. To make matters worse, when she'd examined the boy's school records, none of the group tests or any other information in his file supported the doctor's conclusion.

"She wants to meet today." Homer mopped his head with a bright red handkerchief. "She'll be here for a Promfest meeting after school, and wants to meet right before that. She says two would be convenient."

"Maybe for her." Skye plucked her calendar out of her tote bag and flipped it open to October fourth. "I have an appointment at the grade school with the kindergarten teachers at one. I don't think I can make it back here by two."

"You can talk with teachers anytime." Homer waved away her objection, turned, and walked away, hollering over his shoulder, "Dr. Wraige wants us to humor this woman and get her off his back."

The rest of the day passed as it had begun—badly—and Skye had a throbbing headache by the time she arrived for the Idell meeting. As she took her seat, she glanced around the table, noting that only Mrs. Idell made eye contact, and her glare intensified Skye's pain. None of the staff, which included the principal, nurse, social worker, special education teacher, and English chairperson, looked up from the papers they were all studying.

Homer cleared his throat and said, "Let's hear your information, Ms. Denison."

Mrs. Idell nodded as Skye summarized what the psychiatrist had written, and she smiled when Skye noted that on the group ability test Travis had scored in the superior range. On the group achievement tests, he was above grade level.

But the woman's glare returned when Skye brought up her concern over the lack of assessment data in the psychiatrist's report, and she snapped, "Are you telling me you think you know more than a medical doctor?"

"That's not what I said." Skye kept her voice even. "I said that considering that Travis has a superior IQ, is achieving at a commensurate level, and is passing all his classes, a learning disability is not indicated according to the state and federal guidelines as they exist now."

"So you're excluding him from services?"

"Not necessarily. Perhaps the psychiatrist did have testing done, and perhaps those results do indicate that Travis is

LD, but that information is not in the report you gave me, and the doctor has not returned my calls."

"You're telling me we spent twenty-five hundred dollars"— Mrs. Idell's voice shrieked like a noon factory whistle—"and you're not going to give my son the help he needs?"

"Not at all. What I'm saying is that I need to see some details so I can figure out what type of services he requires." Skye scooted her chair as far away as possible from the irate woman.

"I'm sick of jumping through hoops for you and this sorry excuse for a school." Mrs. Idell pounded on the table. "Either Travis starts receiving help tomorrow morning, or I'm going to make all of you sorry—especially you, Ms. Denison."

CHAPTER 6

Moments Like These

"That went well." Homer sneered. He and Skye had moved to her office after Mrs. Idell had stormed away. "Just stick the little bugger in special ed. It would serve him and his mother right."

Skye closed her eyes in an attempt to find her happy place, counted to ten, and bit her tongue, but she still blurted out, "Have I been talking to myself for the past four years? We can't simply slap a student in special education. We need data to back up the decision. And it would not 'serve him and his mother right.' He needs counseling, which I've offered to provide on numerous occasions, and she and her husband need parenting classes, which you refuse to let me suggest to them."

"Okay, okay, already." Homer scowled. "You know I was only kidding." He paused in his pacing and stared down at Skye, who was seated behind her desk. "You're not usually this touchy. Something wrong?"

"No." Skye blew out a lungful of air. "Everything's fine. I'm sorry I lost my temper."

"Good. We don't have time for you to be having some sort of breakdown."

"Right." Skye kept a straight face. "The school year must go on."

"Glad you're on board." Homer resumed his pacing, then spun on his heel and marched over to Skye. "Okay, here's what we'll do. Since you have such a bad history with the Idells, I'll assign Jackie to be case manager. From now on she'll handle all parent contact. You keep trying to pin down that damn psychiatrist."

Skye frowned, a protest on her lips, then reconsidered. Homer had a point. She had never managed to establish a rapport with the Idells; it made sense to let Jackie try. "That's a great idea." Skye hid a small grin. Besides, if the new social worker failed, it would prove that it wasn't only Skye with whom the parents had problems.

"Then it's settled. I'll have a talk with Jackie and bring her up to speed." Homer stood. "She's doing a fantastic job. I'm sure she can fix this mess, too."

Homer scurried from the room before Skye could respond. She stared at the closed door for a second, then glanced at the wall clock. Her headache was nearing migraine level, and she had to be at the Promfest meeting in fifteen minutes.

She opened her bottom drawer and stared at its contents. Nestled side by side were a bottle of Aleve and a fresh package of Double Stuf Oreos—she had finished off the previous cookies last Friday. Would a pill or a cookie get her through the meeting without her head exploding?

Who was she kidding? She'd been eating a half dozen Oreos every afternoon this past week. Skye had ignored Jackie when she'd kidded Skye about being addicted. But now as Skye reached for the medicinal chocolate wafers with the oh-so-soothing cream center, she wondered if Jackie might be right.

No, Skye comforted herself. *Of course not. Everyone knows that a balanced diet consists of a cookie in each hand.* With that assurance in mind, she twisted the first one apart and licked the frosting out of the middle. Sighing, she felt herself relax for the first time since she'd arrived at school. After devouring five more of the healing cookies, she was ready to face the Promfest committee.

Annette Paine had complained about the picnic table–type seating in the cafeteria, so this meeting was being held in the home ec room. The chairwoman probably wouldn't consider it much of an improvement. Although there were regular chairs, the room was crowded with sewing machines, stoves, washer/dryer combos, and refrigerators.

Actually, Skye didn't think the queen bee would be satisfied with anything less than a suite at the Ritz-Carlton. Skye smiled meanly, thinking, *Welcome to the world of public education, where the motto is "Thou shalt not spend the taxpayers' money on comfort or decor."*

Although Skye arrived a few minutes early, nearly every seat was already taken. There were only two empty spots, and one was next to Zinnia Idell. *Shit!* Skye's gaze moved to the other opening. *Crap!* That seat was next to Kurt Michaels—much more agreeable company, but potentially just as dangerous. Skye shook her head. She was being silly. Kurt probably flirted with all women. Still, Wally had thought there was something shady about the reporter, and his instincts were usually on target. She hesitated; there were no good options.

Before Skye could decide what to do, Annette moved to the front of the room and called the meeting to order. She shot Skye an irritated look, and Skye scurried over to the seat next to Kurt.

As she pulled in her chair, he gave her a teasing smile. "Good choice."

"What?"

"I hear Zinnia Idell would like to kill you."

"How did you hear that?" Skye's tone was irritated. *Geesh, the whole brouhaha only happened half an hour ago.*

"She got here fifteen minutes ago, and has been telling anyone who would listen how awfully you and the school are treating her." Kurt kept his voice low as Annette asked for the last meeting's minutes to be read.

"Great." Skye slumped down, trying to become invisible. "No wonder they're all looking at me funny."

Kurt leaned closer and whispered in her ear, "Pretend you don't notice."

"Easy for you to say."

"Anyway, I was saving this place for you."

"Me? Why?"

"Because I wanted you to sit next to me."

"Oh." Skye stopped herself from smoothing her hair. Had she even combed it since that morning? "Sorry, I still don't have any gossip for you, so I can't pay my debt yet."

"I'm a patient guy. I can wait." Kurt flashed his dimples. "Something will come up."

Annette moved on to the treasurer's report, and Skye asked Kurt, "What are you doing here, anyway?"

"Same as last time. Looking for a good story."

"Here?" Skye shook her head. "You know the definition of a committee, don't you?"

He shook his head.

"A group that keeps minutes and wastes hours." Skye grinned. "You write about this stuff and you'll put your readers to sleep."

"I'm not interested in the meeting per se, but the conversations before and after are usually good for a paragraph or two."

"Oh." Did that mean he was going to write about what Mrs. Idell had said?

"No." As he had the day he fixed her tire, he seemed to read her mind. "I'm not putting Zinnia Idell's ravings in my column."

"Thank you." Skye tuned her attention back to the meeting.

Annette was now exhorting people to work on the haunted house. Skye sank lower in her chair, attempting to avoid eye contact with the woman, but Annette's stare had zeroed in on her. Skye was frantically trying to think of a good reason she couldn't volunteer when the home ec room's door flew open, and Jackie hurried in.

Annette snapped, "You're late, Ms. . . . ?"

"I'm Jackie Jennings, the new social worker." Jackie smiled apologetically. "I'm so sorry; there was a crisis, and the kids come first."

"Yes, of course they do. Take a seat, Ms. Jennings." Annette waited as Jackie sat next to Mrs. Idell. "I was asking for volunteers to be a part of our haunted-house fundraiser."

Jackie's hand shot into the air. "I'd love to help."

"Super." Annette turned to Evie Harrison and handed her a clipboard with a pen attached. "Here. Make yourself useful and send the sign-up sheet around."

As Evie complied with an exaggerated smile, Skye said to Kurt, "I'm amazed that Evie agreed to be Annette's assistant. I thought she'd quit the committee after Annette forced her out of the chairmanship."

"I asked her about that, and Evie said she was doing it just in case Annette couldn't fulfill her duties. Evie wanted to be positioned to take over." Kurt raised his right eyebrow a fraction. "She still has hopes of getting her daughter elected prom queen, and I'm going to find out what her plan is."

"Interesting." Skye teased, "I'll keep my eye on your column for breaking news."

Annette had been watching Evie pass around the haunted-house sign-up sheet, and as woman after woman waved it away, she glared and said, "My own husband will be taking time from his busy dental practice to play the role of Frankenstein, and my lovely daughter will be sacrificing her dance lessons in order to be the zombie cheerleader captain."

Skye was surprised. Dylan Paine was her dentist, but she hadn't realized he was Annette's husband. They seemed like an odd couple—he was cheerful and easygoing, and she was intense and never seemed satisfied.

Annette continued, "Our newest committee member,

Jackie, is a wonderful example, and our initial volunteers have done a magnificent job building the haunted house. Now it's time for the rest of you to do your parts. We need ticket sellers, sound and light techs, actors, and people to perform a myriad of other little tasks. I expect everyone here to step up to the plate and take one of these jobs."

Skye scowled at the mention of Jackie's name. What in the heck was she doing here, anyway?

Forty minutes later, after announcing that their next fundraiser would be the Christmas House Walk, making a wish list of business donations, and bullying everyone into agreeing that the Promfest colors would be baby blue and silver, Annette ended the meeting.

As the crowd surged toward the door, Skye made her way to Jackie and tapped her on the shoulder. "Hi, I'm surprised to see you here. Usually only one faculty member attends this type of committee meeting."

"Uh . . ." Jackie blinked. "Well . . . Homer told me you hated this assignment, and, uh, I said I'd do it."

"He didn't mention that to me when I saw him right before coming here."

"Oh." Jackie edged backward. "Maybe I misunderstood. But I can't back out now."

"Sure you can."

"I'm not going to."

"Suit yourself." Skye shrugged, walked away, and joined the line of people trying to exit.

Kurt materialized by Skye's side, his thigh and arm brushing hers. "So that's the new social worker everyone's talking about."

"That's her." Skye felt an unwelcome sizzle from his touch. "What are they saying about her?"

"She seems to have made quite an impression in a short time. People think she's charming. They say she's ready to do anything she can for you." Kurt craned his neck. "What's the holdup over there?"

Skye peeked around the group in front of them. "Annette

is checking everyone against some list before they're allowed to leave."

"Good thing I'm not in a hurry." A mischievous gleam lit his denim blue eyes.

"Yes. You should circulate." Skye kept her gaze focused on the woman in front of her. "I'll bet you'd overhear a lot of good gossip."

"The only thing everyone's talking about is what a pain in the butt Annette is being about Promfest. Everything has to be her way or the highway." He gave Skye a sexy little grin. "But thanks for looking out for me. I kind of thought you didn't approve of my writing, but maybe my delightful personality has won you over."

"That must be it." Skye attempted to infuse her words with sarcasm, but felt her cheeks flame. She looked away and was relieved to see that only one person stood between her and the exit.

"So, what are you doing after—"

Skye stepped up to the door, and Annette's voice cut off whatever Kurt had been about to say. "Ms. Denison, I see you haven't signed up to help with A Ghoul's Night Out. You were doubtlessly distracted by the *Star*'s handsome new reporter when the sign-up sheet was being passed."

Skye narrowed her eyes. What was Annette implying? "Well, I . . . uh . . . that is—"

"It's probably an oversight," Annette cooed. "After all, considering how magnanimous your colleague Jackie is being with her time, I'm sure you'll want to be equally generous."

Shoot! It hadn't occurred to Skye that with Jackie volunteering so publicly, there was no way she could refuse to help without looking bad. "Right."

"Super." Annette smiled, revealing pointy canines. "Here's the sheet."

At the thought of being inside a haunted house, Skye's heart raced and her pulse pounded. She took a deep breath and told herself it would be fine. She'd just make sure she signed up for something outside the actual building. She peered at the list. Nearly all the jobs had been taken. The only places with blanks were under "Cast." Her options were either a witch or Countess Dracula.

She knew she'd never survive being closed up in a casket—the one time she'd hidden in a real one, she'd nearly hyperventilated—which left being a witch. Her pen hesitated above the blank line. Did she really have to do this? Then she recalled Homer praising Jackie: *She's doing a fantastic job.* And what had Kurt said? *She seems to have made quite an impression.* Not to mention Annette's earlier pronouncement: *Jackie is a wonderful example.*

Skye shook her head. She was being ridiculous. It had been twenty-eight years since her bad experience in a haunted house. As she often told the kids who complained about something that had happened long ago, it was time to get over it. She was too old to be afraid of things that went bump in the night. Taking a firm grip on the pen, she resolutely signed her name on the line next to *Witch #3*. Skye could only hope that she would be stationed near an exit.

Skye handed the clipboard back to Annette, and before she could step out the door, Annette trilled after her, "Rehearsals are seven p.m. Wednesday and Thursday. On Friday, the dress rehearsal is at six and we open for business at seven. Please be prompt."

It was Friday afternoon, and Skye caught herself smiling as she sat at her desk, trying to whittle down the endless piles of paperwork that seemed to grow every time she left the room. Jackie was scheduled to be at the junior high for the rest of the day, and for once Skye had the office to herself. She thought of the Oscar Wilde quote, "Some cause happiness wherever they go; others whenever they go." Clearly Jackie fell into the latter category, at least from Skye's perspective.

Another positive was that the haunted-house rehearsals had been less awful than she had feared. And, while she wasn't looking forward to the opening that evening, her dread had diminished. She was one of a trio of identically dressed witches who would pop out at different locations in the haunted house, giving the impression that a single witch was disappearing and reappearing.

The other two witches, Nina Miles, a parent whom Skye knew slightly, and Hope Kennedy, a teacher from the elementary school, were a lot of fun. Skye had been a bit embarrassed when their dresses had to be padded so all three of them would appear to be the same size, but neither Nina nor Hope had made a fuss. In fact, since they all appeared remarkably similar once they were in costume, they'd all had a good time fooling people. They even startled themselves— when one popped up unexpectedly on another, it was like looking in a mirror.

A Ghoul's Night Out was being held in an old white stone building on an isolated corner at the end of Basin Street. The American Legion had occupied it for years, but had recently built a brand-new hall outside of town. After scoping out the witches' assigned spots, Skye had managed to obtain the one closest to the door that opened onto the hallway were the restrooms were located.

Having done what she could to mitigate her anxiety, Skye had put the upcoming experience out of her mind. She was concentrating on a particularly difficult part of the report she was writing when her office door thumped open and Jackie and Justin strolled in, laughing.

Her concentration broken, Skye blurted, "What are you doing here?"

"Gee, I'm sorry. Did you need the room to yourself?" A creased formed between Jackie's brows, but she quickly smoothed it out. "The parent didn't show up for our appointment, so I figured I'd get some work done here. But I could go sit in the teachers' lounge if it's a problem."

"Oh. No. That's okay. You're welcome to stay." Skye bit her lip. What else could she say—that she wanted to be alone? She'd sound like a poor imitation of Greta Garbo.

Besides, it wasn't as if she were testing a student and could demand that Jackie give her privacy.

"Thanks." Jackie turned to her companion, an enigmatic expression on her face. "Justin, tell Ms. Denison what you were telling me."

"Hi, Ms. D." Justin pulled a chair up to Skye's desk. "We were just talking about the history of the building that the Promfest haunted house is using."

"What about it?"

"I was doing some research for an article for the *Scoop*, and it turns out the old American Legion hall is really haunted." Justin paused for effect. "Or at least, some people claim it is."

"What do you think?" Skye asked cautiously, preferring to allow the students to come to their own conclusions.

"All I know is that a lot of people have heard or seen something creepy there, but you know how rumors fly in this town."

Skye nodded and picked up her pen, not wanting to hear any more about the haunted building, especially right before she had to spend time alone in the dark there.

"Justin, tell her the whole story," Jackie urged. "It's such a hoot."

"Well." He looked a little uncomfortable, and nervously jiggled his foot. "From what I've heard, back in 1935, when the building was an opera house, the star, a beautiful woman with long black hair, caught her husband, the male lead singer, with the blond understudy and freaked out. She picked up an ax that had been a prop in one of their shows and chopped off the other woman's head, then turned on her husband and buried the ax in his . . . uh, private parts."

"Wow." Despite not wanting to hear the story, Skye was enthralled. "I wonder why I wasn't aware of that. I'll have to ask my grandmother if she knows anything about it. She's the right age."

Justin shrugged. "Anyway, when the star came to her senses and saw both victims lying at her feet in a pool of blood, she couldn't live with what she had done, so she climbed to the roof, tied a noose around her neck, and jumped off."

"Oh, my." Skye shook her head. "So now she haunts the building?"

"Ever since then, all three of them have been seen and heard. When the opera house closed, everyone thought that would be the end of it, but it wasn't. In the 1950s the building became a dance hall, and strange things started happening again. Ladies claimed that when they looked in the bathroom mirror they saw a beautiful woman with long black hair wearing a white dress covered in blood."

A shiver ran up Skye's spine. "That sounds a lot like one of the scary games my friends and I used to play at slumber parties, where we stared into a mirror until we convinced ourselves we saw an evil spirit."

"I've heard of that game," Justin agreed. "But the men say that they've heard both crying and voices arguing." He took a breath and added, "When the dance hall closed, the weird stuff stopped. Then in the 1970s the building was bought by the American Legion and it all started up again."

"Of course," Skye muttered.

"During the next twenty-five years, before the American Legion moved to their new place, the caretaker said he saw ropes dangling from the roof, but they disappeared when he went up to check. Both members and guests reported seeing bloody axes leaning against the wall in the woman's bathroom, and a man saw a pretty blonde covered in blood, running down the hall outside the restrooms."

Great, Skye mumbled to herself. *In the exact location I so carefully chose.* To Justin she said, "That should be an interesting article. Make sure you have some direct quotes to back up your story."

Skye had managed to keep Justin from seeing how much his story had upset her, but as soon as he and Jackie left, Skye buried her head in her hands. Why had she ever agreed to be a part of A Ghoul's Night Out? All the fears she had managed to suppress came rushing back. Sighing, Skye opened her bottom desk drawer and reached for the Oreos. As she bit into the crunchy chocolate, she wondered if there were enough cookies in the world to calm her down this time.

CHAPTER 7

Oh, What a Night

Holy water, crucifix, garlic—check. Salt—check. Taser, flashlight, cell phone—check. Skye sat at her kitchen table inventorying the contents of her backpack. What else should she bring? She was prepared to fight off vampires, witches, and bad guys, but she needed something for werewolves.

Regrettably, she didn't have any silver bullets for her shotgun. *Hmm*, maybe she should stop by the Brown Bag Liquor Store and pick up a six-pack of Coors Light. Wasn't its nickname the Silver Bullet? If the beer didn't kill the werewolves, at least it would get them drunk.

What worked against ghosts? Although Skye secretly thought her own house was haunted, she had never attempted to get rid of the apparition. Mrs. Griggs had been a benevolent spirit, causing trouble only if Skye tried to get intimate with Wally. Given that they had moved their more amorous activities to his place, there had been no need to drive the ghost away.

Unfortunately, the ghosts at the American Legion hall did not seem to be of the Casper persuasion, and the only idea Skye could come up with was exorcism. Was it too late to ask Father Burns to perform a quick one at A Ghoul's Night Out?

She glanced at the kitchen clock. Five thirty. Only fifteen minutes before she had to leave. Probably not enough time to convince a priest to make a haunted-house call.

Skye considered calling Vince and asking him to adopt Bingo if she didn't make it out of the Promfest event alive tonight. She knew her mother wouldn't care for her pet. May's dislike of all animals, especially cats, was legendary.

Intellectually, Skye knew she was being silly. She was no more in danger at A Ghoul's Night Out than she was at school. But emotionally she felt she was opening herself up to the unknown—giving herself over to someone or something else's influence. And she hated not being in control of the situation.

Taking a deep breath, she pushed her chair away from the table and stood. As ordered by Annette, Skye had applied green makeup to her face, and was dressed in black tights and a leotard. Over them she wore a knee-length sweater coat—no way was she prancing around in public with her curves jiggling. She would exchange the sweater for her costume in the privacy of the bathroom once she got to the hall.

Skye was shrugging on her backpack when the phone rang. She'd better let her machine answer it—the Promfest chairwoman was not someone you kept waiting. But her curiosity wouldn't let her ignore the call entirely, so she hurried into the parlor to listen.

After the fourth ring, Wally's smooth baritone said, "Skye, are you there? Pick up."

She grabbed the receiver. "I'm on my way out the door. I have to be at the haunted house by six or Annette Paine will kill me."

"I'm glad I caught you before you left." Wally's tone was tense and distracted.

"Why?" Skye felt a stab of anxiety. "What's wrong? Are you all right?"

"I'm fine," Wally's voice was neutral. "It's my dad. My cousin just called. My father collapsed at work and is in a hospital."

"That's terrible." Carson Boyd ran his multimillion-dollar corporation from its headquarters in west Texas. Skye had met him for the first time last April, when he'd come to Scumble River on business. It had been an enlightening encounter on several levels. First, because Wally had never told her that he was heir to a fortune. Second, because Carson had come into town in disguise. And last, because Wally's dad had tried to convince Skye to trick his son into returning to El Paso and taking over the family empire. "Do the doctors know what's wrong with him?"

"No."

"Is there anything I can do?"

"No. I'm on my way to O'Hare. I was able to get a seat on a plane that leaves at nine."

"Oh." Skye felt a stab of . . . she wasn't sure what. Rejection, maybe. "That was lucky." Why hadn't he asked her to go with him? Was he waiting for her to offer? She wanted to be by his side through good times and bad. No matter how estranged father and son were, if Carson was seriously ill, Wally would be devastated, and Skye wanted to be there for him.

"I'm not sure how long I'll be gone. The doctors were still working on Dad when my cousin called, so he had no idea how bad it is."

"Let me know as soon as you find out." Skye twisted the cord around her finger, trying to decide whether she should offer to go with him.

"I will." Wally's tone was remote. "Keep your cell on. I'll call you on it."

"I will, but you know reception around here is iffy at best."

"Then it'll go to your voice mail." Wally sounded slightly irritated. "You have figured out how to retrieve your voice mail, haven't you?"

"Of course." Skye crossed her fingers and reminded herself to have Justin show her one more time. She frowned. Why did she have such a hard time with technology? According to the IQ test she'd been given in graduate school, she was smart, but cell phones, computers, and stuff like that never seemed to work for her.

Wally broke into her thoughts. "Okay. I have to hurry if I'm going to make my flight. I'll be cutting it close as it is."

"Right." Why was Wally so stiff? *Duh!* Because he was concerned about his dad, and distracted with the logistics of getting to him. Skye mentally slapped herself. It had been four years since her ex-fiancé jilted her, and she'd thought she was over her insecurities, but evidently they still existed. "Be careful. Traffic will be bad on a Friday night."

"Well . . ." There was a pause; then Wally said, "I'll talk to you later."

She didn't like that he was using his cop voice, not the warm and loving tone with which he usually talked to her. Come to think of it, he had acted the same way when his father had visited last spring. What was it about his father's presence—either physically or in spirit—that changed Wally's personality so much? Was it because he didn't see himself as a man who would inherit millions of dollars? Skye knew he didn't want anyone in Scumble River to know about his wealthy background.

"Have a safe trip." Another pause, and then she said, "Your father will be in my prayers."

Ick. That had been awkward. After she hung up, Skye chewed her lower lip, then reached for the phone, having decided she *should* offer to go to Texas with Wally. But what if he didn't want her there? She didn't want to make things worse for him when he was so concerned about his father.

Abruptly she snatched her hand back from the receiver. As she told the kids she counseled, if you ask a question you don't want an answer to, expect an answer you don't want to hear. If Wally had wanted her to accompany him, he would have said so.

Maybe once he got to El Paso and found out how his father was doing, he'd ask her to join him. She thought about how she'd feel if she were thousands of miles away and got a call saying her dad was sick. Her only focus would be getting to him, which was exactly how Wally was acting. It was self-centered even to think any of this was about her.

Having come to that conclusion, Skye looked at her watch. *Crapola.* It was five till six; she was going to be late.

It took only ten minutes for Skye to drive to the old American Legion hall, but Annette met her at the door, frown lines etched in her green makeup. "Ms. Denison, what part of *prompt* don't you understand?"

"I'm so sorry." Skye tried to edge around the angry woman, but Annette blocked the entrance. "I received an emergency phone call as I was leaving."

"I see. Nothing serious, I hope." Annette didn't give Skye a chance to answer. Instead she hitched up the tattered and stained bridal gown she was wearing as her Bride of Frankenstein costume and stepped aside. Gesturing with a pointed finger, she ordered, "Hurry into your outfit and take your place." Then she turned sharply on her white stilettos and said over her shoulder, "The dress rehearsal will start in ten minutes—whether you witches are ready or not. No one will ruin A Ghoul's Night Out."

Skye hurried through the haunted house toward the backstage area. The volunteers who had constructed the interior had done an amazing job. Skye couldn't imagine the time it must have taken to build all the sets and props. There were three main sections. The first was a spa that had been turned into a chamber of horrors, the second was a demonic dance club, and the third contained scenes reenacting famous murders by women—Lizzie Borden being the star.

The trio of passageways that brought the attendees from section to section were populated by the more traditional Halloween characters. Skye and her fellow witches were each assigned to one of these corridors. They were to pop out through a door in a false wall, scare the pants off the group walking through, and then run as fast as they could to the opposite end of the hall and disappear behind another panel.

Before reporting to her spot, Skye darted behind the sets and grabbed her costume from a nearly empty rack. The lone costume still hanging there was one of her fellow witches'. Clearly she wasn't the only late arrival. She silently cheered, glad she wasn't alone in incurring Annette's wrath.

Without stopping, she nipped into the outer hallway and ran past the entrance that led to her designated position. When she reached for the knob of the ladies' room door, the hall lights flickered twice.

Skye felt her heart stop until she realized the flickering was only the signal that the dress rehearsal would start in five minutes. Not wanting to be caught in the haunted bathroom when the lights went out for real, she burst through the door, shrugged off her backpack, and dashed into the nearest of the three stalls.

She tore the plastic covering off the witch's dress and threw the bulky garment over her head. While Skye struggled to tug it into place, she thought she heard a strange noise, but the heavy fabric muffled the sound. She mentally shrugged; it was probably the third witch, who, having finally arrived, was also in the bathroom putting on her costume.

At last Skye managed to get into her dress. When her head emerged, she realized the sound she had heard was someone crying. Her stomach clenched, but she took a steadying breath and said to herself, *It is not the ghost. It's a real person and she's upset. Do something.*

Squatting, she looked under the stalls, then toward the sinks and mirrors. Fear knotted inside her. There weren't any feet. If no one else was in the bathroom, who was sobbing?

Skye held her breath and listened. The weeping had stopped. Had she imagined it? She adjusted her costume, stuffed the sweater she'd been wearing into her backpack, and cautiously pushed the stall door open. She was alone. She was loath to look into the mirror—terrified that a bloody woman would stare back. Nevertheless, by telling herself to quit being so stupid, she forced herself to turn toward the glass.

Letting out a sigh of relief, she used spirit gum to attach the prosthetic nose and chin that were a part of her makeup. She was fiddling with a fake wart that was supposed to be worn on her chin when she caught sight of her watch. The dress rehearsal was starting in less than a minute. She swiftly stuck the black pointed hat on her head, ran to the door, and pushed. It wouldn't budge.

She put her shoulder to it and shoved with all of her not inconsiderable weight. It opened a couple of inches, but immediately slammed shut. Someone or something was holding it closed from the other side. Was this a joke? Why would someone want to trap her in the john?

Skye grabbed the flashlight from her backpack, preparing for when the lights went out for good. But she stuffed the light back into her pack when she remembered that the safety inspector had said that the bathroom lights had to remain on throughout the event.

Next she scooped out her cell phone. Whom should she call? As she considered her options, she glanced at the digital display. No signal. *Shit!* Now what? If she didn't get out of there and to her appointed place on time, Annette would have her head on a platter.

Skye looked around. Was there any other way out? There were no windows, and the three small stalls and the larger handicapped one took up nearly all of the space, except for a small area in front of the sinks. Skye nudged open each stall door with her foot. She could see at a glance that the first three were empty, but she had to step inside the bigger one in order to check the entire interior.

She swept her gaze over the area, biting off a scream at the sight of a bloody ax propped beside the toilet. She backed out and swung around. Still no sign of anyone else in the room. Panic welled in her throat, but she forced herself to swallow it. Was she imagining sights and sounds, or were they all real?

Despite her fear, she pushed open the stall door again. The ax was still there, and this time she recognized it as a prop from the Lizzie Borden scene. The blood was red paint. Whoever was playing Lizzie must have brought it with her when she went to use the bathroom, leaned it against the wall to free her hands, then forgotten it.

Skye shook her head. She was letting this whole "haunted" haunted-house thing get to her. Had she imagined the blocked exit as well? She darted over to the door and gave it a mighty shove, nearly falling flat on her face when it swung wide open without any resistance.

The hall was now pitch-black, and it took her a minute or so to orient herself. Fumbling, she once again retrieved the flashlight from her backpack and clicked it on. The corridor was deserted.

Skye took a few steps toward the entrance of her assigned passageway and shrieked. Something had taken hold of her ankle! She gasped, panting in terror, but managed to aim the light downward. A plastic hand had been set up so that a person walking close to the wall would think that someone had grabbed his or her leg.

Damn! Damn! Damn! She should never have volunteered, no matter how bad it made her look in the eyes of the Promfest committee. What had she been thinking?

Eerie sounds poured in from the haunted house's interior, battering at her brittle nerves, and a wave of apprehension swept through her. The pockets of darkness that her flashlight beam couldn't penetrate closed in on her, and she started to shake as fearful images began to build in her mind.

Skye stopped and backed up against the wall. Trembling and unable to catch her breath, she was back in that moment when she was six years old, reliving the terror of her first and, until now, last experience in a haunted house.

She had been fine as long as she had held Vince's hand,

but the moment he had gone off with one of his friends, Dracula had lunged out at her. As she ran away from him, a giant spider had dropped from the ceiling and landed on her head. Shrieking, she had torn herself free and raced into the next room.

There she had tripped and ended up sprawled in a greenly glowing cemetery among tilted tombstones. Before she could get up, a zombie had risen from his grave and was looming over her.

All Skye remembered after that was screaming and screaming. Then she was outside, and Vince was kneeling in front of her, begging her not to tell their mother that he'd left her alone. She never had, but she had threatened to reveal his secret anytime she needed to make him do something for her.

The thought of all the times she had blackmailed Vince throughout the years brought a smile to her lips, and she slowly managed to calm herself down. After she took a few deep breaths, her heart rate returned to normal and she no longer felt like throwing up.

Squaring her shoulders, Skye picked up her backpack—it had dropped to the floor during her panic attack—and forced herself to continue walking down the hallway. Still hoping to be on time for her first appearance (she was the last of the three witches to emerge), she picked up her pace. She was only a few steps from the door leading to her assigned spot when she heard the first scream.

Skye came to an abrupt stop, her heart jumping in her chest. She had gotten used to the fake moans, groans, and shrieks of the haunted house, but what she had just heard was not one of them. It was real.

CHAPTER 8

Moments Like These

W ho was screaming and why? Despite her fears, Skye felt compelled to find out. If someone was in trouble, she couldn't pretend she hadn't heard anything and walk away, or wait for someone else to take care of the problem. She wasn't that kind of person—she helped others even if it meant risking herself.

After the first shriek, there had been a moment's pause, followed by a steady wail. Skye cocked her head and listened intently, turning slowly toward where she thought the sound was originating. Her auditory directional skills were poor, but it seemed as if the screams were coming from behind the wall where she was standing.

That couldn't be right. That was the area where she was supposed to appear and disappear, and given that she was the last of the three witches, it was near the end of the circuit. The only person who should be in that section was herself.

Instantly she stiffened. Could the shrieks be coming from the spirit of the woman with the long black hair? No. These screams sounded all too human. Her pulse beat erratically as she approached the door that led to her designated passageway.

Skye put her hand on the knob, trying to get up the

courage to turn it, but before she could make herself twist
the cold metal sphere, she heard the tippy-tapping of high-
heeled shoes—a sound that could very well be the footsteps
of an opera star's ghost. She choked back a cry. Were they
coming from behind the door or behind her? A chill raced up
her spine. She couldn't tell.

She jerked her hand away from the knob, twisted, and
plastered her back to the wall. Should she hide, try to get
out, face her fears, or all of the above? She had to do something.

A loud moan made her jump, rousing her from her inde-
cision. It was better to take positive action and gain the advantage of surprise than to stand there and wait for whatever
or whomever to come get her.

Skye reached into her backpack and withdrew both the
stun gun and the bottle of holy water, figuring it was best to
be prepared for the natural as well as the supernatural. For
easy access, she tucked the vial into her cleavage, and trans-
ferred the Taser to her right hand.

Once armed, she turned the knob, opened the door a
crack, and peered around the corner. At first she couldn't see
anything in the darkness. She groped for the flashlight she
had stuck in her belt, but it dropped to the floor.

Carefully she squatted to retrieve it, blindly patting the
linoleum until her fingers touched the cold metal. Grasping
the cylindrical base, she felt for the switch and thumbed it to
the ON position. Nothing. She shook it and it came on
briefly, only to sputter out. She tried again, hitting it against
her thigh, and this time it didn't even flicker.

Shit! That would teach her to buy cheap stuff at the dol-
lar store. If she got out of here alive, she was putting a
police-quality Maglite on her birthday wish list, and she was
buying Energizer batteries, not the low-priced generic ones
she usually opted for. The bunny would never let her down.

Unhappily, that didn't help her now. But on the upside,
while she had been trying to figure out what to do next, her
eyes had adjusted to the darkness. The narrow area between

the hall entrance and the door in the false wall was empty. Maybe the screaming hadn't come from there after all. Yes, that must be it. She could still hear faint whimpers but they came from a little farther away, beyond the next partition.

Skye told herself she had to put on her big-girl panties and do what had to be done. Still, as she slipped inside the small space, she left the outer door open for a quick get-away.

She could no longer hear the footsteps or moans. Had the ghost moved on to scare someone else? Or maybe the whole thing had been a part of the haunted-house act of which Skye wasn't aware. With that optimistic thought, she noticed that the door located in the false wall was ajar. She placed her palm against it, but before she could push, a hand wrapped around the edge. Without thinking she yanked the door shut.

A wail of pain rang through the cheap plywood.

Great. She had just pissed off a ghost. No, wait a minute; a ghost wouldn't have felt anything. Gripping her stun gun, she flung open the door. As she burst into the passageway, her head slammed into something solid and unyielding. Her vision blurred and she crumpled to the floor.

For an instant everything went black and she couldn't move. What had happened? *Damn!* Someone must have hit her. Was he or she standing over her right now, ready to plunge a knife through her heart?

Skye's eyelids flew open. She could dimly make out a sprawled body in front of her, and she realized what had happened. They both must have tried to go through the door at the same time and hit their heads. As Skye's vision cleared, she could see that the other person was dressed in a long, cobwebby black gown, wearing stark white makeup and fangs. Who was playing Countess Dracula? Skye searched her memory, but came up blank.

The woman sat up slowly, reached for the flashlight that had rolled a few inches from her hand, and flicked it on. She stared at Skye. Fear, stark and vivid, glittered in the woman's eyes, and her mouth formed a large circle. Screaming, she struggled to her feet and, keeping her gaze on Skye, backed through the door, then turned and ran.

Clearly Skye wasn't the only one spooked by the haunted house. She eased to her feet, her head still swimming. Why had the countess run away like that?

Warily, Skye stepped farther into the passageway. The door had swung shut, as it was designed to do, and it was even darker here than in the outer hallway. Skye took a moment to get her bearings, then reached out and felt along the wall. Somewhere nearby was a panic button that would turn on an emergency light in the passageway, as well as a signal in the control room indicating that there was a problem. And a freaked-out Mrs. Dracula was definitely a problem.

She knew the button was at shoulder level and the size of a doorbell. Shuffling forward, she inched down the narrow corridor while trailing her hand against the rough plywood. If she went too fast, she might overlook the switch.

Where was the blasted thing? Had she somehow gotten turned around? Was she going the wrong way? Or had she missed it? As she took another step, her right foot slid into what felt like a large pile of clothes. Still unable to see in the darkness, Skye crouched. Tentatively, she reached out and touched the mound, then ran her fingers down its length.

Yikes! She yanked her hand back. It wasn't someone's abandoned laundry. It was a person.

Hesitantly, she grabbed what she hoped was the shoulder and shook it. "Hey, get up. Are you all right?"

Skye tried again, but there was no response. She needed help. Jumping to her feet, she continued her search for the light. Her breath was coming in shallow, quick gasps, and by the time her fingers stumbled onto the switch, her chest felt as if it would burst.

She pushed the plastic button and light flooded the passageway. Blinded from the sudden glare, Skye instinctively closed her eyes as she swung around and stepped back to the person on the floor.

When she opened her eyes, she recoiled, then stood frozen in shock. A woman was lying on the floor in front of her, unmoving and corpselike. And she was a dead ringer for Skye herself!

CHAPTER 9

It Might Be You

Sheer black fright swept through Skye. Her mind reeled with confusion. Was she going insane? The situation was jarringly reminiscent of her recurring nightmare—the one in which she was attending a funeral, went up to pay her respects, and instead of finding the deceased in the casket, she saw herself.

Panic, unlike anything she'd ever experienced before, welled up in her throat. Her breath whistling rapidly in and out and her heart pounding like a jackhammer, she sank to the floor. Huddled against the wall, Skye gripped the stun gun and stared at her doppelgänger, trying to make sense of what was in front of her. Several minutes ticked by, but her brain refused to function and she remained paralyzed.

The sound of running footsteps roused her from her stupor. As the initial shock began to wear off, she calmed down. Regaining a fragment of self-control, she realized that the person sprawled a few feet from her was one of the other two witches. During the rehearsals they had discovered that all three of them looked nearly identical once they were in costume and makeup. Only the strange light and her already agitated state of mind had kept her from immediately comprehending the woman's true identity.

Once Skye understood what she was seeing, she crawled over to her double and pressed her fingertips to the woman's carotid artery, feeling for a pulse. There was none that Skye could detect, but she did note a line across her look-alike's throat where the green makeup had been rubbed away. As Skye took the woman's wrist to check for a pulse there, she saw a long rope with green stains clutched in the witch's right hand.

Unable to detect a heartbeat, Skye used the bottom of her skirt to wipe off the makeup from around the woman's mouth. Her skin had a bluish tinge and she didn't appear to be breathing. How long had she been lying there?

While debating whether to remove the woman's prosthetic nose and chin in order to identify her, Skye heard a male voice from outside the door shout, "The signal came from this section."

"Stop. Don't come in here." Skye struggled to her feet and blocked the entrance. Raising her voice, she ordered, "Go back and call nine-one-one. Someone's been attacked and is badly hurt."

The men argued, but after explaining what she had found and asserting her position as a police consultant, Skye dissuaded them from attempting to enter the passageway. She instructed them to post guards at all the outer doors and make sure no one left the building. While one of the men went to phone for help, the other ran off to round up the rest of the security detail to stand watch.

Skye was surprised at how quickly Roy Quirk arrived. According to her Timex, it had taken him less than three minutes. With the chief out of town, and as Wally's second in command, Officer Quirk was in charge. Roy was in his early thirties, and still looked like the football player he'd been in high school.

He nodded to Skye as he stepped inside the passageway, then quickly assessed the scene. Ten minutes later two paramedics burst through the door. Quirk moved aside, giving them access to the woman. From where Skye stood pressed against the wall, she couldn't see what the paramedics were doing, but after only a minute or two they got to their feet, murmured a few words to Quirk, and left.

Quirk flipped open his cell phone and barked out several orders, then turned to Skye. "We need to keep people out of this area. Please move into the exterior hallway."

Skye frowned. She wasn't exactly "people." She was the psychological consultant to the Scumble River Police Department, which made her Quirk's colleague, not some civilian. "I take it that, since the paramedics are gone, the woman's dead?"

Quirk didn't answer; instead he asked, "How long ago did you find her?"

"I'd guess close to fifteen minutes ago, but I can't say for sure."

"Has anyone else been in here?"

"Not since I found her." Skye shook her head. "I persuaded the guys from the control room not to come in. Instead I had them call you and post guards at the exits."

"How did they know you needed help in the first place? Did they just happen by?"

"No." Skye explained about the panic button, then added, "As well as working the sound system and the lights, the men act as a sort of security force for the haunted house."

Quirk made a note on the pad he had taken from his shirt pocket. "Did you touch anything?"

"Yes." Skye recalled her movements. "The door, the wall from the door to the light switch, the switch, her neck, shoulder, and wrist. Oh, and I also wiped some makeup from her mouth with my skirt."

"Son of—" Quirk cut himself off and gave her a sour look. "You contaminated the scene."

"What was I supposed to do?" Skye put her hands on her hips. "It was pitch-black. I didn't even know she was there until I tripped over her. Then I had to see if I could help her."

He clamped his lips shut, took her arm, and led her to the door.

"Did you call the coroner?" Skye persisted. She certainly had no desire to stay with the body, but she suspected Quirk had never handled a murder on his own.

"I've got it all under control." Quirk nearly pushed her over the threshold. "You stay here and don't let anyone but the officials in."

"But I need to tell you—"

Quirk shut the door before she could finish.

She yelled through the wood, "Someone needs to find Countess Dracula." There was no response, and Skye doubted that Quirk had heard her.

The news that something awful had happened spread quickly, and as Skye stood with her back to the door, the cast and crew gathered around her and shouted questions.

"Did you really find a body?"

"Who is it?"

"Were they murdered?"

"I can't say anything." Skye held up her hands in a quieting gesture. "The police have arrived and are handling it."

"Ms. Denison, why did you want to find Evie Harrison?" asked a girl dressed as a zombie cheerleader.

"What are you talking about?" Skye puckered her brow. "I'm not looking for Mrs. Harrison."

The undead cheerleader toyed with the fake knife sticking out of her chest. "I heard you shout that you needed someone to find Countess Dracula—that's Evie Harrison."

"I see." Skye digested that information. She wished she had a list of cast members and their roles. "In that case, I *would* like to find her." Skye raised her voice and said to the crowd, "Does anyone know where Evie Harrison is?"

No one answered, but the cheerleader poked Skye in the arm with a pom-pom. "So why do you want her?"

"I need to ask her something," Skye equivocated, not willing to explain that she had encountered Evie near the body, or that Evie had run off screaming.

"Oh." The teen scratched at the makeup that made one side of her face look as if it had been shredded.

"Why are you so interested?" Skye asked.

"Evie's my mom." The girl bit her lip. "And it's sort of weird that she's not here with everyone else. I thought maybe she was hurt or something."

"You're Cheyenne, right?" The teen nodded and Skye reached out and put a hand on her shoulder. "The last time I saw your mom, she was fine." Skye crossed her fingers. Evie had been physically okay. "Hey, I bet you know everyone here, right?"

"Maybe." Cheyenne's expression became guarded. "So what?"

"Do you know the other two witches? The ones dressed like me?"

"Yeah. I know them. Mrs. Kennedy was my teacher in grade school, and the other is Bree's mom." Cheyenne pointed to a trio of zombie cheerleaders.

"Have you seen either one around here since the police arrived?"

"Not that I remember." Cheyenne turned to go.

"I'll keep an eye out for your mom." Skye took a step after her. "And you let me know if you see Mrs. Kennedy or Mrs. Miles."

The girl nodded, then walked away and joined a group of teenagers who stood in a tight cluster as far from the adults as possible. The kids were laughing and joking, and seemed fine, though a couple of the girls kept sneaking worried peeks in the direction of the door Skye was guarding.

What did she know about the other two witches? Skye mentally went through the Rolodex in her mind, trying to dredge up information. She had met Nina Miles a couple of years ago. Her oldest daughter, Farrah, had been a member of the cheerleading squad whose captain had been murdered. And during that same period, her youngest daughter, Shawna, had cut off the hair of one of her classmates in order to stop the other girl from performing the starring role in the annual dance recital. If Nina was the dead witch, that meant three children were now motherless.

Not that she wanted the body to be that of Hope Kennedy. *Shoot!* She didn't want either of the two women to be the dead witch. She didn't want it to be anyone. What she really wanted was for this to be a nightmare and to wake up.

She pinched herself, but other than a red mark on her arm, nothing had changed: She was still standing in the drafty hallway of the old American Legion hall. The crowd had backed off and was now milling around in small knots. Skye knew they should all be separated and not allowed to talk to one another, but what could she do? There were just too many of them.

As she strained to hear fragments of conversations, several Scumble River police officers arrived, followed closely by Simon Reid, who, in addition to owning the town funeral home and bowling alley, was also the county coroner.

Skye stepped aside and let the officers and Simon through the door. Simon touched her hand briefly as he passed. "Are you okay?"

"I'm fine." She looked up into his concerned golden hazel eyes and tried to smile. "Just a little shaken up."

He patted her shoulder and nodded, then hurried into the passageway.

A few seconds later Anthony, one of the PD's part-timers, came back out and said, "Roy told me to take over for you. We can't do much until County gets here."

Scumble River was too small to have its own crime scene techs, and called on those from the sheriff's department when they needed forensic evidence collected.

Skye nodded. "Does he want me to do anything else?"

Anthony looked uncomfortable. Skye had helped his little sister get the special instruction she needed in school, and he was one of her biggest fans. He stared at his shoes. "Uh, no, not exactly."

"Not exactly?" she prompted.

"Uh, he said he didn't need your help."

"Oh." Skye felt her face flush. She hadn't realized that

Quirk didn't like her, or at least didn't like her working with the police.

"I think maybe Roy is a little, uh . . . I mean, this is probably his first murder without the chief around, and he might be feeling a little . . ."

"Overwhelmed? Defensive? Pressured?" Skye suggested.

"Yeah. All of those." Anthony's eyes glinted with amusement. "Chief Boyd will straighten things out when he gets back. Don't worry. The rest of us know you're okay."

"Thanks." Skye paused, considering whether to mention the Countess Dracula incident to Anthony or wait until she could speak to Quirk again. She hated to put the young man in the middle, but she decided she had no choice. Someone had to locate Evie Harrison. She may very well have witnessed the murder, and there was an outside chance she had committed it.

After Skye finished telling Anthony about her run-in with Evie, and he relayed the message to Quirk, Skye drifted from group to group, checking to see what people were saying and trying to locate Hope and Nina.

The only interesting fact she learned was that another bunch of haunted-house workers had gathered near the front entrance. The police weren't allowing anyone to leave their present locations, so it was impossible to judge who was stuck in the lobby and who was really missing.

It took nearly an hour for the crime scene techs to arrive—the Stanley County seat was located in Laurel, down forty-five miles of winding country roads. Once the techs got there, the Scumble River police started interviewing the people who had been detained. But even after all were spoken to, they still weren't allowed to leave. No one knew why they were being held, but Skye guessed the police wouldn't release anyone until they had identified the victim.

Skye was in the first group questioned, and once she was finished giving her statement, she talked to the people around her. No one had seen anything prior to the police's arrival, or afterward. And no one had seen Nina or Hope either. Skye was trying to think of what else to do when she noticed that Simon had come out into the hallway and was using his cell phone.

After he hung up, she went over to him. "Has the victim been identified?"

"No." Simon looked at her quizzically. "Haven't you talked to Roy?"

Skye was torn. "Uh . . ." Should she admit Quirk was cutting her out of the loop or pretend she was still on the team? "Not really."

Simon tilted his head. "It's not the same when Boyd's not here, is it?"

"Well . . ."

"I suppose Roy's within his rights. After all, you're a consultant. If he doesn't think he needs your help, he doesn't have to include you."

"But—"

"But he'd be a fool not to utilize your talents," Simon said matter-of-factly.

Skye was too surprised to do more than nod. She would have bet good money that Simon didn't place much value on what she did for the police department, that he disapproved of her involvement in investigations. She narrowed her eyes. Which of her other assumptions about Simon were wrong?

"I'm guessing Roy's lack of an invitation is not going to deter you from looking into this case," Simon said.

The denial died on her lips when she saw the devilish look in his eyes. "I can help. I'm familiar with the people and the haunted-house setup."

"So, what do you want to know?" Simon took her arm and steered her to a more secluded area.

"You said the victim hasn't been identified yet, but were you able to determine a time of death?"

"According to the liver temp, between when you found her and thirty minutes prior."

Skye rummaged in her backpack for a notepad and pen, handing superfluous items to Simon as she searched. He raised an eyebrow when she produced the string of garlic, and bit his lip to stifle a grin when she pulled out the crucifix. At last she found what she was looking for and allowed Simon to give back what he'd been holding.

Amusement and tenderness flickered in his expression when he said, "Being here really scares you, doesn't it?"

"A little." She was glad the green makeup hid the flush she felt creeping up her neck.

"I remember your telling me how much you hated haunted houses after what happened to you when you were little. Why did you volunteer?"

Skye couldn't meet his eyes. "I was trying to get over my phobia." How could she admit she'd been prompted by her insecurity regarding the new social worker? Especially since Simon was apparently dating Jackie.

Simon didn't look convinced, but he let it drop. "What else do you want to know?"

"What are they doing to identify the victim?" Skye asked. She had told Quirk who the other two witches were supposed to be, but she hadn't been able to tell whether he thought that information was important or not.

"I overheard them saying they found Hope Kennedy and she was fine, but no one has seen Mrs. Miles."

Skye was thrilled that the teacher was okay, but felt her heart sink at the news that Nina was missing. There couldn't be a good outcome, but she'd held on to the hope that a terminally ill stranger had wandered into the haunted house, donned the witch costume and makeup, and died of natural causes.

Simon went on, "I called Xavier, and he's bringing over makeup remover and rubbing alcohol to loosen the spirit gum holding on the prosthetics." Xavier Ryan was Simon's assistant at the funeral home. "Once we reveal her face, we'll ask Mr. Miles to take a look. Roy told Anthony to call and have him come over."

"Poor man." Skye shook her head and tried not to think

about how awful it would be for him. "What reason did Anthony give Mr. Miles for asking him to come?"

"Roy told Anthony to say there was a problem at the haunted house and he should come right away, then hang up." Simon rubbed his chin. "Not to give him a chance to ask for details."

"You know his daughter is here somewhere. She's one of the zombie cheerleaders. Quirk needs to take her aside now, before she hears something."

"Anthony said something to that effect, but Roy didn't want to alert anyone, so he refused."

Skye's mouth tightened. "I understand his reasoning, but Bree's an eighteen-year-old girl." Roy Quirk was really beginning to annoy her. "It's not right for her to find out about her mother through the grapevine." Wally would get an earful when he called.

"I'm sure once Mr. Miles makes the identification, Roy will have an officer bring the girl to her father."

"Maybe I should go find her and sort of stand nearby until that happens."

"That's probably a good idea." Simon ran a hand through his short auburn hair. "But Roy's not going to be happy I've told you all this."

"I'll be subtle." She gave Simon a conspiratorial grin. "Besides, Quirk isn't the boss of you."

Simon chuckled softly, but broke off when Xavier approached and handed him a small paper bag. Xavier nodded to Skye, then said to Simon, "Here's the makeup remover and rubbing alcohol you wanted. Give me a call if you need anything else. I'll be waiting in the hearse."

When Skye had first met Xavier, his pale blue lashless eyes magnified behind old-fashioned horn-rimmed glasses had made him seem reptilian, but she had come to like and respect Simon's soft-spoken assistant. He was a widower, and his daughter, Frannie, was a freshman in college.

Skye thought Xavier was probably lonely with her gone—or maybe not. Frannie had been one of Skye's favorite students, but she was extremely intelligent and curious, not always the easiest qualities for a parent to deal with.

Simon touched Skye's hand. "I've got to return to the victim. Once we make the identification, I'll be transporting the body. Will you be okay?"

"I'll be fine." Skye squeezed his arm. "Thanks . . . for everything."

After Simon left, Skye scanned the area for Bree Miles. Four girls were dressed as zombie cheerleaders, and Skye wasn't sure which one was Bree. She could eliminate Cheyenne Harrison and Linnea Paine, but the other two were unfamiliar to her. Luckily, since they were all huddled together, it didn't matter.

Skye dragged a chair over to a spot against the wall next to the group and pulled a book out of her backpack, pretending to be engrossed in the novel. Although it was only October, the girls were talking about the prom.

Skye shook her head. Cats were the only ones that were supposed to have nine lives, but teenagers certainly carried on as if they did, too. The girls had to have heard that someone had died, yet as far as Skye could tell, the big topic of conversation, after who was going with whom to the prom, was the dress each wanted and how much it would cost.

A half hour went by, and Cheyenne was describing an elaborate copper-colored strapless dress with a mermaid hem, made by some designer named BCBG for only seven hundred dollars, when an angry-looking man in his early forties marched over and said, "Bree, get your things. It's time to go home."

"But, Dad, Mom said I could stay out until midnight."

"A woman's been killed." Mr. Miles pulled the girl aside and said so softly that Skye had to lean forward to hear, "They thought it was your mother."

"But isn't Mom home sick with the flu?"

"Yes." Mr. Miles propelled the girl toward the outside door, and Skye followed, hugging the wall. "And we need to get back there before some busybody hears the rumor and calls to offer their condolences on her death."

"Yeah. She'd freak."

As Mr. Miles and Bree waited at the exit for the officer on duty to check with Quirk before he let them out, Bree asked, "So, who *was* the dead woman?"

Mr. Miles looked around, and Skye quickly averted her gaze so he wouldn't guess she was listening. But as soon as he turned back to his daughter, Skye moved closer.

"You can't tell anyone," he said in a low voice, "but it's Linnea's mother. Mrs. Paine."

Skye swallowed a gasp. Annette Paine! She was the last person Skye would have guessed. Tears slid down her cheek. Annette may have been overbearing, but she was also a mother and a wife. Her death would create a void in many lives.

Skye felt a stab of guilt. She hadn't liked Annette, had made fun of her obsession with Promfest, but no one deserved to be murdered. Wiping away the wetness under her eyes, Skye squared her shoulders. She would make sure Annette's killer was found and brought to justice.

The first question Skye needed to answer was this: Why in the world had Annette been dressed as a witch when she was supposed to be the Bride of Frankenstein? Both the witches and Mrs. Frankenstein wore green makeup, so all Annette would have had to do was stick on the prosthetic nose and chin. Still, how had she had time to change costumes, arrive at Skye's assigned spot, and get herself killed?

CHAPTER 10

A Night of Mystery

A few minutes after Mr. Miles and Bree left the building, an officer came into the hallway and spoke to Frankenstein, aka Dylan Paine, Annette's husband. Funny, Skye didn't remember seeing him among the crowd as they had waited for the county crime techs to arrive, or even after everyone had been interviewed. How could she have missed a six-foot-four green monster?

As Skye watched, Dr. Paine nodded a few times at what the policeman was saying, then pointed to the trio of zombie cheerleaders. Both men went over to the group, and Dr. Paine whispered into Linnea's ear. She looked puzzled, but followed her father and the policeman through the door leading to the inner passageway.

Fifteen minutes later, Simon emerged wheeling a gurney that held a black body bag. Skye made her way to his side and walked with him toward the exit, speaking softly. "Was the witch Annette Paine?"

He gave a brief nod.

"Did they discover anything else?"

"Not that I heard." The low volume of his voice made it clear that what he said was for her ears only. "The crime techs are still working."

"Any sign of Evie Harrison?"

"I didn't see her." Before Simon pushed the gurney through the door, he paused and asked, "Are you okay to get home by yourself?"

"I'm fine."

"Then I'll talk to you tomorrow."

Skye watched as Simon and Xavier loaded the body bag into the back of the hearse. She was astonished at how easily she and Simon had fallen back into their former roles. They had broken up over a year ago, and she'd been dating Wally for nearly that long, yet it had felt right to be working as a team with Simon.

She reassured herself that this marked the beginning of a new friendship with her ex, nothing more. Certainly it had nothing to do with her relationship with Wally. She relaxed. It felt good to be at ease with Simon again.

Another half hour went by before everyone was dismissed. Skye was among the last to leave. She had loitered in the bathroom as the women had taken turns getting out of their costumes and wiping off their makeup, hoping to overhear something, but nothing had been said that she didn't already know.

Speculation about the night's events ran wild. No one seemed to have heard that the dead woman was Annette Paine, and no one mentioned Evie Harrison's absence. With some of the haunted-house workers held in the lobby and others kept in the hallway, and with many people leaving as soon as they were allowed to, Skye wasn't surprised that everyone was still in the dark.

Because she'd been late, Skye had been forced to park at the very back of the lot, and the asphalt appeared endless as she trudged to the farthest corner. Clouds covered the moon, and the chilled, damp air made her shiver. She pulled her sweater coat more tightly around her, wishing she had worn a heavier jacket. She felt achy and exhausted, but her thoughts kept turning to the dead woman. Who would want to kill Annette Paine? Yes, she could be a royal pain at times, but enough to cause someone to commit murder?

Abruptly something clicked in her mind, and a terrifying realization washed over her. What if Annette wasn't the intended victim? The killer could have been after anyone who was supposed to have been dressed as a witch. The murderer could have been after Nina or Hope or . . . Skye gulped, facing the undeniable and horrible fact that *she* might have been the killer's target.

The idea that someone might want to see her dead made Skye stumble, but a hand reached out and steadied her before she fell. Screaming, she pulled loose from the grip and took off running.

She was digging frantically through her backpack for the car keys when a voice yelled after her, "Skye, wait. Stop. It's me. Kurt. Kurt Michaels."

She turned her head, but kept running until she recognized the man chasing her. She paused with her hands on her knees, gasping for breath. She really, really had to get back to swimming in the mornings.

Kurt caught up with her. "Sorry. I didn't mean to scare you like that."

"What are you doing skulking around a dark parking lot at ten o'clock at night?"

"Waiting for you." He offered her an easy smile. "By the way, what happened in there? I heard the call on my scanner, but they didn't say what was wrong, only that you had requested the police and an ambulance. Then the coroner showed up with the hearse."

"I can't talk about it." Skye was glad they hadn't put the murder out over the radio.

"Sure you can." Kurt put a hand on her arm and tried to steer her to a black Land Rover parked next to her Bel Air. "Why don't we go get a drink at the Brown Bag and you can tell me all about it."

She shook his hand off again. "What part of 'no' don't you understand?"

"The whole word." The corners of his eyes crinkled attractively when he grinned. "It's not a part of a reporter's vocabulary."

"Have it your way." Skye found her keys and, after dropping them twice, unlocked her car. "But I'm going home. There's a hot bath there and a glass of Diet Coke with my name on it."

"Your hands are shaking. I don't think you're in any condition to drive." He inserted himself between her and the open car door, blocking her access. "If you don't want a drink, we could get coffee."

"Get out of my way or I'll Taser you." Skye reached into her backpack and pulled out her stun gun. "I'm really not in the mood for this."

"Okay. Okay." Kurt held up his hands and backed away. "But I am driving you home."

She started to shake her head, but she noticed that his blue eyes had changed to a steely gray, and he no longer looked like the flirtatious, carefree reporter she had come to know. She couldn't quite put her finger on it, but he seemed different . . . older. He stood straighter, his shoulders squared, and his features had lost any hint of boyishness.

He took her silence as refusal and said, "You're pale, you're trembling so hard I'm afraid you'll accidently pull the trigger on that stun gun of yours, and you can barely stand up."

"Don't pretend to be my friend and concerned about me." He was even more attractive at this moment, and Skye was afraid he'd persuade her to tell him everything that had happened. "You just want a story."

"I do want to be your friend." He gave Skye a long look. "I want a story, too. Surely those things aren't mutually exclusive."

Skye handed him the keys. "Fine." The thought of trying to navigate the dark, twisting road between the old American Legion hall and her house was overwhelming.

"But I'm not talking to you." He was right: She wasn't in any shape to drive.

"Okay, whatever you say."

As he started the Chevy, he commented, "I really love this car. I don't suppose you'd consider selling it. I always wanted a vintage Bel Air."

Skye ignored him. He wasn't getting her to talk that easily.

"So, do you think A Ghoul's Night Out will be open tomorrow?"

She shrugged, praying that the answer was no. She never wanted to step foot in that building again, especially while it was still decorated as a haunted house.

"It'd be a shame to waste everyone's work." Kurt shot her a quick glance.

"True."

"I'll bet it will be open." He twisted the wheel to avoid a pothole. "No way will Annette Paine let anything short of a nuclear war stand in her way. Closing down a big money-maker like this would ruin her. She'd be impeached, and Evie would get to be the Promfest chair."

"I doubt Annette will care." *Crap!* The words had popped out of her mouth before she could stop them. "I, uh, I mean that—"

"Why would Annette all of a sudden stop being obsessed with this fund-raiser?"

Skye bit her lip.

"Did something happen to Annette? Was she the one in the body bag?"

Skye closed her eyes.

"Don't try pretending you're asleep." Kurt pulled the Bel Air over to the side of the road. "Not after dropping that bombshell."

"I can't tell you." Skye gritted her teeth. "Now, start this car moving or I'm getting out."

"I'm truly not trying to be a jerk about this, but I need to know what happened."

"No, you don't *need* to know." Skye unbuckled her seat belt. "You *want* to know."

"You're wrong."

"First, the paper doesn't even come out until Wednesday, and I'm sure the police will make a statement in plenty of time for you to get the story in that edition." Skye fingered the door handle. She really didn't think she had the energy to walk home, but she wouldn't let him bully her into saying anything more.

"What's second?" Kurt reached across her and rebuckled her seat belt.

"Second." Skye held up two fingers. "Second, freedom of the press does not mean the press gets to trample all over other people's freedoms."

"I agree."

"You do?" Skye was so startled she forgot what her third reason had been and instead asked, "Since when do reporters think that any other freedom is as important as the First Amendment?"

"Not all reporters are blind to the implications of what happens when that freedom is abused."

"The ones I've met have been."

"Are you sure?"

Skye groaned and rested her pounding head on the back of the seat. "I've had a terrible day and I'm really tired." She wasn't up to participating in a philosophical discussion. "Won't you please just drive me home?"

"Okay." Kurt sighed and started the car. "But I hope there doesn't come a time when you're sorry you refused to tell me what I need to know."

"I hope so, too." There was an expression on his face she couldn't read. Was he threatening her? His words gave that impression, but his body language seemed to be saying something else.

Skye could see her driveway ahead when Kurt said, "Look, I promise what you tell me is off the record. Just nod. Is Annette Paine dead?"

Not sure why she was giving in, Skye nodded.

"Was she murdered?"

Skye shrugged—though she was fairly sure Annette had been murdered. Why else would she be clutching a rope that had clearly been tightly pressed across her neck at one time?

"Shit!" Kurt pounded the steering wheel.

Skye nodded again. The whole thing was, indeed, shitty.

They were both silent as Kurt stopped the Bel Air in front of her house; then Skye said, "Thank you for driving me home. Go ahead and take the Bel Air back to the American Legion. I'll get someone to give me a ride there to pick it up tomorrow."

"What about the keys?"

"Put them under the floor mat and lock the doors." Skye got out of the car. "I've got another set."

"Okay." His thoughts were clearly elsewhere. "I'll talk to you tomorrow."

"Not if I can help it," she muttered to herself as she waved, watching him make a three-point turn, then drive away in a cloud of dust. Kurt Michaels was a dangerous man—smart, attractive, and he had a silver tongue. Any one of those traits could get her in trouble; all three together spelled heartache for some unsuspecting woman. Skye vowed to avoid him in the future.

The steps leading to her front porch looked like Mount Everest as she started her climb. She concentrated on putting one foot in front of the other, and when she reached the top, she took a deep breath. Before she could exhale, she heard the porch swing squeak.

She whirled around and stared into the darkness. "Who's there?"

Running footsteps answered her.

CHAPTER 11

It's a Jungle Out There

"Ms. D, where have you been?" Frannie Ryan flung herself at Skye. "I've been waiting hours and hours for you."

Frannie was a little taller than average, and a lot curvier than was fashionable. During Frannie's years at Scumble River High, Skye had tried to help the size-fourteen adolescent navigate the size-four high school world. When Frannie left for college a month ago, Skye had prayed that the girl's hard-won confidence wouldn't be lost.

"Frannie, you scared the heck out of me." Skye extracted herself from the teenager's hug.

"It's just that I'm so glad to see you." Frannie's brown eyes were shiny with tears that she quickly blinked away; then she said, "And it's freezing out here."

"Yeah, two weeks ago it was in the seventies; then we had a hard freeze Tuesday night and the temperature hasn't warmed up much since then." Skye observed that Frannie wore only a T-shirt, jeans, and a fleece hoodie, none of which were warm enough to spend much time outdoors in during an Illinois October. "Wasn't it cold in Chicago?"

"Not as bad." Frannie twisted a glossy brown lock of hair

around her finger. "You know the lake effect keeps it warmer there."

"Right." Skye noticed that Frannie had cut and flatironed her nearly waist-length waves. Her hair now hung in a straight curtain to the middle of her back. Skye decided to ignore the girl's change in appearance and ask the more important question. "Are you home for a visit?" Not that that would explain why Frannie was camped out on Skye's porch so late at night, but she had to start somewhere.

Her teeth chattering, Frannie stammered, "I-it's a long story. Can we go inside?"

"Of course. Let me find my keys." Skye reached into her backpack and started digging through her possessions before it dawned on her that her house keys were on the same ring as her car keys. "Shoot."

"What's wrong?"

"Kurt has them."

"Who's Kurt?" Frannie narrowed her eyes. "If you broke up with the chief, why didn't you go back to Simon?"

"We are not having this discussion now. Or ever." Skye knew that Frannie desperately wanted her and Simon to start seeing each other again. With Frannie's father working for Simon, and her not having any siblings, she regarded Simon as the big brother she'd never had.

"But—"

"No." Skye silenced the teen with her most quelling teacher look. "We need to figure out how to get inside. Then we can talk."

"Don't you keep a key hidden outside somewhere?"

Skye shook her head.

"Who has a spare?" Frannie took a cell phone from the pocket of her jeans and tried to hand it to Skye. "We can call someone."

"No, I'm afraid we can't." Skye pushed the phone away. Her parents had left that afternoon for their trip to Las Vegas, and no one else had a key.

"Can you pick the lock?" Frannie was aware of some of Skye's more unusual talents.

"Not these. I put in dead bolts to keep someone from doing that very thing." Skye thought of an alternate solution: Frannie could drive Skye to the American Legion hall, where Skye could unlock the old Chevy with a hanger. "Do you have your dad's truck?"

"No. Sorry. A guy from my dorm was going home for the weekend and dropped me off."

"Darn." Skye paced the length of the porch several times, then shook her head. "I can't think of anyone to call to pick us up and give us a ride to my car. Uncle Charlie will already be in bed, Vince will still be out partying, and Owen would have a fit if I called Trixie this late. I guess we'll have to break a window." She led Frannie to the back of the house, took off her sweater coat, and draped it around the teen's shoulders.

"This is sure a funny-looking trellis." Frannie wrapped her hands around one of the wrought-iron rungs. They were covered with dead vines, but still appeared sturdy enough to support a person's weight.

"It was designed to act as a fire escape in an emergency," Skye explained. "During the summer, when the plants are all leafy and green, you can't tell it's a ladder."

"That's so cool."

Skye looked up at the second-story balcony. The waning crescent moon glinted off the glass panes of the French doors. She removed the flashlight from her backpack and tucked it into her cleavage. It might not be able to provide any illumination, but it was the perfect tool for knocking a hole in a window.

Putting her foot on the first rung of the trellis-cum-ladder, Skye said to Frannie, "Go back around to the front door. I'll let you in as soon as I get inside."

Once she reached the top, Skye hoisted a leg onto the balcony and took the flashlight from her décolleté. She advanced to the door and put her arm back to swing the makeshift club at the pane, but a faint mewing sound stopped her short. *Shoot.* She didn't want Bingo to get cut from flying shards.

Trying to scare him away, she tapped on the window, but he strolled nonchalantly to where the two doors met. He got on his back paws and stretched his front feet toward the knob. It was a lever-type handle that, if pressed either up or down, disengaged the lock.

Could she get Bingo to open the door? She grasped the handle to wiggle it, hoping the cat would bat it hard enough to unlock it, and nearly fell as the French door swung open. Had she forgotten to lock it? Another explanation was that Bingo had opened it sometime earlier. Either way, at least she didn't have to break any glass, but it was time to put dead bolts on those doors.

Skye pulled a pair of jeans over her tights, then ran down the stairs, tugging a sweatshirt on over her leotard. As soon as Skye pulled open the front door, Frannie burst over the threshold and headed toward the kitchen.

Skye followed her and watched as she peered into the refrigerator, complaining, "There's nothing in here to eat."

"Sorry. I haven't been to the grocery store in a while." Skye held out a couple of cans. "Tomato or chicken soup?"

Frannie made a face. "Anything else?"

Skye tried the freezer. "Frozen peas, a mystery casserole, and ice cream."

"We got a winner." Frannie grinned. "I'll take the ice cream."

"I thought you were cold."

"It's never too cold for ice cream."

Skye grabbed the container, pried off the lid, and scooped the contents into two bowls, marveling that the manufacturers actually thought a pint of ice cream held four servings. She added spoons and joined Frannie at the table.

"Phish Food. My favorite," Frannie said as she dug into the Ben & Jerry's. Through a mouthful of chocolate and marshmallow she asked, "So, who is this Kurt guy? Where were you all night? And why do you look like crap?"

Not taking offense—Skye was well aware she looked awful—she explained about the reporter, the haunted house, and her role as a witch. She omitted finding Annette dead. Wanting to change the subject, Skye asked, "Why didn't you and Justin go to the prom or the Promfest last year?" She knew that the teens hadn't been dating when Frannie was a junior, but they'd been a solid couple by her senior year.

"Money, mostly." Frannie dug out a chocolate fish from the ice cream and crunched it between her teeth. "It costs a fortune to go to the prom—at a minimum you need a dress and shoes, and your hair done."

Frannie had worked evenings and summers at the bowling alley's grill since it had opened, and had saved every penny she made for college.

"I'm sure your father would have been happy to pay for that stuff," Skye commented.

"Maybe, but you know Justin's folks didn't have the money for a tux, flowers, and a limo," Frannie pointed out.

It was only recently that Justin had been able to find work as a bagger at the local supermarket, and his parents didn't have any extra cash. Justin's dad was on disability, and his mother was too depressed by her husband's illness to cope with anything else.

"But Promfest is free, and a lot of kids who don't go to the prom go to that. I hear it's a lot of fun. Why didn't you two go?" Skye persisted.

"No Prom Bucks." Frannie finished her ice cream and put the dish in the sink. "What with his job, his work with the Vietnam vets, and taking care of the house, Dad didn't have time to volunteer." She came back to the table. "And can you see either of Justin's folks doing anything to earn him PBs?"

"Hmm, that's a flaw in Promfest that I hadn't thought about. We need to do something about it."

"Right." Frannie blew out an exasperated puff of air. "Like those ex–prom queens who run Promfest care about kids like us. They're happy we don't attend. Leaves more prizes and goodies for their precious offspring. Those bi— uh . . . witches are vicious. You should see the stuff they pull trying to get their sons and daughters elected king and queen."

"Like what?"

"They try to either bribe or blackmail us into voting for their kids, and if that doesn't work they go after our parents. Jobs have been lost and loans turned down."

"You're kidding." Skye was shocked.

"It would help if it was a secret ballot, instead of a show of hands."

Skye was silent. She'd had no idea. But now that she did, she'd make sure the upcoming vote was confidential.

"You watch, this year is going to be a bloodbath." Frannie shook her head. "Mrs. Paine will do anything to have Linnea crowned queen. And Mrs. Harrison feels the same way about getting Cheyenne the title."

"But why?"

"Why do people want Prada purses and Corvettes?" Frannie rolled her eyes. "They want everyone to envy them. Their self-image is at stake."

Hmm. Could that be the motive behind Annette's murder? Heck, it would fit as a motive to murder Nina Miles, as well. They both had daughters in the running for prom queen. There was something wrong with that logic, but Skye was too tired to figure out what. It was getting late. Time to ask the hard question.

"So, much as I miss you and am happy to see you, why are you here?"

"Because my father's going to kill me."

"Do I want to know why?" One advantage to Frannie's being out of high school was that Skye didn't have to worry about doing the right thing as Frannie's school psychologist. Instead, she could be the girl's friend.

"Probably not, but since I need you to tell Dad for me, you have no choice."

"What do you need me to tell him?" Warning bells were sounding in Skye's head. "And why can't you tell him yourself?"

"Because he won't yell at you, and by the time he sees me, he'll have calmed down."

"Your father is about the calmest man I know." Sometimes Skye wondered if Xavier had a pulse. If she hadn't seen him out in the sunlight, she would have sworn he was a vampire.

"That's the problem." Frannie leaned forward. "He never gets mad, so when he does, it's worse than if he did it all the time."

Skye could understand that—she hated dealing with people who stuffed all their emotions down deep inside them, then blew like Mount Saint Helens once they finally let go— but she still wasn't going be the one to tell Xavier Frannie's bad news.

"Your dad loves you more than life itself," Skye reassured Frannie. "It must be something pretty terrible if you think he'll go nuts."

She tried to imagine all the things an eighteen-year-old girl could say to her dad that would cause him to have a meltdown. Pregnancy? *Eek!* That would be bad in so many ways. What else? Had she wrecked the car? No, Frannie didn't have a vehicle at school. That left only one possibility.

"Tell me you're not quitting college," Skye pleaded. "You've only been there a month."

"But I hate it." Frannie's bottom lip quivered. "I don't have any friends, and the classes are a lot harder than high school. I've never gotten lower than an A-minus in my life, but I got a D on my first biology test."

"Give it time. Now that you realize it's harder, you'll study more and bring up that grade. And, once you find the right group, you'll make friends. Remember, it took you a while in high school, too." Skye scooted her chair closer to Frannie's. "Hey, I just thought of something. My sorority, Alpha Sigma Alpha, has a chapter at Loyola. Maybe you could go through rush and—"

"Get real," Frannie cut her off. "No sorority will invite me to pledge. Those peroxide monsters don't want someone my size in their house. I'm guessing you looked different in college than you do now."

"Yeah," Skye joked, "I looked about a hundred years younger." At Frannie's disappointed expression she quickly added, "Okay. Yes, I was thinner, but ASA isn't like that. We're more concerned about personality and values and a good fit with the other sisters."

Frannie grunted, then exhaled in a long whoosh of air. Her expression clearly stated that she thought Skye was hopelessly out of touch with reality.

"Really." Skye tried to convince the girl. "And I could put in a good word for you."

Frannie bit her lip. "It's not only the grades and the friends. . . ."

"Then what?"

"I miss it here. I hate the city. I thought I'd love it, but I'm scared all the time. We've been told not to even walk to the library by ourselves. Besides, I miss my dad and Justin and you."

"Oh. But your scholarship . . ." Skye wasn't sure how to respond. She wasn't all that fond of the city either, but she'd lived in one for more than a month before making that judgment. And if Frannie dropped out of Loyola, she'd be giving up a full ride. Could Xavier afford tuition somewhere else? "It's just that opportunities are never lost; someone will take the ones you miss."

Frannie shrugged.

Skye tried again. "I guess all I'm saying is, you might want to give it a little more time before you make such a big decision."

Frannie shrugged again, then said, "Could you just call my dad?"

CHAPTER 12

Got to Be There

It took forever to track down Xavier. It was nearly one o'clock in the morning before he arrived to pick up Frannie, and after two when the father and daughter finally drove off together. Then, before going to bed, Skye made the mistake of checking her answering machine.

The first message was from Wally, a terse, "There's still no word on why my father collapsed." A pause. "You need to check your cell. I keep getting a busy signal. Talk to you tomorrow."

Shoot! A busy signal? What was wrong with her cell phone?

The second call was from Vince. His voice sounded funny, but all he said was, "I need to talk to you. I'll stop by when I get done with work tomorrow."

Afterward, Skye lay in bed staring at the ceiling. She took turns picking at the various worries in her life as if they were scabs. First, there was Wally's father. Was he okay? How would Wally handle it if he wasn't?

Next, her thoughts turned to the murder. Was Annette really the target, and would Quirk be able to solve the case? What if the killer had really been after Skye or one of the other witches? Would he try again?

Then there was Frannie's decision to quit college. Would she truly drop out? Did she plan to go somewhere else? And if she didn't, would she end up working dead-end jobs for the rest of her life?

Last, there was Vince's mysterious message. What could be wrong with her brother?

It was nearly dawn before Skye fell asleep, and she didn't wake up until after one thirty in the afternoon. As she sipped a cup of Earl Grey tea, she turned the radio on to WSRE— the voice of Scumble River. Annette's mysterious death dominated the local news.

Shit! She wasn't surprised the information was out so quickly, but Kurt had better not have been the one to leak the story. Now the murderer knew the identity of his victim. If Annette hadn't been his intended target, his real quarry was now in danger.

Skye ate a handful of dry cereal. She really had to go to the grocery store. She'd better call Trixie to see if her friend could give her a ride to the old American Legion hall to pick up her car. But first she needed to talk to Wally.

While she got dressed, she punched in his number. It immediately went to voice mail, and she left a message for him to get in touch with her as soon as he could.

Next she dialed Trixie, whose first words were, "Why do I always miss all the excitement?"

"Yeah. Right." Skye snorted. "It's oh, so much fun wandering around a haunted house tripping over dead bodies."

Trixie ignored Skye's statement and peppered her with questions.

Skye finally managed to say, "Give me a ride to my car, and I'll tell you everything."

Once Skye explained why her car was at the American Legion hall, Trixie said, "I'll be right over."

Fifteen minutes later, Skye met Trixie in the driveway, and as she hopped into her friend's Civic, Trixie demanded, "Spill."

"You really had to be there." Skye buckled her seat belt.

"Last night was one of the worst, the longest, and the most bizarre nights of my life."

Clearly unsatisfied with Skye's answer, Trixie said, "That's the point. I wasn't there. So tell me already."

"I guess it all started when Justin told me about the ghosts."

"Oh, my God!" Trixie squealed. "This is even better than I thought."

Skye filled her friend in, concluding with, "Anyway, after the police let us go, guess who was waiting in the parking lot for me?"

"Simon."

"No. He had to go with the body. The new reporter in town, Kurt Michaels."

"Oh, he's a hunk. I hope you were nice to him."

Skye described their conversation and drive home. "Don't you think that was odd?"

"He's definitely hiding something. Maybe he's an FBI agent."

"Investigating what?" Skye snickered. "Illegal haunted houses?"

They both laughed.

Skye finished up with, "Oh, yeah. Frannie was waiting for me on my porch when I got home, *and* she's decided to quit college. And to add icing to the cake, there was a mysterious message from Vince on my answering machine. He said he needs to talk to me and is coming by after work."

"What do you think that's about?"

"My optimistic side hopes he's going to tell me he and Loretta are getting married."

Trixie frowned. "And your pessimistic side?"

"Hopes that whatever the problem is, it's something I can fix before Mom and Dad get home from Vegas."

Trixie was silent for a moment, then brought the conversation back to the murder. "Do you think Annette was the intended victim, or do you think it was supposed to be one of the three women everyone thought would be dressed as witches?"

"I don't know." Skye shrugged. "I can't imagine why anyone would want to kill me—other than a crazed parent."

"Could one of the parents you've worked with be that angry?"

Skye considered Mrs. Idell and nodded reluctantly. "I guess it's possible. I'm pretty sure a disgruntled parent slashed my tire."

After Skye explained about the note she had found on her car, Trixie said, "We need to find out if anyone had a reason to want either Hope Kennedy or Nina Miles dead."

"That's a good idea." Skye bit her lip. "I'll try to find out if Quirk is concentrating on Annette, or if he's looking into the other witches' enemies, as well. But he told me to stay out of it—"

"Men are like horoscopes," Trixie cut Skye off. "They always tell you what to do and are usually wrong."

Skye giggled, then completed her interrupted sentence. "So, I'm not sure how to get that information."

"You need to call Simon. With both your mom and Wally gone, he's your only contact at the police department."

"That's not a good idea."

"Why?"

"What if he thinks I'm trying to get back together with him?"

"Then maybe your reporter friend has dug something up. Call him."

"That's not a good idea either."

"Again, why?"

"Because I don't want him to get the wrong idea either." Skye felt her cheeks color, and quickly added, "Besides, he'd probably end up getting more info from me than I would from him."

"Then I guess it's you and me, Sherlock." Trixie stomped on the brake pedal, threw the little car into reverse, turned it around, and headed in the opposite direction. "Let's go talk to Nina and Hope."

No one was home at Hope Kennedy's house, so Trixie and Skye drove over to Nina Miles's. Nina lived in the expensive part of Scumble River, where each of the houses was situated on several acres of land. It was ironic that they all backed up to an old graveyard. The homeowners had fought long and hard to have the bodies moved, but had lost the battle. At the time, Skye had wondered why they had built their houses there to begin with, if they didn't like living next to a cemetery. It wasn't as if the tombstones had popped up overnight.

Trixie parked in the circular driveway, and she and Skye climbed up the steps leading to the impressive double doors. The house had an ultramodern design with lots of angles, and as Skye rang the bell she craned her neck at the window that jutted overhead.

When Bree answered the door, she asked, "Ms. Frayne, what are you doing here? Did I miss a cheerleading practice?"

As well as being the school librarian and cosponsor of the student newsletter, Trixie was also the cheerleading coach.

"No, Bree." Trixie shook her head. "We need to talk to your mom about something."

The girl looked apprehensive. "Am I in trouble?"

"Not at all," Skye reassured the teenager. "Is your mom home?"

"Yes, she's watching TV."

"May we talk to her?" Trixie asked.

"Sure, come on in."

Bree pointed them down a hallway and disappeared. As Skye and Trixie rounded the corner, Skye could see Nina sitting on a couch in the family room.

Nina tried to gather up the used tissues surrounding her when she spotted Skye and Trixie, saying, "Please excuse the mess; I can't seem to shake this bug."

"Don't worry about it." Skye waved away the woman's

apology. "We're sorry to bother you when you're not feeling well, but we have something important to discuss with you."

"Of course, please have a seat." Nina motioned to the overstuffed chairs facing the sofa.

Skye wasn't sure how to start, but Trixie said, "We're here about Annette Paine's murder."

"Murder?" Nina coughed. "I thought the police didn't know how she died yet."

"From what I saw, I'm pretty sure it was murder." Skye said.

"What did you see?" Nina demanded.

"Sorry, I can't say," Skye answered. "But I'm not sure she was the intended victim."

"Why?" Nina sneezed and blew her nose.

"Well, you know she had on your costume?"

"Yes."

"So, whoever killed her could have thought he was killing you, or Hope, or me."

"I hadn't thought about that." Nina frowned.

"Can you think of anyone who would want to kill you?" Skye asked. "Does someone gain a lot of money if you die, or does anyone hold you responsible for something that happened to them?"

"No." Nina shook her head. "I'm a stay-at-home mom. No money of my own. And I can't believe anyone would hate me that much."

The three women were silent until Trixie asked, "Did you know Annette very well?"

"We hung around in the same circles, but we weren't friends." Nina grimaced. "Queen bees don't have friends, just minions."

Skye leaned forward. "Can you think of anyone who would want to kill Annette?"

"Anyone who ever had to be on a committee with her, or deal with her for any reason." Nina shrugged. "She treated everyone equally badly."

After a few more minutes of chitchat, Skye and Trixie excused themselves. It was nearly four o'clock, and Skye needed to retrieve her car and get home before Vince arrived.

Skye had just pulled into her driveway when Vince's black Jeep threw up a plume of gravel and skidded to a stop next to her car. Vince was four years older than Skye, but his golden good looks and carefree attitude usually made him seem like the younger sibling. However, today every one of his thirty-eight years showed on his face. His butterscotch blond hair was matted as if it hadn't been combed since the previous day, and his emerald green eyes were bloodshot.

Skye got out of the Bel Air and walked over to Vince as he exited his vehicle. She pulled him down to kiss his unshaved cheek—he was a good six inches taller than her five-foot-seven height. "That must have been quite a party last night," she teased.

"No party."

Skye's stomach clenched. What in the world was wrong with Vince, the ultimate good-time guy? "Did your band have a gig?" By day Vince owned and operated Great Expectations hair salon; by night he was the drummer for a popular local rock group.

He shook his head. "We haven't been taking as many bookings lately."

"Why?" Skye tugged her brother up the front steps, through the door, and into her kitchen.

"The guys are all getting older. They want to spend more time with their wives and girlfriends."

"Oh." Skye was shocked. She'd gotten to know the members of Vince's band pretty well a while back, when their lead singer had been murdered, and they had not struck her as stay-at-home family men. "Uh, so, you want something to drink?"

Like Skye, Vince was not much of a drinker, but today he rummaged under her sink and grabbed a bottle of tequila that had been left over from a party last fall. "Got any lime?"

Skye nodded. She liked lime with her Diet Coke, and still

had a couple in the crisper drawer, although they were past their prime. As she sliced one, Vince got down a pair of shot glasses from the cupboard over the stove, blew the dust out of them, and sat at the table.

Skye joined him, putting the bowl of lime quarters in front of him. He poured the liquor into the glasses and pushed one over to Skye. Vince squeezed lime juice onto the side of his hand, added salt from the shaker on the table, and licked, then downed the entire contents of the shot glass in one gulp.

Skye tried to frame the right question, but Vince broke the silence first, saying in a raw, hurt voice, "Loretta dumped me last night."

"What?" It was the last thing Skye had expected to hear. She wouldn't have been surprised if Vince had been the dumper, but her handsome brother was rarely, if ever, the dumpee.

"She said we just aren't right for each other. We have different goals, different dreams."

"Maybe she meant you aren't serious. Are you? Serious, I mean, about her?"

He poured another shot and stared at the golden liquid before answering, "Maybe."

"Did you tell her that?"

"Not exactly."

"What exactly did you tell her?" Skye knew Vince was fairly verbal for a guy, but he was still a guy. "What is the basis of your relationship with her?"

He shrugged. "We didn't talk about that."

"Do you want to have a serious, maybe-leading-to-marriage, relationship with Loretta?"

Vince half nodded, then shook his head. "It's no use. What she really meant was that she's an important criminal attorney and I do hair for a living. Her family is rich and powerful, and ours is blue-collar. The only place we have any influence is in a town of three thousand people."

"Loretta's not like that."

"I knew you'd take her side."

"I'm not taking her side, but she is my friend and I know what she's like." Skye put her hand over Vince's, stopping him from taking another drink. "But you're my brother. I'll always be on your side."

"Well, she's made up her mind." Despair and anger were mixed in his voice. "And there's nothing I can do about it." He slumped back in his chair.

Skye wondered if she should try to speak to Loretta. Probably not. At least, not if she wanted to keep their friendship intact. Still, maybe just a friendly call to say hi might be in order.

Vince threw back another shot of tequila, wiped his mouth, and said, "Let's talk about something else."

"Okay." Skye moved the liquor bottle out of her brother's reach. "But no more of this."

"So." Vince tipped his chair so he was balanced on the two back legs. "What's this I hear about you and Wally breaking up?"

CHAPTER 13

These Are the Times

"What?" Without thinking, Skye picked up the glass in front of her and downed the contents. The straight tequila burned like liquid fire. Choking, she gasped, "Where . . . did . . . you . . . hear . . . that?"

"All the Saturday regulars were talking about it today." Vince dropped his chair back down on all four legs, stretched across the table, grabbed the bottle of booze, and poured himself and Skye another shot.

Vince's regulars were the ladies that still got their hair "done" every week. Most wore styles that had been all the rage in the fifties and sixties, when poodle cuts, beehives, and the ever-popular bouffant were considered cutting-edge. Colors ranged from pure white to ash blond, with the occasional blue rinse for extra-special occasions. These women were the Internet of Scumble River. They had invented a form of instant messaging long before Skye and Vince were born.

"You'd think they'd be talking about Annette Paine's murder, not me," Skye snapped once she stopped coughing.

"They had plenty of time for both." Vince smirked. "Besides, they find you more interesting than a dead body."

"Great."

"The radio didn't say it was murder. How do you know so much?" Vince demanded.

Skye explained her involvement, then asked, "What did your regulars say about Wally and me?" Could Wally have broken up with her behind her back? How would he do that? Did he take out an ad in the *Laurel Herald News*? He couldn't have put it in the *Scumble River Star*—the local paper came out only on Wednesdays.

"When Sally stopped by the police station yesterday to bring her son, Anthony, his supper, Thea told her that Wally up and left town last night without giving them any warning. She also informed Sally that Quirk claims he is under orders not to tell anyone where the chief was going or why he left or how long he'd be gone."

Skye felt her heart start again. "I know where Wally is and why he's there. And I certainly understand his desire not to have the whole town know his business. Just because he had to go out of town doesn't mean we broke up. How do people come up with this stuff?"

"Search me." Vince twitched his shoulders. "But Masie, the waitress at the diner out on the interstate—you know, the place with the homemade pies—blabbed to Hilda this morning while they were both waiting for their prescriptions to be filled at Bate's Pharmacy that late last night when she was coming home from work, she saw *you* parked on the side of the road with that new reporter from the *Star.*"

"It wasn't that late," Skye protested. "After the police let us all go, he drove me home. He stopped the car to ask me a few questions, hoping to get a story for the paper. We were there all of two minutes. Nothing happened."

"Hey." Vince put his hands up. "I believe you. I'm only warning you what's going around town."

"Thank God Mom is in Vegas."

"Like no one called her." Vince grinned. "You can be sure one of her friends—Hester or Maggie or Aunt Kitty, or maybe all three—has let her know about it by now."

If that were true, Skye could only hope May was on a

winning streak at the slot mchines, or her mother would be on the next flight home. In any case, she vowed to screen her calls. She was not talking to her mother until Wally was back home and the rumors had died down.

"You haven't heard the best part yet." Vince's good humor appeared to have returned.

Skye cringed. Nothing like seeing his sister in trouble to cheer up her brother. "What?"

"Miss Letitia said that while she was at the podiatrist's office this morning to get her toenails trimmed—she has that awful fungus—Priscilla Van Horn, who was there for her bunions, told Miss Letitia that Wally was seeing Annette Paine on the sly. Priscilla said she heard that Annette told you about the affair and you threatened to leave Wally. So Wally killed Annette for ruining his life. Then he left town to avoid being arrested, and you were so distraught that you spent the night with Kurt Michaels."

"Good Lord! These women should be writing for the tabloids."

"Yeah. But you did dump Simon, and before the sofa cushion had cooled off, you took up with Wally."

"Shit! Shit! *Shit!*" Skye closed her eyes. Just when you thought there was nothing else in your life that could crash and burn, the ashes of your previous disasters caught fire and burst into flame.

"Yes. You are in deep doo-doo."

"This is so unfair," Skye whined. "How many women have you inked in, then a few weeks later crossed out of your little black book? And no one talks about you like this."

"Hey, it's not my fault there's a different set of rules for men and women in small towns like Scumble River." Vince shrugged. "Get over it. You need to do something about these rumors ASAP."

"What am I supposed to do? Hold a press conference?"

"Not altogether a bad idea." Vince snickered, then turned serious. "You know, you could talk to some of the media about the murder and get out your side of the story."

"No." She pressed her fingers against her temples. "People who get in bed with the media usually get screwed."

"But you need to nip the rumors in the bud before Mom and Dad get home."

"I agree completely. But there has to be a better way to do it than trying to manipulate the press." Skye thought a moment, then asked, "Who's the reigning queen of gossip with Mom gone?"

A second later they both said, "Aunt Minnie."

Skye asked, "Do you have any plans for supper?"

Vince shook his head, taking her non sequitur in stride.

"Are you hungry?"

"Starving." Vince made a pitiful face. "With Mom out of town, there's no one to bring me lunch."

Skye bit her tongue. This wasn't the time to remind him that a thirty-eight-year-old man should be able to make a sandwich, stick it in a brown paper bag, and bring it with him to work.

"Okay, then here's the plan." Skye got up. "We'll go get something to eat at the Feed Bag—I'm driving, since you've had so much to drink. Afterward we'll drop by Aunt Minnie's and give her the real scoop."

"Which means two minutes after we leave her house, all of Scumble River will know."

"Exactly."

"Are you going to let her in on why Wally's out of town?" Vince asked.

"I probably shouldn't if he told Quirk not to tell."

"Wouldn't he be more concerned about stopping all the talk than keeping his privacy?"

"You'd think so, wouldn't you? And I'm sure he had no idea that by keeping his destination and reason for leaving a secret, he was, in fact, fueling the gossip he was trying to avoid." Skye bit her lip. "Still, maybe I'd better check with Wally before I visit Aunt Minnie."

"That sounds like the smart thing to do." Vince eyed her thoughtfully. "Can you call him?"

"I'll try his cell again, but I already left him a message to call me ASAP, and if he's in the hospital he probably has his phone switched off."

"He's in the hospital?" Vince sounded shocked.

"It's a long story, and you can't tell anyone, but . . ." Skye filled Vince in on her Friday, starting with Wally's call.

"Is the Promfest committee still putting on the haunted house?" Vince asked when she finished.

"Not this weekend. There was a message on my answering machine from Evie Harrison when I got up this morning. The police haven't released the scene yet, but they told the committee that A Ghoul's Night Out can reopen by next Friday."

"Are you going back?"

"I don't want to." Skye's voice was unsteady. "I'll have to think about it." Vince shot her a concerned look, but she changed the subject, telling him about Frannie's bombshell, and ending with, "Not one of my best nights."

"Nope." Vince's expression had returned morose. "Sounds as if neither one of us should have gotten out of bed yesterday."

"Probably not." Skye gazed out the window. "Maybe not today either."

After Skye and Vince ate at the Feed Bag, she drove a sobered-up Vince back to his car, dropped him off, and considered her next move. She hadn't been able to get hold of Wally—as she had predicted, his cell was switched off. She'd left another voice mail, but he hadn't gotten back to her yet, so the visit to Aunt Minnie's had to be postponed.

Kurt hadn't phoned, and neither had Simon. She was both relieved and annoyed. She didn't want to lead Simon on, or slip and give Kurt more information, but lacking the two men's input, she had no idea what was going on in the murder investigation.

Hmm. Who else could tell her what she needed to know? Skye checked her watch. It was close to seven. Given that in the chief's absence Quirk was in charge, he would have taken the day shift, which ended at three. So, who would be working afternoons? With any luck, Anthony would be on duty, but even if it were one of the other part-timers, she might be able to get the lowdown. And if all else failed, there was always the dispatcher, who often knew more than all the officers combined.

With that plan in mind, she headed to the police station. It was housed in the same redbrick building that also contained the city hall and town library. During the weekday, the parking lot was often crowded, but on a Saturday night Skye had her choice of spots. She pulled the Bel Air in between a purple Gremlin and a white Ford Focus. It didn't bode well that neither vehicle looked familiar.

When Skye pushed open the glass door, a series of chimes announced her arrival. She waved at the dispatcher, who sat at a desk to Skye's right; a shoulder-height counter with bulletproof glass reaching to the ceiling separated the woman from the reception area.

May's friend Thea and cousin Char were the only dispatchers Skye knew well. Thea generally worked days with Wally, May worked afternoons with Quirk, and Char worked midnights.

Recently two weekend dispatchers, Silvia and Betty, had been hired to work twelve-hour shifts on Saturday and Sunday. Skye was pretty sure the one on duty tonight was Silvia, but they both were medium height and weight, with short brown hair and glasses.

Skye knocked on the glass, and Silvia—or maybe it was Betty—nodded, and buzzed her through the security door at the end of the counter.

Once inside, Skye poked her head around the corner and said, "Hi. Who's on?"

"McCabe." The dispatcher made a face, but didn't turn her head. She was expected to type data into the computer, monitor the radios, and answer the phones simultaneously.

That explained the purple Gremlin. It was a car only Otto

McCabe, an inept county deputy who moonlighted in Scumble River when no one else was available, would drive and/or think was cool. Quirk would have been the worst on-duty officer to run into, but McCabe was a close second.

"Is he out patrolling?"

"Yeah. He's making the circuit. He should be back before long."

The circuit was from one end of Basin Street to the other, and was patrolled mainly to keep an eye on the numerous bars that were scattered down its length.

"Mind if I wait?" Skye didn't like McCabe, but he was dumb enough to let something slip if she needled him.

"Make yourself at home."

As Skye stepped into the dispatcher's tiny cubicle, she could make out the nameplate pinned to her uniform. It said, SILVIA; Skye had been right. "Anything interesting happening out there?"

"Nope." Silvia continued to focus on the computer monitor. "Been pretty quiet, not like last night."

"Yeah." That was the opening Skye was looking for. "Phew. Last night was way too exciting."

"You were there, right? You found the vic?"

"Yep."

"That must have been scary, being in a haunted house and stumbling across a dead body."

"I was terrified." Skye slid a glance at the woman behind the desk, but she was still busy checking data on the screen. "Have they gotten any leads yet?"

"When I took over from Char this morning, she said Quirk had Dr. Paine in the interrogation room all night, but let him go around six."

"I wonder if Quirk found out anything."

"I doubt it." Silvia shrugged. "He was like a bear with a pinecone up his ass."

Skye blinked, trying to get that picture out of her head, and before she could ask any more questions she spotted Otto McCabe as he strolled through the garage entrance into the station's coffee/interrogation room. It seemed strange to see him in the navy Scumble River police uniform rather than the tan Stanley County one.

"There's McCabe." Skye quickly rose from her chair. "I'd better catch him before he goes out again. See you later, Silvia."

McCabe stood in front of the soft-drink machine. He repeatedly stabbed the Jolt button with his index finger, but no can of soda fell down the chute and into the slot.

Skye sidled up behind him and said, "That stuff will kill you."

McCabe twisted around, his hand on the gun on his hip. He bore an unfortunate resemblance to Barney Fife from the old *Andy Griffith Show*, and Skye wondered whether he, like Barney, was allowed to have only a single bullet; and if so, did he keep it in his shirt pocket as the TV character had?

Once McCabe saw Skye, he scowled. "You got no business sneaking up on an armed man like that. I could have shot you dead."

"Sorry." Skye put up her hands. "I had no idea you were so jumpy. Maybe you should lay off the caffeine."

"I'm not jumpy. I'm alert." McCabe hitched up his pants and bristled. "You gotta be on your toes at all times in this job. You can't let the perps get the drop on you."

Skye restrained herself from pointing out that on a Saturday night in Scumble River the only "perps" McCabe was likely to run into would be drunks. And they'd be out on the roads causing accidents, not in the PD's coffee room.

McCabe waited a few seconds for her to speak, and when she didn't, he tugged at the collar of his uniform shirt. "What are you doing here, anyway?"

"I stopped by to pick up some papers that the chief wanted me to look over." Skye crossed her fingers. "You did hear that the police department hired me as their psychological consultant, didn't you?"

"Sure I did. Nothing gets past me. I got my ear to the

ground and my eye on the prize." He puffed out his chest and thrust his head forward. "You working the murder?"

"Yes." She was working on the case, just not officially—yet. She would be as soon as she talked to Wally. "I was tied up today with some family business, so I didn't get a chance to discuss things with Officer Quirk. Did he brief you when you came on duty?"

"Sure. Me and Roy go way back."

"And?" Skye asked, trying to sound nonchalant.

"It's a mess. With all the costumes and people running around in the dark, no one has an alibi."

Skye couldn't believe her luck. "Yeah." McCabe was spilling everything. "That's a problem. Any idea of a motive for the killing?"

"Nah." McCabe gave up on the soda machine and poured himself a cup of coffee instead. "No one seemed to like the vic, but no one seemed to hate her enough to kill her either." He leaned a skinny hip against the counter. "That's something you'd probably work on, right?"

"Right." Skye wondered if Quirk knew about the battle for the Promfest leadership, not to mention the battle for whose daughter would be crowned prom queen. She doubted he read Kurt Michaels's gossip column. "Did Roy say whether Evie Harrison was questioned?"

"Harrison . . . Harrison. I don't rightly remember, but the name sounds familiar."

"Well, concentrate." Skye stepped closer. "Didn't you take notes?"

"Hey." McCabe's expression turned suspicious. "If you're the psychological consultant, why are you asking me? Why don't you look at the file?"

Skye backed off. "I wanted to save some time." *Shoot.* He was smarter than he looked.

"Where's the gall-darn fire?" He took a sip of coffee. "The body's not going nowhere."

Skye's voice was knife-edged. "Even *you* must know that

the more time goes by, the less likely the case is to be solved."

"Don't be lecturing me, missy." McCabe took off his hat and hit the side of his leg with it. "I'm a professional peace officer."

"It sure doesn't look that way." Skye shook her head. "Maybe if the chief knew that you are unaware that time is of the essence in a murder investigation, you would no longer be working for the Scumble River PD. Heck, maybe the new sheriff might be interested as well."

McCabe's Adam's apple bobbed like a rowboat on Lake Michigan. "Now, Skye, you wouldn't tell him that, would you?" His tone had swung from pompous to pleading.

"Well . . ." Skye realized she had the deputy over a barrel. "No, not if you can remember what you heard about Evie Harrison."

"Right. No need to bother the chief . . . or the sheriff." McCabe backed toward the exit. "I'm sure when you and Wally are together, you have better things to do than talk about me."

Skye raised an eyebrow, but let that comment pass. "So, then, what's the scoop on Evie?"

"They found her in her car." McCabe put his hand on the doorknob. "She was drunker than a skunk and says she doesn't remember anything after putting on her costume and taking her position at the haunted house."

"Did they give her a Breathalyzer or test her blood?"

"She wouldn't blow into the Breathalyzer." McCabe opened the door. "And the law says we can't force her. If she was operating a moving vehicle, she could lose her license for refusing, but since she wasn't, there was nothing we could do. You need a court order for a blood test."

"Does Quirk believe her?"

McCabe nodded.

"Okay, one more question."

McCabe froze. "What?"

"Is Quirk considering the fact that Annette Paine might not have been the intended victim?"

"Nope." McCabe had nearly disappeared into the garage; only his pointy nose was still in the coffee room.

"So Quirk is sure the murderer meant to kill Annette?" Skye probed.

"She's the vic, and it's her murder he's investigating." McCabe slammed the door, after muttering, "I can't spend all night here jawing with you. I gotta get back on the road."

A few seconds later Skye heard the squad car's engine roar to life and its tires squeal as McCabe tore out of the garage. Lost in thought, Skye walked over to the soda machine and whacked it above the coin return with the heel of her hand. A can of Jolt fell into the dispenser. She scooped out the high-voltage cola, popped the top, and took a long swallow. She felt an instant caffeine surge, and her nervous system went on red alert, but she shrugged. What the heck, she wouldn't be able to sleep tonight anyway.

If Quirk is only concentrating on investigating people who might want to kill Annette, and she wasn't the intended victim, there's a one-in-three chance that the next dead body to turn up might be mine.

CHAPTER 14

Stand by Me

"Hello?" Skye squinted at the clock radio. It was six a.m. She'd been asleep for only three hours, having, as she predicted, tossed and turned for most of the night. Who could be calling her at this ungodly hour? *Shoot!* She should have let the machine pick up. What if her mother had decided to nag her long-distance?

"Hi, sugar. Sorry to wake you, but I wanted to make sure to catch you at home." Wally's silky voice smoothed over her like expensive body lotion. "I got your messages too late to call you back yesterday. Is everything okay?"

"I'm glad you called. I miss you." Skye ignored Wally's question. She'd tell him all about the murder and the rumors in a minute, but first she wanted to shake off her sleep-deprived fog and focus. "How's your dad?"

"He seems to be doing fine," Wally answered. "In fact, he's trying to talk the doctors into letting him out of the hospital."

"It's wonderful that he's feeling that much better. Does that mean you're coming home soon?"

"I'm not sure. I wish I were, but things are still up in the air here. Dad wants me to stay. And the doctors can't figure out why he collapsed in the first place."

"Oh." Skye was surprised by the depth of her disappointment. "Could it have been exhaustion? Your father struck me as someone who would work twenty-four/seven if he could."

"That's one of the things they're considering, but they want to run more tests. At this point, it's a process of elimination."

"Well, it's good that they're being thorough." Skye adjusted the pillows behind her back so she could sit up more comfortably. "That way when they say he's all right, you'll know they're sure and you won't have to worry that they missed something."

"Right." Wally's voice was oddly gentle. "How did you make out with the haunted house? Did you overcome your fear or has it been as terrible as you expected?"

"Haven't you talked to Roy?"

"No. He's next on my list." Wally sounded concerned. "What happened? Did some of the kids get out of hand?"

"I wish." Skye blew out a long breath. "Annette Paine was murdered."

"What!" Wally bellowed. "Son of a B. Why didn't Quirk call me?"

Should she tell Wally her theory behind Quirk's silence? No. She didn't want to sound whiny. "He probably didn't want to bother you."

"Why do I think that's not his entire motive?" Wally asked. "So, tell me, from the beginning, what's happened in the thirty-six hours I've been gone."

Skye launched into a detailed explanation, ending with, "I talked to Otto McCabe last night, and—"

Wally broke in, "Don't tell me Quirk called in McCabe to work."

"Oops." Skye hadn't realized that McCabe was on Wally's "Do Not Call" list. Now when Wally talked to Quirk, it would seem as if Skye were a tattletale. "Uh, could you pretend you don't know that? I don't think Quirk likes me too much to begin with, and his thinking I've been snitching to his boss isn't going to help matters." Skye bit her lip. "In fact, you need to pretend you haven't heard about the murder."

"No." Wally's voice was firm. "We're not playing that game. If Quirk has an issue with you, we'll deal with it. He needs to understand I hired you as the psych consultant because of your skill as an investigator, not because of your skill in bed—although that's outstanding, too."

"Wally!" Skye felt her cheeks flush.

"Just the facts, ma'am," he said with a trace of laughter, then turned serious. "But back to my point. If Quirk resents you, the three of us will take care of that when I get back, but that doesn't give him the right to try to make an end run around either of us."

Skye was silent, not sure what to say. Although she was thrilled by Wally's fierce loyalty, she didn't want to be the reason he and his best officer argued.

Wally seemed to read her mind. "Whatever happens, none of it is your fault."

"Thank you." Skye snuggled under her blanket, pretending it was Wally who was keeping her warm. "My Catholic guilt gets out of hand once in a while."

"Once in a while?" Wally chuckled. "Anyway, what were you saying about McCabe?"

"Oh, yeah." Skye gathered her thoughts. "As I mentioned, Annette was dressed as one of the trio of witches, though she was supposed to be the Bride of Frankenstein. So I think it's reasonable to question whether she was the intended victim or not, but McCabe claims that Quirk isn't looking in that direction."

"Hmm." Wally paused. "You said that once everyone was in costume, all three of the witches looked exactly alike?"

"Yes."

"Do you wear masks?"

"No, but the makeup includes a fake nose and chin," Skye explained. "The resemblance is so uncanny, I don't think our own mothers could tell us apart. Which is why I was so freaked out when I found the body. For a nanosecond I thought I was looking into a mirror."

"Shoot. That must have been downright creepy." Wally's voice held a hint of a Texas twang. "I sure wish I could be there with you, sugar."

"Me, too." Skye felt slightly alarmed. She had never heard any trace of a Texas accent in Wally's voice before. She hoped he wasn't getting too used to being back in his home state.

"Unless there's something you don't know—which could be the case, since it doesn't sound as if Quirk is sharing information with you—Roy may very well be going down the wrong road."

"Yes. And it could be a detour that gets someone else killed—maybe me." Skye's voice quavered.

"Can you think of anyone who would want you dead? How about that parent? The one you think left you the note and slashed your tire?"

"I guess. But she'd have to be really crazy, because I don't have that kind of power—the principal or superintendent can overrule any of my recommendations."

"Then if it's not Annette, it's probably one of the other two women," Wally soothed. "But when I talk to Quirk, I'll mention that you received a threatening note a couple of weeks ago." Wally's tone became authoritative. "He *will* look into the other possible victims. And he *will* include you in the investigation."

"That would be wonderful." Skye hoped Wally was able to control Quirk even thousands of miles away, but she had her doubts. "It would be a relief to know he was at least bearing in mind other possibilities."

"Consider it done."

"Great." She was sure it wouldn't be as easy as that, but she changed the subject. "Are you spending all your time at the hospital?"

"Pretty much," Wally grumbled. "It's so frustrating trying to get answers. The doctors say Dad seems fit as a fiddle. All the tests so far have come back negative, and they're running out of stuff to do."

Out of the blue, a thought popped into Skye's mind. Could Carson Boyd have faked his collapse? When she had met him last spring, he had been determined to get Wally to go back to Texas and take over the family business, even if it meant deceiving his own son. Could his illness be part of a scheme to lure Wally home? But what would that accomplish? She pushed the thought aside and said, "I'm sure your father appreciates your being there."

"I suppose."

"Last March you mentioned that your cousin is your dad's second in command at CB International. Did you two grow up together? Are you close?"

"He's ten years younger than I am, so not really," Wally answered without elaborating, then asked, "Any other excitement in town since I've been gone?"

"Frannie is quitting college, and Loretta dumped Vince."

"So, a typical Scumble River weekend."

"Very funny." Skye rolled her eyes. "You should do stand-up."

Wally sniggered. "Maybe I'll give it a try sometime."

"Sure. Next time the Brown Bag has open-mike night, right?"

"Right." Wally took a deep breath. "Guess I'd better let you go so you can get ready for church."

"Yep. It's about that time." It was already seven. If she was going to get a seat at the eight-o'clock Mass, she did need to get going, but she didn't want to hang up. "Call me tonight?"

"Definitely. Around ten?"

"Perfect."

There was a pause, and when he spoke again his voice was gentle. "Be careful. I couldn't stand it if anything happened to you."

"I will." Skye hung up slowly, hating to break their connection. Once the receiver went dead she whispered, "You be careful, too. I have a bad feeling your father is getting ready to rope and tie you like a calf at a rodeo."

Skye kept the feeling of warmth and caring she had gotten from her conversation with Wally wrapped around herself as she showered and dressed for church, but as soon as she arrived it evaporated.

She usually managed to nab a seat in the back, preferring to be one of the observers rather than one of the observed, but in order to do that she had to get there at least twenty minutes early. Wally's call had put her behind schedule, which meant she had to walk the entire length of the aisle to the very front. She could feel the congregation's eyes following her every step, like a herd of hungry cows watching the bale of hay being put in their feed trough.

In Scumble River, people attended church for different reasons—some to worship God, others to exchange the latest gossip. Skye was sure the latter group's focus today was the haunted-house murder.

Her relief at sliding into a pew was short-lived when she saw that her seatmates were Dylan Paine and his daughter, Linnea. Skye leaned toward them and whispered how sorry she was for their loss. Dr. Paine nodded, keeping his expression neutral, but Linnea burst into tears. Skye patted the girl's hand and made comforting sounds. As they stood for the processional, Dr. Paine put his arm around his daughter and handed her a handkerchief. Skye was reminded that Annette may have been an annoyance to some people, but her daughter was certainly grieving for her.

As always, Mass was both soothing and uplifting, and Skye felt herself unwind. Father Burns achieved a perfect balance between demonstrating concern for Annette and her family, and exuding confidence that good would triumph over evil.

Clearly he knew of his flock's tendency to spread stories, because he ended the service with a gentle admonishment: "Let us all pray; Lord, please keep your arm around my shoulder to keep me safe, and your hand over my mouth to keep me compassionate."

As the recessional played and Skye made her way down the aisle, she noticed that Dr. Paine and his daughter were stopped time after time, by people shaking his hand and hugging Linnea.

Sadly, Father Burns's reprimand had little effect. Once Annette's family departed, the rumor mill revved up, and Skye overheard several groups of people at the rear of the church swapping theories about the murder.

They were all so busy getting their own opinions across, no one seemed to notice Skye, and she was able to slip behind them. She hoped that they might give her a lead, so she pretended to read the bulletin board on the back wall. Using only her peripheral vision, she kept her face averted, but her ears tuned in to what was being said.

A man dressed in a shiny polyester suit and cowboy boots stated, "Junior told me that the haunted house was black as the inside of a bull, and no one was where they were supposed to be, so anyone could've killed her."

A grandmotherly-looking woman sighed. "But who would want to kill a pretty girl like that?"

Girl? Skye rolled her eyes. Annette hadn't been a girl since Ronald Reagan was president.

The woman standing next to the polyester cowboy patted her hair, which was teased and sprayed into the shape of a helmet. "Pretty is as pretty does," she interjected. "Annette liked to get her own way and could be real nasty if things weren't going how she wanted them to."

"I think it's terrorists," the man in the boots replied. "Wally should call in Homeland Security. Those Mooselimbs hate American women."

Skye blinked. It sounded as if he thought Bullwinkle, armed with a tree branch, had killed Annette.

Helmet Hair poked him in the side with her elbow. "You think everything is terrorists, Burt. Every time the chickens don't lay as many eggs as you figure they should, you want to call the FBI."

"Thelma's right, Burt." A man with slicked-back hair and a mean mouth said. "Why would terrorists kill an over-the-hill prom queen?"

"Yeah." Thelma stuck out her chin. "Besides, everyone knows it was her husband."

"What in tarnation are you talking about? Why would Dr. Paine kill his wife?" Burt shot Thelma a dirty look. "Did she disagree with everything he said and try to make him look like a fool?"

"Because Annette caught him messing around. I heard she threatened to divorce him and take half of everything," Thelma answered with a malicious look in her porcine eyes. "And while he may want to trade his forty-year-old wife for two twenties, he doesn't want to trade his fancy lifestyle for the one he'd get after she took him to the cleaner's."

"That would do it." The grandmotherly woman nodded. "Guys like that want their first wives to just disappear. They act like she had nothing to do with their success, and they don't care if their kids have to eat cereal three meals a day, as long as the men don't have to skip a golf game or give up their plasma TVs."

Burt protested: "If Dr. Paine is such a sleaze, how come everyone keeps him as their dentist?"

"It's like that joke: What do you call a male slut?" Thelma paused, then said, "A man." She cackled at her own witticism. "If he was a woman and behaved that way, no one would go to him, but a man can screw his brains out and no one cares." She shrugged. "Besides, he's a great dentist."

Voices rose as everyone in the group offered an opinion and Skye slunk away. The info about Dr. Paine had been enlightening, but she was fairly sure she had heard everything these four had to say. Maybe some other group would have more information she could use.

Skye walked down the steps and out the double doors. Another knot of people had gathered on the front lawn. She stopped near them, half-hidden by a large evergreen, and pretended to use her cell phone.

The three thirty-something women were talking about Evie Harrison, and Skye's ears perked up. The leader of the trio was Andrea Pantaleone, a tall, lean brunette whom Skye had met a year and a half ago during the Route 66 hundred-mile yard sale. Andrea had been the health inspector assigned to the event, and Skye had found her both observant and intelligent. It would be interesting to hear what she had to say.

"It's a shame about Annette Paine." Andrea shook her head. "I didn't like her, but I hate to see anyone that young die."

The other two women nodded.

"I don't know why everyone is acting so surprised to hear that Evie drinks." Andrea folded her arms. "She's done it since high school."

"It's one of those nonsecret secrets," a shorter, slightly thinner woman stated. "Everyone knows, but no one says anything. Now it's out in the open." She turned to the third woman and demanded, "Isn't that right, Kay Lynn?"

"That's because no one wants to hurt her husband. He's so distinguished." Kay Lynn *tsk*ed. "And with him being a minister, it's hard on him, having a drunk for a wife."

"I wonder if Evie killed Annette and then blacked out." Andrea asked the middle woman. "Laurie, didn't you tell me that she was really ticked off about the whole head-of-Promfest thing?"

"Yes," Laurie agreed. "She was really mad at Annette about that, but then she just let it go and even agreed to be Annette's assistant. I think Annette had something on her and threatened to tell."

"You're probably right," Andrea concurred. "And I bet Evie stayed on the committee to keep Cheyenne in the running for prom queen. If you're not one of the Promfest movers and shakers, no way will your daughter be elected."

Kay Lynn nodded, and Skye decided it was time to leave.

If she stuck around much longer, someone was sure to notice and start grilling her about finding the body.

Because she had been so late getting to Mass, Skye'd had to park across the street. She stood at the corner, waiting for a break in the stream of cars pouring out of the lot. Finally an older sedan paused. The sun visor was down and a scarf obscured the lower half of the driver's face. All Skye could see was a hand motioning for her to go.

Waving back, Skye stepped off the curb. While she walked, she dug her hand into her purse, feeling for her key ring. As she pulled it out of her bag, she glanced downward to separate the car key from the others on the ring. Immediately she heard an engine rev, and when she looked up, a chrome grille was roaring toward her. She stood frozen. A nanosecond later she flew into the air, sailed across the asphalt, and landed on the side of the road.

CHAPTER 15

Show Me the Meaning

"I'm fine, really." Skye got up, brushed the dry leaves and dirt from her shins, and looked herself over. Her clothing had survived her fall better than she had. Her hands and her knees were scraped and bloody, but her skirt was pristine.

A concerned group of parishioners surrounded her, and Skye heard one man mutter, "We never used to have crazy drivers in Scumble River. There're too many outsiders here these days."

"What happened?" Skye directed her question at the three women she had been eavesdropping on a few minutes prior. They had managed to work their way to the front of the crowd, and stood facing her.

"You were nearly run over." Andrea ripped open a packet of Wet Ones. "Here, you'd better clean up before you stain your nice outfit."

"Thanks." Skye gingerly wiped the blood from her palms. "I remember a car stopping to let me cross the street, but when I got to the middle of the road, it seemed to speed up and I couldn't move."

"Yeah." Kay Lynn dug through her purse and produced a small tube of antiseptic ointment. "You were doing a deer-in-the-headlights imitation."

"Then suddenly I was airborne." Skye couldn't stop talking, her heart was racing, and it felt as if she had chugged a triple espresso.

"You were lucky." Laurie handed Skye a couple of Band-Aids. "Some guy came out of nowhere and pushed you out of the way."

Kay Lynn gave a ragged little laugh. "I thought you were roadkill for sure."

Skye looked around the circle. "Where's the guy who saved me?"

Everyone glanced at his or her neighbor until Andrea answered, "He must have left."

"Does anyone know who he was?" Skye asked. "I want to thank him."

The group shook their heads.

"Did anyone get the license number of that car?" Skye tried again.

"No," Andrea admitted. "We didn't really see the whole thing. Only the back of some guy shoving you out of the street and a big car roaring away. Did anyone see anything else?" she asked the others, who all shook their heads.

"But I did call the police." Laurie added, "They should be here any minute."

As if her words had conjured it up, the distant sound of a siren grew louder. Everyone waited in silence as a squad car pulled up next to them and Roy Quirk got out.

He frowned when he saw Skye. "I should have known you'd be here."

"Hey, I'm the victim." Skye was in no mood for any of his crap. "Someone nearly ran me over; then instead of seeing if I was okay, the driver fled the scene."

"Whoa." Quirk took a pad and pen from his breast pocket. "Start from the beginning."

After Skye told him what she remembered, he asked the people standing around, "Did any of you get the make, model, or license plate of the car?"

They shook their heads.

"Anyone recognize the driver?"

More shakes of the head.

"Can anyone identify the guy who pushed Miss Denison out of the way?"

Everyone remained silent, except Kay Lynn who volunteered, "He had a great butt. I'm positive I'd recognize it if I saw it again."

"Thank you." The muscle beneath Quirk's right eye twitched. "I'll be sure to get in touch with you if we ever have a rear-end lineup."

The crowd snickered.

"Since you didn't see anything, you all can leave now." Quirk made shooing motions with his hands. "And when I say now, I mean immediately."

After the group dispersed and she was alone with Quirk, Skye asked, "So what are you going to do? I could have been killed."

"Not much we can do with no witnesses or evidence." He shrugged. "It was probably some old lady who mistook the gas pedal for the brake."

"You don't think it might have something to do with the murder?" Skye couldn't believe he wasn't admitting those events could be connected. "Didn't Wally tell you that a couple of weeks ago I received a threatening note and my tire was slashed?"

"Yeah. He told me." Quirk's face turned an ugly shade of red, and his eyes blazed. "I don't appreciate your running to him every time you don't get your way."

"What are you talking about?" Skye sputtered. Why was Quirk getting so huffy and defensive? "I might be the intended victim."

"There's no evidence that the killer was after anyone but Annette Paine. I'm not going to let you sidetrack the few resources I have from that investigation and send everyone on a wild-goose chase." Quirk got into the car. "I know you like being the center of attention, but it's not going to happen while I'm in charge."

"But—" Skye cut herself off, took a calming breath, then said, "I've been threatened, almost run over, and Annette was in a costume she wasn't supposed to be wearing."

"Your 'threatening' note was probably from some kid you'd ticked off, and lots of people knew Mrs. Paine was dressed as a witch. She threw a very public fit when Mrs. Miles didn't show up, and she made it clear she would take her place."

"Oh." Skye hadn't known that. "But why was she in my assigned spot?"

"You arrived late and have a reputation as a bit of a flake." Quirk started to close the squad car's door. "My best guess is that she was checking up on you."

He flashed Skye a smirk that she wanted to rub off his face with an electric sander. The word *butthead* clamored to pass her lips, but she bit her tongue. Mouthing off wouldn't do any good. And although Quirk was patronizing her, he was telling her details of the case he would otherwise refuse to share.

Before driving off, he said, "Whoever murdered Mrs. Paine probably followed her, and when he or she saw she was alone—since you weren't where you were supposed to be—he killed her."

Shit! Skye hobbled toward her Bel Air, her knees aching from her fall. Could Quirk be right? Had her tardiness given the murderer the opportunity he or she needed? Maybe Annette was the intended victim after all. Maybe the driver of the car that had nearly mowed her down really was a confused senior citizen.

Engrossed in thought, Skye opened the door of her Chevy and began to slide inside. Before she had settled into the seat, a deep-timbred voice asked, "Are you okay?"

Her scream was loud enough to make the statue of Saint Francis in front of the church come to life. Skye put a hand to her chest, trying to slow down her heartbeat so she could speak. "You can't be here. Get out right now." All she needed were new rumors floating around about her having an affair with Kurt Michaels.

"That's a cold way of greeting the man who saved your life." The reporter grinned back at her from the Bel Air's passenger seat.

"*You* were the one who pushed me out of the way?"

"Yep."

"Did you see who was driving or get the license number?" Skye asked. "Why didn't you stick around?"

"No, no, and I didn't stay because I didn't want to have to deal with the cops." Kurt relaxed against the seat back and rested his right ankle on his left knee. "There were enough people around to help you if you were hurt."

"Why?"

"Why what?" His response seemed automatic.

"Why didn't you want to deal with the police?"

"It's no big deal." Kurt examined the crease in his jeans. "Quirk and I just don't see eye-to-eye."

"About what?" Skye felt as if she were playing Twenty Questions and losing.

"Things going on in town."

"Like the murder?"

"Like the murder." Kurt's warm hand closed over Skye's. "I'll bet he thought your almost getting run over just now was an accident."

Skye nodded.

"What do you think?"

"I don't know." She shrugged. "I thought it might be re-lated to Annette's death, but then Quirk told me a couple of things that make me wonder."

"Like what?"

"Like maybe it was someone who mistook the gas pedal for the brake." Skye half turned to face the reporter. "You read about that in the paper all the time."

"True." Kurt ran his fingers through his thick blond hair. "But happening so soon after the murder . . . I don't buy it as an accident. Maybe the murderer thinks you saw something and can identify him or her."

"That's an interesting theory." An idea glimmered at the edge of Skye's mind. "You know, Annette's husband was at Mass today, and I heard that he was playing around on her. If he killed her, maybe he was the one who tried to run me down." Skye frowned. "No, Linnea was with him. Surely he wouldn't think a hit-and-run was an appropriate father-daughter activity."

"No," Kurt agreed, "but about ten minutes before you came out of the church, I saw Linnea get into a car with a group of friends." Before Skye could respond, Kurt asked, "What else did Quirk say that made you think it was just an accident?"

"He said a lot of people knew Annette was dressed as a witch."

"Oh." Kurt thought for a half second, then said, "So what? A lot of people may have known, but all it takes is one who didn't know."

"That's right," Skye agreed. "I hadn't thought of that. I'm sure people who were on time and already in their places didn't know."

"Right." Kurt leaned back and put his tennis shoe–clad foot on the dashboard. "Quirk could still be barking up the wrong victim."

"Great. Just when I thought I wouldn't have to be scared anymore." Skye shook her head. "After my little chat with Quirk, I know he's not going to look into any other possibilities, which leaves Hope, Nina, and me dangling like worms on a hook. If the murderer wants any of us, all he has to do is snap us up."

"If Quirk won't investigate, we'll have to." Kurt turned to face Skye. "My boss says you're the Scumble River Nancy Drew. Let's use those talents."

"I'm guessing the reason you're so gung ho is that you're hoping for an exclusive."

"That's one thing I'm hoping for." Dimples appeared in

Kurt's cheeks. "A chance to spend more time with you is an added bonus."

Skye felt a surge of attraction, and frowned at him. "Let's keep this on a professional level."

"Why?"

The single word sent a shiver down her spine. "Because I'm already seeing someone, as you very well know."

"It doesn't look as if you're engaged." He reached across her and captured her left hand, pretending to examine it closely. "Are you?" He kissed her wounded palm before releasing her hand.

"No, but that's not the point."

"My philosophy is, until you walk down that aisle and say 'I do' in front of a preacher, things can change." His voice had taken on a velvety timbre, like a country singer crooning a sexy ballad.

She drew her brows together. With Wally out of town and Quirk acting like a jerk, she needed an ally who knew how to get people to open up and spill their secrets. Trixie was good, but she didn't have Kurt's training or the opportunities that being a reporter afforded him. From what Skye had read in his column, Kurt was a whiz at persuading Scumble Riverites to tell all.

"Look." Kurt cut into her thoughts. "Flirting is harmless, and if it could develop into something more, don't you want to know that before you find yourself married to the wrong guy?"

Skye reluctantly nodded. "But it won't develop into something more."

"Probably not, but at least we'll have some fun."

Skye chewed her thumbnail. Lives could be in danger. Maybe her own. "Okay." She could handle Kurt. He was like an overgrown puppy, cute but harmless. "Here are the ground rules. One, we can't be seen together—there's already gossip. Two, no touching. And three, nothing in the paper until we nail the killer."

"Fine." Kurt's blue eyes twinkled. "Here are my rules.

One, I don't care about gossip. Two, you can touch me any-time you want. And three, anything I find out, I print."

Skye's face was set in hard, tight lines. "Either we com-promise or we don't work together."

"Compromise isn't generally in my vocabulary, but I can compromise on that."

"You are so not funny." Skye blew out an exasperated breath. "Here's my counteroffer. I really don't want to be gossiped about, so we're careful about being seen together, okay?"

"I can live with that."

"If I touch you, you can touch me back, but you can't ini-tiate contact."

"Sounds good."

"We talk over any info before you publish it, and if it would mean that the killer might get away or not be con-victed, you don't put it in the paper until I say so."

"Deal." Kurt held out his hand.

Skye shook.

"See? I knew you wouldn't be able to resist touching me." Kurt's look was teasing. "Now I get to touch you."

"No." Skye backed away, but there wasn't very far she could go without getting out of the car.

"Yes." Kurt leaned forward.

Shoot. He was going to kiss her. Right here in front of the church. Truth be told, she was a little curious. She hadn't kissed that many men. There had been her high school boyfriend, the guy she dated in college, the one she met in the peace corps, her ex-fiancé, Simon, and Wally.

Each one had been better than the guy before him. Could Kurt top Wally? She closed her eyes. She could feel his breath on her face and she resigned herself to the inevitable. But instead of masculine lips pressed against hers, Skye felt a gust of wind. She shivered and her eyelids flew open. Kurt was standing outside the car.

He smiled. "I'll take a rain check on my touch." He leaned down. "In the meantime, why don't you look into

Hope Kennedy's enemies, and I'll see what I can discover
about Nina Miles. We both should try to find out what skele-
tons Annette had in her closet."

"Okay." Kurt started to walk away, and Skye called after
him, "Wait a minute. I locked my car before going into
Mass. How did you get inside?"

"You drive an old ragtop." He reached in his pocket and
showed her a folded length of metal clothes hanger. "Piece
of cake."

Shoot! Shoot! Shoot! Skye pounded the steering wheel as
she drove home. Why did she get the feeling she had sold
her soul to the devil with the blue jeans on?

The remainder of Skye's Sunday was a waste. When
she'd talked to Wally before church, she'd forgotten to tell
him about the gossip and get his permission to tell her aunt
about his real reason for leaving town, so she wasn't able to
take care of that chore. And neither Hope Kennedy nor Evie
Harrison was answering either the door or the phone. The
only task she had accomplished was grocery shopping.

Eight o'clock Monday morning, Skye sat at her desk in
the high school and stared bleary eyed at Travis Idell's file.
The psychiatrist was still not returning Skye's calls, and
Mrs. Idell was growing more and more enraged by the
school's lack of action. She was now threatening to bring the
matter to due process, which had thrown Homer into a tizzy.

He had threatened and cajoled Skye, but she had stood
firm, agreeing only to review the file once more. Now, as she
looked over the paperwork in Travis's folder for the fifth
time, she was again amazed that a professional had allowed
an assessment of such poor quality to leave his office. She'd
seen some badly written reports in her time, but this one was
a doozy.

Her favorite line was, *Travis appears to have a slight
case of dyslexia, and because of this the principle has suspended him from school on several occasions.*

However, no matter how amusing she found the report,

the bottom line was that there was nothing in it to support the idea that Travis had a learning disability. She had already explained to Homer that if everyone else on the PPS team agreed Travis qualified for service, the team could put him in special education. At that point, she would write a dissenting opinion, but her statement would not interfere with the placement.

She knew Homer would have grabbed at this chance to pacify the Idells if she hadn't also pointed out that if, later on as an adult, Travis felt being placed in special ed had harmed him, he could come back and sue the district and the individuals who had signed off.

Her warning had made the principal think twice about taking the easy way out, which was when he had ordered Skye to reconsider her position. She had, and now she needed to tell Homer she hadn't changed her mind.

Skye glanced at the clock. School had been in session for only ten minutes, which meant Homer was probably still sipping his first cup of coffee and playing Free Cell on his computer. Maybe he'd be in a decent mood.

She reached reluctantly for the phone. The next-to-last thing in the world she wanted was to suffer through a due-process hearing, but the very last thing was to wrongly place a student in special education.

She was dialing Homer's extension when the PA burst into life and Homer's voice blared from the speakers: "Teachers, please follow evacuation plan A. Repeat. Evacuation plan A. This is not a drill."

CHAPTER 16

Escape

"Chemical bombs." Homer held his head and slumped in his chair. "Here in Scumble River High."

"I'm so relieved that I read about those types of bombs in the newspaper a few weeks ago, and recognized them before someone got hurt," Jackie said, a brave smile on her face. "Though I put myself at risk, I was happy to do it to protect our precious students."

Jackie and Skye sat in the visitors' chairs in front of the principal's desk. It was eleven o'clock and they had been allowed back in the building only a few minutes ago. While waiting outside with the students for the school to be cleared, Skye had talked to a member of the county's bomb squad and had learned that the bombs discovered in the cafeteria, gym, and lobby had been made using two-liter pop bottles. If the top had been unscrewed and the contents exposed to air, a chemical reaction would have taken place, forming a dangerous gas and a caustic liquid.

For once the school's small size worked in its favor. The county squad had thoroughly inspected the building in less than three hours, and was satisfied that there were no other bombs present. Nevertheless, the superintendent had decided to close the high school for the rest of the day. All the teachers and other staff members were busy making calls and supervising the dismissal, but Homer had ordered Skye and Jackie away from the phones and into his office.

"This is it," Homer moaned. "It's time for me to retire."

"Sir." Jackie leaned forward. "You can't mean that. What would we do without you?"

Skye held back a giggle. Homer threatened—or promised, depending on your perspective—to retire at least three or four times a school year.

"Hell, I don't know and I don't care," Homer snapped, instantly sitting up and throwing off his 'poor, pitiful me' routine.

Skye snickered. The social worker hadn't learned yet that Homer was one of those rare individuals who didn't respond well to positive reinforcement.

Jackie tried again, apparently not being a quick study. "What I meant, sir, was that the school needs you—now more than ever, in our time of crisis."

"Yeah. Right," Homer growled, and bounded to his feet. "What we really need is for you two to figure out who planted the bombs."

Skye raised an eyebrow. "Isn't that a job for the police?" She had spoken briefly to Quirk, who was looking less and less like he enjoyed being in charge.

"With your boyfriend out of town, I doubt the Scumble River PD can find their asses using both of their hands and a butt-sniffing dog."

"While I think the Scumble River police officers are very good"—Jackie leapt out of her chair and into the conversation—"they do have a lot on their plate with the murder and all, so if you think we can help, I, for one, am happy to be of service, sir."

"You will both make this your number one priority." Homer rewarded Jackie with his version of a smile, then glowered at Skye. "I want every student with any hint of discipline problems interviewed."

"But—"

"Yes, sir," Jackie cut Skye off. "I'll clear my calendar for the rest of the week."

"Week? Are you nuts?" Homer roared. "I want the little booger behind these bombs found by the end of school tomorrow." He swiveled and pointed at Skye. "You, talk to that newspaper staff of yours. Those brats seem to be able to dig out all the secrets around here and are perfectly willing to spill them."

Homer had never quite recovered from the exposé Xenia, the *Scoop's* bad-girl reporter, had done on one of the cheerleaders.

"Okay." Skye got up. "But I think Travis Idell should be the first student we interview. This smacks of one of his stunts, and he did get an A in chemistry."

"Fine. I would love to pin this on that little twerp. Maybe that would shut up his parents." Homer jerked his thumb at Jackie. "But you talk to Travis. If it's not him, all we need is for Skye to stir up his folks even more."

"Yes, sir." Jackie nearly saluted. "I'll see him as soon as he arrives at school tomorrow."

Homer's hairy brows met above his nose, forming a caterpillar-like shape. "So, why are you two still standing here?"

Jackie raced Skye to the door. Opal handed them two stacks of files as they passed her desk. Silently they walked to their office and got to work. It was one forty-five when they finished reviewing the three years of discipline records. They had discovered forty-two students who had been involved in serious incidents and who still attended Scumble River High; adding the student newspaper staff to their list of interviews gave them an even fifty kids to see the next day.

Realizing there was nothing more she could do at the high school, Skye headed over to the elementary school to talk to Hope Kennedy. After she and Trixie failed to find the teacher on Saturday, Skye had tried to get in touch with her all day Sunday, but Hope hadn't answered the door or the telephone.

This afternoon Skye was in luck. When she stopped at the office to sign in, Fern Otte, the grade school secretary, told her that Hope's class had just gone out for afternoon recess. Knowing that this would be Hope's first break since lunch, Skye headed down to the teachers' lounge.

Both the lounge and the faculty restrooms were located in the basement of the old building. Skye wound her way through huge rolls of construction paper, stacks of athletic equipment, and shelves of cleaning supplies. The mixed odors of sweat and ammonia made her sinuses close, and as she pushed open the door to the lounge, she announced her presence with a loud sneeze.

Hope had been facing a bulletin board at the back of the empty room, but at Skye's disquieting entrance, she spun around. She clutched a Styrofoam cup to her chest, and a stream of coffee arced across the floor.

Hope and Skye each put their hand to their heart and said at the same time, "Oh, I'm so sorry."

Skye grabbed a handful of paper towels from the nearby sink. "I didn't mean to scare you." She knelt to sop up the spattered liquid.

"Not your fault." Hope joined her on the floor, wiping droplets that were out of Skye's reach. "I'm a little jumpy since the murder."

"Me too." Skye got to her feet and threw the sodden mess she was holding in the trash can. "That's actually what I wanted to discuss with you. I tried to get hold of you over the weekend, but you were never home when I called or stopped by."

"After what happened Friday night, I wanted to get away for a while, so my husband and I decided to go visit his mother in Saint Louis." Hope poured herself another cup of coffee. "I didn't hear your phone messages until late last night when we got home." She sat at the closest of the three long tables running the length of the room. "I figured you wanted to chat about the murder. Right?"

"That's right." Skye felt she and Hope were on friendly enough terms to come to the point. She had worked with Hope for several years, and helped her with a couple of problem students.

"I thought it was an uncommonly smart move on the part of the police department to sign you on as a consultant," Hope said. "Although you solved several of their major cases, I'm surprised their male egos didn't get in the way."

"Thank you. It's really sweet of you to say that." Skye felt her cheeks redden. She wasn't used to compliments. "I guess Wally is secure enough in his own manhood not to be threatened by my help."

"Chief Boyd does seem like an extraordinarily easygoing guy."

"Most of the time." Skye smiled, then brought the conversation back on track. "Has Quirk talked to you since Friday?"

"No." Hope's brown eyes sharpened. "Isn't he keeping you informed?"

"I've spoken with him," Skye said carefully, not sure how much she should reveal about Quirk's attitude toward her. "But he says he doesn't need my help."

"And Chief Boyd's out of town." Hope put together the pieces.

"Right." Skye decided to be straightforward. "Wally's told Quirk that I'm part of the team, but Quirk has other ideas." Skye was counting on the fact that Hope was both levelheaded and not a gossip. "The thing is, I think he may be on the wrong track."

"You think Annette might not have been the intended victim."

Skye nodded.

"And you're trying to figure out if one of the other witches was the murderer's target."

Skye nodded again.

Hope took a thoughtful sip of coffee. "Do you have any enemies?"

"A few parents aren't too happy with me." Skye shrugged. "But I find it hard to believe someone would try to kill me over a special-ed placement—beat me up, sue me, try to get me fired, maybe, but murder seems a little excessive." Skye tilted her head. "How about you?"

Hope ignored Skye's question and asked one of her own. "Have you checked out Nina Miles?"

"I talked to her Saturday, but she said there was no reason for anyone to want to harm her." Skye looked at Hope intently. "Why? Do you know something about her?"

"Only that she's a part of that same group of women that runs the high school Parent-Teacher Organization—the one that Annette and Evie were fighting to control." Hope looked at the wall clock. "I've got to get going. Recess is almost over."

"You never answered my question." Skye followed her to the door. "How about you? Do you have any enemies?"

"Yes."

"What?" Skye's eyes widened. "Who?"

Hope took a deep breath. "You've got to promise you won't tell anyone."

"Except the police, right?"

"Only Wally."

"But he's out of town. How about Quirk?"

"No!" Hope turned, an edge of panic in her voice. "He's the one I'm afraid of."

As Skye got into her car after school, she couldn't stop thinking about Hope's final words before she stepped into her classroom: *Quirk would love to see me dead.*

Skye had been able to push her concern aside for the next couple of hours while she was writing a psych report back at the high school, but once she was alone in the Bel Air, her anxiety level ratcheted higher and higher, like a ski lift lurching to the top of a slope. She gripped the steering wheel and tried to figure out her next move.

Skye had planned to stop at the Harrisons' house on the way home, since Evie was still not answering her phone, but Hope's statement was now her top priority. She had to talk to Wally ASAP, and she didn't want to do it on a cell phone that might lose its signal at any moment.

Once Skye was inside her house, she went directly to the kitchen and picked up the receiver. After dialing, she grabbed a can of ginger ale from the fridge. She'd felt queasy and light-headed all afternoon.

Wally answered on the fourth ring. "Everything okay?" His voice was tense.

"Well"—Skye cursed caller ID—"there hasn't been another murder." She barely restrained herself from adding *yet*. She needed to work herself up to telling him about Quirk. "How's your father?"

"They still don't know what caused him to collapse, but since he appears to be fine now, the docs say it was probably exhaustion. They're releasing him tomorrow, and I've arranged for a live-in nurse to start Friday. He's agreed to work from home, and she'll keep an eye on him."

"That's wonderful." Skye hoped that meant Wally was coming back soon. "I'm so glad he's okay. I know all this waiting and wondering must have been awful for you both."

"I've got a flight into O'Hare on Saturday and should be in Scumble River by late evening."

"That's fantastic." Skye's spirits lifted. This was the first good news she'd had in quite a while.

"So, what's up?"

Skye hesitated. Maybe she should wait until Wally got home, but that was still five days away, and a lot could happen before then.

"Are you there?" Wally asked, irritation in his voice.

"Uh, yes, sorry."

"No, I'm sorry. I'm just so frustrated. I wish I could split myself in half."

"I understand." Skye took a sip of soda; her mouth felt like the bottom of Bingo's litter box. "Unfortunately, what I have to tell you won't make you feel better."

"I had a hunch that was the case. Quirk already told me about the chemical bombs at the high school."

"It's not about that." Skye's heartbeat felt irregular, and her head was pounding. "It's about Quirk."

"He's still not including you?" Wally demanded, seeming almost happy to have a target for his frustration.

"No, he isn't, but that's not why I'm calling." Skye tried to order her thoughts. "I talked to Hope Kennedy today. She was one of the witch trio."

"And?"

"And it turns out Quirk has a reason to want her dead."

"Fu—" Wally stopped, then asked, "Why?"

"Fred isn't her first husband. When she was sixteen, she got pregnant and her parents forced her to marry the baby's father."

"Quirk?"

"No, his older brother," Skye answered.

"Surely, after all this time, Quirk's not still mad at her for divorcing his brother?"

"No. He's mad at her for killing him."

"What?"

"It was self-defense." Skye took a deep breath and went on. "Quirk's brother, Ray, was a druggie. About a month before the baby was born, he got hold of some PCP, went berserk, and started beating her. She grabbed a rifle and shot him."

"This happened, what, twenty years ago?"

"Eighteen."

Wally paused, obviously doing the math. "So, her son, Ross, is Quirk's nephew?"

"Yeah, but Fred adopted him when he was a baby, which is another reason Quirk is pissed. When she changed the baby's name to Kennedy, he told her it was as if she not only killed his brother, but also erased his very existence."

"But why would he wait eighteen years to murder her?" Wally asked.

"Quirk's mother is terminally ill, and she wants to see her grandson before she dies. She's never made any attempt to be a part of his life before, and Ross said no."

"Why would Quirk be upset with Hope for that?"

"Hope refused to try to talk Ross into it." Skye swallowed, then added, "So Quirk told her that he'd see her dead in hell for all she's done to his family."

"Which would explain why Quirk doesn't want you poking around. If he killed Annette thinking she was Hope, the last thing he wants is your convincing everyone Annette was the wrong victim."

"Yep." Skye was relieved that she and Wally were on the same page. "And you know, I was just thinking how quickly Quirk arrived at the haunted house the night of the murder."

"Like maybe he was already there?"

"Yeah." Skye thought about the situation, then asked, "So, are you going to call in the sheriff to take over?"

"Damn! I hate to. A lot of people say they want to kill someone, but they don't actually go through with it. And he might have gotten to the scene so fast because he was patrolling in that area. I don't want to ruin Quirk's career if he's innocent." The stress in Wally's voice was evident. "If the nurse can start Wednesday, and if I can get a flight home that afternoon, I'd rather handle this myself." Wally paused. "In the meantime, don't give Quirk any reason to think you're still investigating, and tell Hope to make sure she's never alone."

"I already told her that." Skye understood how Wally felt. After all, Quirk was innocent until proven guilty, and having a motive didn't make him a killer.

After several minutes of silence, Wally asked, "Is there something else?"

"No." Skye blew out a breath. "I guess I'm waiting for the other shoe to drop—and in this case it feels as if there might be three feet."

"I know what you mean."

Once Wally hung up, she decided to lie down. She was too ill to drive to Evie's. Skye's head was swimming, and she felt as if she could vomit at any moment. Had she caught the flu from Nina?

CHAPTER 17

Everything You Want

Skye and Jackie met with Homer Tuesday morning before the first bell. His first question was, "How long is this going to take?"

"We each have twenty-five students on our list to interview, and it will take at least fifteen minutes per kid, maybe more, which means over six hours for us to see them all." Skye answered.

"So, you can finish by the end of the day," Homer stated.

Skye shook her head. "I can only stay until eleven." She hoped Homer wouldn't have a hissy fit. "Since this is an emergency, I'll skip my time at the grade school this morning, but Jackie and I both have to be at the junior high's PPS meeting at eleven thirty. Neva says they have a serious issue to discuss."

Homer bared his teeth in a sarcastic smile. "What? Neva needs help redecorating her office again?"

"She didn't tell me what it is, so I have no idea." Skye had found that the junior high principal usually had her own agenda, and trying to change it in any way was not a good idea.

"That still gives us three hours," Jackie chimed in. "We can get half done."

Homer's face turned the color of a boiled lobster, and he waved his hands in the air as if they were claws fighting off a diner intent on devouring his tail. "You two will stay until you've talked to every last delinquent on your list."

"Let's call Neva." Skye stepped around Homer and picked up the phone on his desk. "Maybe she'll postpone the meeting until Wednesday."

"No." Homer cursed softly under his breath. "If you think it's that important, go, but come back here as soon as that meeting is finished."

"Definitely." Jackie beamed at him. "I'll bring sandwiches so we can eat at the PPS meeting and not have to stop for lunch. We can probably be back here by one, and I'm sure we can finish by three."

"I doubt it." Skye knew better than to promise Homer what she couldn't deliver.

"Oh, come on, Skye," Jackie admonished. "Stop being so negative. We can do it if we really try."

Skye gritted her teeth. Jackie was *seriously* annoying her. Skye had tried to be friendly to the woman, but it was time for an alternate approach—avoidance. From now on, unless they had to both attend the same meeting, Skye resolved to steer clear of Jackie. Whenever Jackie was in their shared office, Skye would go somewhere else.

The junior high's art room smelled of turpentine and glue. Scraps of construction paper were scattered on the faded blue linoleum. The windows rattled as gusts of wind buffeted them, and cold air seeped around the frames, causing the student drawings thumbtacked to the bulletin board to rustle.

Principal Neva Llewellyn sat at the teacher's desk. The other members of the Pupil Personal Services team sat at small tables for two arranged in an arc facing her. When Skye entered the room, no one was speaking.

Skye slid into an empty seat beside Madeline Weller, the special-education teacher. Ever since Wally's ex-wife, the former special-ed teacher, had left town, they'd had a new one every school year. For some reason—perhaps the low salary, poor working conditions, or lack of respect—it was hard to keep good educators in Scumble River.

Madeline was fresh out of college, slender and petite. She looked about thirteen, and Skye had been meaning to ask how she was doing. Her caseload consisted of students with behavior disorders and learning disabilities, and most of them were boys.

Neva shot Skye an annoyed look and said, "Now that we're finally all here, let's begin."

Skye checked the wall clock; she was fifteen minutes early, which would have usually ensured her being the first to arrive. What was going on?

Neva nodded to the special-ed teacher and said, "Ms. Weller, please tell the team what you reported to me yesterday morning."

In a soft voice, the teacher said, "I coach the eighth-grade pom-pom squad." She cleared her throat. "Yesterday the girls were all excited."

Skye watched Neva's expression darken and wondered what was coming.

"They wouldn't tell me what was going on." Madeline's face clouded. "I knew it must be something big, because they were all giggly. So, I, uh . . ." Madeline's cheeks reddened. "I eavesdropped."

Jackie asked, "What did you hear?"

"A group of five girls has decided to get pregnant." Madeline's big blue eyes rounded in dismay. "They said they'd seen a Web site that said how cool it was to all have babies at the same time and raise them together."

"Did you call their parents?" Skye asked Neva. Surely the principal hadn't waited for this meeting before taking action.

"Of course," Neva snapped. "But several of the mothers and fathers weren't certain how to handle the situation. It's not as if they can put the girls in chastity belts or force contraceptives down their throats."

"Do you want me to talk to the girls?" Skye offered.

Before the principal could answer, Jackie waved her hand in the air. "Not to step on any toes"—she smiled at Skye—"but I should be the one to talk to them."

"Why?" Neva looked at Jackie.

"Well, no offense, Skye, but social workers are better trained in counseling. Most school psychologists just test and consult."

"That isn't true, Jackie, at least in my school psych program." Skye kept her expression neutral. "But if you'd like to handle this situation, I'll step aside and concentrate on the high school's problem."

Neva sat back in her chair and frowned at Skye. "Shouldn't I be the one to decide that?"

"Right." Skye backpedaled quickly. "I meant I'd do whatever the team thinks is best."

"Since it's obvious Jackie is eager for the job"—Neva crossed her arms—"and this isn't Skye's top priority, I'd prefer Jackie to handle it."

Skye feared her head was going to explode. Homer thought his chemical bombs should be number one on her list. Neva thought her wannabe mommies should be. Skye couldn't wait to hear what the grade school principal considered to be her main concern.

"I'll get right on it." Jackie beamed.

Skye's patience was wearing thin. "You told Homer we'd be back at the high school this afternoon to finish up the interviews there."

"I thought you said you were going to handle that." Jackie tossed her hair. "Since I'm needed here."

"I meant I'd take the lead." Skye's stomach clenched. "But if you don't do any of the interviews, it will take twice as long and Homer won't be happy."

"It seems fair to me." Neva's forehead wrinkled. "Homer can't expect to monopolize both of you." She pushed back her chair. "Jackie, after you finish with the girls, brief me before you leave."

"Yes, ma'am."

"Thank you, everyone." Neva stood, indicating the meeting was over. "See you next week." She put her hand on Skye's arm as she attempted to leave. "I need a word with you before you go."

Skye nodded, stepped aside, and waited.

Once everyone had left, Neva shut the door and said, "I'm very disappointed in you, Skye."

Her pulse quickened. *Shit!* She had worked hard to gain the principal's trust. "I'm sorry to hear that."

"I expected you to be the one eager to talk to those girls. Instead, you're late to the meeting and then act as if our problem isn't as important as the high school's."

"I certainly didn't mean to imply that." Skye fought the urge to cry. "It's just that Jackie and I already promised Homer our time."

"I understand your concern, but I don't think that's the real reason."

"It is." Skye was confused. "Really."

"Maybe you think it is, but unconsciously, I think you're a little jealous of Jackie." Neva tilted her head. "Before she was hired, you were the one everyone turned to for assistance. Could it be that you perceive she's taking your place and you resent it?"

"No." Skye disputed Neva's theory. "I'm glad for the help." But was she? Skye pushed that doubt away.

"Fine." Neva shrugged her shoulders. "Now, about your being late. You know I don't tolerate tardiness."

"I wasn't. I was here at quarter after for our eleven-thirty meeting."

Neva raised an eyebrow. "But the meeting was rescheduled for eleven, at your request."

Skye stood frozen, stunned by Neva's words. Was she losing her mind, or was someone out to get her? "I most certainly did not reschedule the meeting."

*   *   *

"What do you mean, there are still eighteen kids you haven't seen?" Homer grabbed the edge of his desk and glared at Skye, seated opposite him.

Tuesday's dismissal bell had rung ten minutes ago, and Skye was in Homer's office giving him a rundown on what she had discovered—which was nothing. None of the students she'd interviewed seemed to have any knowledge of the chemical bombs or their creator.

"I told you this morning we couldn't possibly see them all today, and since Jackie stayed at the junior high after PPS to deal with the situation there, I could only see eight kids this afternoon."

"Are you blaming Jackie? She called me and said that you insisted she stay there, that you could handle the interviews here." A scowl twisted Homer's heavy features. "I expect you to be finished and to have found the culprit by noon tomorrow." He spoke sharply. "Am I making myself perfectly clear?"

"If Jackie's back to help, that shouldn't be a problem."

Homer's response was an animal-like grunt. He picked up the phone and started dialing, dismissing her with a wave of his stubby fingers.

Skye headed back to her office to work on a report that was due the next day, but she was happy to see Trixie leaning against the wall near her door when she arrived. Reports could be written at home, and her friend was always good for a laugh.

Trixie handed Skye a Diet Coke and said, "Wait until you hear what I saw at the grocery store yesterday."

"What?" Skye felt a spark of anticipation. Trixie was a great storyteller.

"I was in the produce aisle getting some fruit for this week's lunches, and I saw Dr. Paine over by the deli counter."

"His wife dies on Friday and he's buying salami on Monday?" Skye *tsk*ed.

"If you think that's bad, wait until you hear the rest of it."

Trixie plopped into the chair facing Skye's desk. "So, I start to walk over to him to tell him how sorry I am about Annette, but another woman gets to him first."

Skye settled into her seat. "Who was it?"

"I thought she looked familiar, but couldn't remember why. Anyway, she said hello to him, and he said, 'Do I know you?' "

Skye popped the top of her soda can and nodded for Trixie to continue.

"The woman said to him, 'You're the father of one of my kids.' "

"Holy smokes!" Skye's eyes widened.

"You haven't heard the half of it." Trixie's brown eyes twinkled with amusement. "He stared at the woman for a second or two, then said, 'Oh, my God! Are you the stripper from that club near O'Hare? The one that I banged on the couch during my buddy's stag party?' "

Skye had just taken a drink of soda and it spewed across her desktop as she whooped. After catching her breath and mopping up the mess, she asked, "What did the woman say?"

"She said, 'No. I'm your daughter Mallory's fifth-grade teacher.' "

They both laughed until tears ran down their cheeks; then Skye's face sobered, and she said, "I forgot all about Annette's other daughter. I wonder if I should go over to the grade school tomorrow. Homer wouldn't let me see if any of Linnea's friends wanted to talk about Annette's death, but maybe Caroline would want me to talk to Mallory's classmates."

"Wouldn't she have called you if she thought she needed you?" Trixie asked. When Skye nodded, Trixie added, "Besides, I heard you already have your hands full with the chemical bombs here and the wannabe mommies at the junior high. What's up with that?"

Skye filled her in, concluding with, "Then Neva said I

had phoned and left a message requesting that the meeting be moved from eleven thirty to eleven."

"How weird." Trixie took a sip of her Dr Pepper. "Maybe the secretary misunderstood whoever called."

"That must be it." Skye opened the bottom drawer of her desk and grabbed the package of cookies. Her stomach was growling. Jackie had failed to bring the promised sandwiches to the PPS meeting, and Skye hadn't had anything to eat since seven a.m.

"Do you think Neva believed you?"

"She said she did, but she's a hard one to read." Skye offered the Oreos to Trixie.

"No, thanks." Trixie reached into the jar on Skye's desk and pulled out a piece of Halloween candy. "Sounds like Jackie is really diving right into things around here. She must be a big help to you."

"Yeah, she's Johnny-on-the-spot." Skye muttered, twisting the Oreo apart. "Too much so. Let's talk about something else." Skye took a lick of the cream center. "Ick. I think these cookies have gone bad."

"Throw them away." Trixie peeled the wrapper from a tiny Milky Way. "What did Vince want to talk to you about?"

"Right. We haven't spoken since Saturday." Skye tried another Oreo, this time taking a bite of the intact cookie. They seemed okay as long as she ate them whole. "As I feared, Vince's news was bad."

"He dumped Loretta?"

"Other way around."

"No!" Trixie's eyes widened. "That's got to be a first. Why?"

"She gave him the old 'we're too different' speech, but I suspect there's more to it. I need to call her and find out."

"Maybe you shouldn't." Trixie's expression was doubtful. "You don't want to ruin your friendship."

"You could be right."

After a long pause, Trixie said, "What's happening with the murder?"

"I overheard some info at church I'll follow up on. Your story about what Dr. Paine said in the grocery store pretty much confirms what they were saying about him." Skye filled Trixie in on the gossip about the dentist and about Evie Harrison, ending with, "And I was nearly run over by a car after Mass."

"Oh, my God. Were you all right?" Trixie gasped.

"Just a scraped knee and palm," Skye reassured her friend. "Kurt Michaels pushed me out of the way. Quirk blew the whole incident off."

"What a jerk." Trixie looked worried. "We need to find out if Annette was really the intended victim. Any ideas on how we can do that?"

"Kurt and I discussed it, and he's going to help." Skye gave Trixie a summary of her conversation with the reporter, finishing with, "So, he's going to check Nina Miles out—see if she tells him anything she didn't share with us—and I'll talk to Evie. We'll both look into Annette." Hope had made Skye promise not to tell anyone about her history or Quirk's threat, so she couldn't share that info with Trixie.

"Don't you think it's odd that Kurt's around whenever something happens?"

"Not really. He's just doing his job." Skye hadn't mentioned his flirting. She pushed aside the memory of his almost kissing her, and told herself the reason for keeping it from Trixie was that he was only teasing. "Besides, with the police department not giving me any information, I need his help."

Trixie raised an eyebrow, but didn't pursue the matter. "What do you want me to do?"

"Evie and Nina have daughters at the high school, and Hope has a son. Maybe you could chat with them. Kids usually know more than their parents think they do, and you could run into them more casually than I can."

"Okay." Trixie stood. "I'll let you know if the kids have anything interesting to say."

After Trixie left, Skye ate the last cookie in the package and threw the cellophane away. Happily, she had purchased Oreos at the grocery store Sunday after church, and thus there was a new package in the bottom of her drawer for the next day. It had gotten so that she couldn't get through the afternoon without her cookie fix.

As Skye carefully wiped the crumbs from the top of her desk, and made sure none had fallen to the floor—Homer would kill her if she attracted ants—she thought about how she could approach Dylan Paine. She needed to find out if the dental Don Juan had murdered his wife.

How do you get to see a dentist? By developing a toothache. A few seconds later, Skye had Dr. Paine's receptionist on the phone, and was reassuring the woman that although her tooth was throbbing, and Dr. Paine wasn't reopening his office until the day after tomorrow, she didn't want a referral to another dentist. The woman reluctantly said that Dr. Paine could see Skye at four p.m. on Thursday.

Skye wrote the appointment on her calendar, picked up her purse, and stood. As she got to her feet, she felt dizzy and a little nauseated. The half dozen cookies she had eaten on an empty stomach must not have agreed with her.

Skye resolved to go straight home and rest—as soon as she made two stops. First she'd go to Evie's house to ask her what Annette was holding over her head, then to Aunt Minnie's to make sure the correct version of Wally's absence was circulating on the grapevine. When they'd talked Sunday night, she'd gotten Wally's okay to reveal the info about his reason for being out of town, but Skye hadn't had a chance to visit her aunt until now.

Evie lived in a beautiful old Victorian next to her husband's church. A fifty-something man in a clerical collar answered Skye's knock. "Yes?"

"Hello, Reverend." Skye smiled at the handsome minister. "May I speak to Evie, please?"

"I'm sorry—she's not receiving visitors today." He tried to shut the door.

Skye put her foot in his way. "Could you tell her it's Skye Denison, about Promfest?"

"I'll tell her you stopped by." His icy blue eyes dared her to cause a scene. "But she's resting now, and I won't disturb her."

Skye refused to be intimidated. "Will you give her a note from me?"

He inclined his head, and Skye noticed that his thick white hair didn't move. She hurriedly grabbed a legal pad from her tote, then searched its depths for a pen. Reverend Harrison sighed and handed her the one from his shirt pocket.

Skye admired the sleek Mont Blanc as she wrote:

> *Dear Evie,*
> *I need to talk to you ASAP. Call me by tomorrow or I'm dropping out of the haunted house.*
> *Skye Denison*

As soon as she handed Reverend Harrison the folded page, he shut the door in her face. It sure seemed as if Evie was avoiding Skye. What did the woman have to hide?

CHAPTER 18

Something in the Air

A ringing phone woke Skye from a disturbed sleep. She still hadn't felt well when she got home from her aunt's, and had stretched out on the love seat in the sunroom trying to get her head to stop spinning. She must have dozed off, because according to the clock on the VCR it was now eight p.m.

She struggled to get up, her neck and back aching from sleeping on the too-short surface. Stumbling to the kitchen, she snatched the receiver off the hook.

A male voice said, "Hello. Uh, this is Xavier Ryan."

"Oh, hi, Xavier." Skye tried to clear her mind. "Is Frannie okay?"

"Depends on your definition of *okay*."

Uh-oh. "What's up?" Skye wedged the receiver between her ear and shoulder and moved over to the sink.

"She absolutely refuses to go back to Loyola."

"That's a shame." Skye turned on the cold water and splashed her face, trying to focus. "Does she have an alternative plan?"

"Yeah." Xavier's tone was sarcastic. "She's going to get her old job at the bowling alley back."

"That's it?"

"That's as far as she's thought it through."

Skye sank into a kitchen chair. "Maybe she needs a little time to figure out what she wants."

"No." Xavier's voice was firm. "She needs to get her rear end back in college."

"Well, uh, good luck with that."

"Can you talk to her?"

"I doubt I could change her mind," Skye stalled. "And I'm really not feeling well tonight."

"Oh." There was a silence; then Xavier said, "Well, the thing is, she's already on her way to your house."

"I see."

"She thinks you'll take her side." Xavier cleared his throat. "I wanted to make sure you and I were on the same page."

"And you want her in school?"

"Right."

"If it doesn't have to be Loyola, I could suggest Joliet Junior College." Skye got up and put a filter in the coffee machine's basket. Her head still felt fuzzy, and she needed to be able to think straight if she was going to convince Frannie to do something she didn't want to do. "Maybe if she can commute, she'd be willing to give college another try."

"Yeah, that might work." Xavier sounded relieved. "Call me when she leaves and let me know how it went. Okay?"

"Sorry, no." Skye was not getting caught in the middle. "You two can talk about it when she gets home."

While she waited for the coffee to brew and Frannie to arrive, Skye checked her messages. There was one from her mother demanding to know if she had broken up with Wally and was now dating Kurt. Skye deleted that one with no intention of returning May's call.

The second one was from Loretta. All it said was, "Meningitis, menopause, mental illness—ever notice all problems begin with *men*?"

Skye hit the DELETE button again. No way was she returning that call either.

The last message was from Simon. He said he had some info about the murder and he'd get in touch with her the next day. *Hmm.* That sounded promising.

It took several hours to convince Frannie to give JJC a chance, but when Skye pointed out to her that she'd need transportation from Scumble River to Joliet in order to attend, the girl gave in. Frannie had been bugging her father to buy her car since she'd turned sixteen. Once Frannie left, Skye went to bed and fell immediately asleep.

When she woke up Wednesday morning, Skye felt as if she had a hangover, but she forced herself to get up and go to work. Jackie and Skye interviewed students all morning, but none of the kids seemed to know anything about the bombs. Homer was not happy with their lack of results. And when the principal wasn't happy, no one in the school was happy.

Trixie hadn't had any better luck when she talked to Bree Miles, Cheyenne Harrison, and Ross Kennedy. None of the three had revealed any useful information. Linnea Paine was still out of school, so Trixie hadn't been able to speak to her.

To top it off, at noon Skye had found a note in her box from Evie Harrison, which read:

> *Skye,*
> *I don't have time to talk to you. With Annette gone, I'm now Promfest chair and am just too busy. I'll contact you when I have a chance. Stop calling me and showing up at my house or I'll tell Officer Quirk you're harrassing me.*
> *Evie*
> *P.S. Don't even think of quitting A Ghoul's Night Out. Remember, my husband is on the school board, and if you mess this up for me, even your uncle Charlie won't be able to save your job.*

Skye was livid at Evie's threats, but knew she'd better lay off for a while. She couldn't risk Quirk knowing she was still investigating, just in case Roy was the killer. And she couldn't risk getting fired. Her résumé was only now recovering from the last time she was sacked.

Driving home after work, Skye brooded that the day had been a total waste. She hadn't accomplished anything in either of her roles—as school psychologist or as police consultant. The only bright spot was that Wally was due home that evening.

Bingo greeted her at the door, and after petting him she started up the stairs to change into more comfortable clothes. Before she made it to the top, the doorbell rang. Sighing, she went back down. When she looked out the peephole, her first instinct was to turn away. On her porch, standing shoulder-to-shoulder, were Simon and Kurt.

Crap! Double crap! Just what she needed. Pasting a smile on her face, she swung the door open and said, "What brings you two here together?"

"We arrived at the same time, but we aren't together," Simon explained.

"Oh. Well, come in." Skye stepped aside and the men walked into the foyer.

Kurt glanced around, then said, "I need to talk to you in private."

"So do I." Simon moved to Skye's side.

"Uh, okay. Kurt, please wait for me in the parlor." Skye took Simon's arm and led him down the hall.

Once they were in the kitchen Simon said, "Why don't I come back later? I'll take you out to dinner and we can talk then."

Not wanting to seem to be reading too much into his offer, Skye shook her head. "Sorry. Not tonight. I may be coming down with something. I've been feeling sick on and off for the last couple of days."

"You mean you get better, then get sick again?" Simon

questioned, a look of concern in his eyes. When she nodded, he asked, "What are your symptoms?"

"My head hurts, my mouth is dry, my heart races, and I feel dizzy and nauseated."

"You need to see a doctor." Simon crossed his arms. "Let me drive you to the urgent-care clinic in Laurel."

"No. I'll be fine. If I'm not better by the weekend, I'll go." Skye took a step back. "But I would like to lie down, so can you give me the condensed version of what you wanted to tell me?"

"Annette's death is being ruled accidental."

"What? How? Why?" Skye heard herself stammering, and closed her mouth in order to give Simon a chance to answer.

"The county crime techs found hemp fibers caught in eyebolts that were screwed opposite each other on the walls, so the evidence suggests that the rope you found Annette holding was originally strung across the passageway. It had green makeup embedded in it, and it matches the mark on her neck. The theory is that she was running in the dark hall, slammed into the rope, which knocked the breath out of her, and as she fell she grabbed the rope, which then tore loose."

"And that killed her?" Skye asked.

"No. But it brought on an asthma attack, which is what she died from."

"I knew asthma was serious, but I had no idea someone like Annette could die from an attack."

"Over four thousand people a year die because of asthma," Simon explained. "And Annette had several risk factors. She'd had asthma since she was a child, and her doctor said she wasn't compliant with her medication, had a poor awareness of her own reduced ability to breathe, and frequently ended up at the emergency room. Running into the rope in the dark probably caused her to panic, and a stressful or emotional situation can worsen asthma."

"And being in a costume she didn't expect to wear, she

didn't have her inhaler," Skye guessed. "But wouldn't it take her a long time to die?"

Simon shook his head. "A fatal attack can take only a few minutes."

"Hmm." Skye pursed her lips. "Okay, the asthma might have been what killed her, but why was the rope there, and why was she running? Did someone hang it as a trap and then chase her?"

"None of the crew admits to putting up the rope, and no one can come up with a good reason for it to be there, or remembers it being there on their final check of the setup." Simon shrugged. "But didn't you say part of the witches' act was to run down the hallway as fast as possible in order to 'disappear' at the other end?"

"Right. I'd forgotten that."

"The rope was strung fifty-five inches from the floor, which is throat level for a woman who's somewhere between five-six to five-eight. It makes me think that the rope was meant as a trap for someone that height running down the hallway, as you were supposed to do. You would have collided with the rope and, at the very least, sustained a nasty rope burn across your face or neck. And maybe you would have cut off your air supply enough to pass out."

"So the trap was set for someone my height."

"Annette was in that height range, too, as were the other two witches and about a quarter of the females working at the haunted house."

"But they weren't nearly mowed down by a car last Sunday," Skye muttered.

"What?"

Skye explained about the hit-and-run after church, then said, "So either the rope was supposed to choke someone— me or one of the other witches—or maybe the murderer knew about Annette's asthma and was trying to trigger a lethal attack. And if that's the case, who would know her weaknesses better than her husband?"

Simon's expression was thoughtful. "Too bad Quirk has closed the investigation."

Skye felt faint, and she gripped the back of a chair to steady herself. Had she wrongly accused the officer and dragged Wally back here for nothing? Or was Quirk so quick to close the case because he didn't want any further investigation that might point to him?

"You really need to see a doctor." Simon put his arm around her.

"I'll be fine." Skye summoned up a smile. "Don't worry. All I need is a good night's rest."

"I know your folks and Wally are all out of town. If you need something tonight, call me." Simon gave her another squeeze, then released her. "I promise not to jump to any conclusions."

"Thank you."

Once she showed Simon out, Skye went into the parlor. Kurt had been looking at the objets d'art in the étagère, and when Skye entered, he tapped the glass and said, "I really like this vase."

"You have good taste. It's one of a series made by Frank Klepper, a Dallas-based artist who worked in ceramics during the early 1930s. It's called *Curtain of the Dawn.*"

"I thought it was from the thirties. I tend to collect more from the twenties, but occasionally something a little more recent catches my eye." His gaze roved lazily from her head to her feet; then he grinned.

"Glad you approve," she said dryly. It was hard to feel sexy when she might upchuck at any moment. "You said you had something to discuss with me?" She felt herself sway.

"Hey, are you all right?" Kurt's expression became serious, and he helped her to the settee.

"I think I'm getting a bug." Skye rested her head on the seat back and closed her eyes. She'd be fine if only the room would stop spinning.

"Guess that means no kisses," Kurt teased. "Don't want to get your germs."

"Look. I feel lousy, so if you have something important to say, say it. Otherwise, I need to lie down."

"Sure. Sorry." Kurt sat next to Skye and put his hand on her forehead. "It doesn't feel like you have a fever, but you are pale."

She was touched by his concern. "Maybe it's something I ate."

"Can I get you something? Alka-Seltzer? Pepto-Bismol? I could run to the pharmacy."

"No, thank you." He was much more attractive when he wasn't playing the fool, and despite feeling rotten, Skye found herself extremely conscious of his appeal.

"So, did you find out anything?" Kurt asked.

"Not much." Skye quickly told him about the scene Trixie had witnessed at the grocery store between Dr. Paine and his younger daughter's teacher, and then about Evie's refusal to talk to her. She didn't tell him about Hope's fear of Quirk or what Simon had told her, since both had sworn her to secrecy.

"Interesting. I'd heard Paine was a womanizer, but didn't know he was that slimy." Kurt raised an eyebrow. "I wonder what Evie's hiding."

"I wish I knew." Skye twitched her shoulders. "Maybe she'll talk to you."

"I'll give it a try, but don't hold your breath."

Skye made a face, then asked, "What have you found out?"

"Annette's only interest was her social standing. She didn't owe anyone money, and people thought she was bossy and annoying, but no one seemed to hate her enough to kill her."

"Except maybe her husband." When Kurt nodded, she asked, "How about Nina Miles?"

"If she was supposed to be the victim, it was self-defense. Nina was probably boring the murderer to death."

"Oh?" Skye felt the corner of her lips turn up. "Not your most entertaining interview, I take it?"

"She seems to have no life of her own. All she could talk about was her three daughters. Her oldest daughter, Farrah, seems to be a bit of a disappointment. But her middle one, Bree, is the most popular girl in high school, and her youngest, Shawna, is going to be a Broadway star. It seems without her, the dance school in town couldn't even put on a recital, since she helps all the other girls with their performances."

"Yeah, and if she doesn't get the leading role she scalps the competition." Skye told Kurt how Shawna had cut the hair of a fellow third grader in order to dance the lead in *Rapunzel*.

"Why am I not shocked?" Kurt's dimples appeared. "Though Nina's main obsession right now is getting Bree voted prom queen." Kurt scratched his head. "The prom isn't until May, right? Seven months away?"

"Right, but the moms have turned it into a yearlong competition."

"Maybe those women are killing each other."

Skye had wondered that herself when Frannie mentioned how intense the prom queen and king competition had become, but now that she had thought about it more, she said, "They wouldn't do that."

"Why not? Nina sounded pretty ruthless. I doubt she'd let a little thing like murder stand in her way. After all, she admitted to blackmail. Do you know these moms have parties for the kids who are in the running for king and queen, and take pictures of any behavior that they can use against them?"

Skye shook her head. She hadn't known, though she wasn't surprised. "But murdering one of the other candidates' mothers wouldn't help get her daughter elected, because the victim's daughter would get the sympathy vote." Skye struggled to her feet. "Now if one of the *girls* ended up dead, that would be a different story."

Kurt raised his eyebrows. "And I thought the people I covered in my last job were twisted."

"Who were they?" Skye guided Kurt toward the front door and opened it.

"Politicians."

After Kurt left, Skye checked her messages and found one from Wally. He hadn't been able to arrange for his father's nurse to start early. Since he wouldn't be home until late Friday night, he had spoken to the new sheriff, who had agreed to keep an off-the-record eye on Quirk until Wally got back to town.

Skye blew out a frustrated breath, then headed upstairs to lie down. The only good thing about feeling sick was that she didn't have the energy to be scared.

Skye felt much better in the morning, and since she had recovered health-wise, she decided to work on her lingering depression by wearing one of her new fall outfits. She chose olive twill slacks, a matching T-shirt, and a short olive, rust, and brown jacket. To complete the look, she slipped on chunky gold earrings, a bangle bracelet, and the brown Coach pumps she had found on sale for seventy percent off at TJMaxx.

Because of the weekly PPS meeting at seven thirty, Skye's schedule called for her to spend Thursday mornings at the elementary school. The team met in the special-ed room, which was about half the size of the other classrooms. It held only twelve desks—arranged in three pods of four each—and the student chairs of molded orange plastic were designed for the height and build of six- and seven-year-olds.

The sole adult chair was behind the teacher's desk, and although Skye was the first to arrive, she knew better than to try to claim it. Some battles weren't worth fighting.

Next to appear was Abby, the school nurse. She and Skye immediately started to take the chairs off the tops of the student desks, where they had been placed at the end of the previous day.

They were removing the last two when the special-education teacher, Yvonne Smith, came in. As usual, she was dressed in a full denim skirt and an oxford-cloth blouse—today's was blue. Yvonne was what most people pictured when they thought of an elementary school teacher—round and soft, with a halo of gray-brown curls and a smiling face.

Next to turn up was Belle Whitney, the speech therapist, who took a seat next to Abby. Belle looked like a can of Reddi-wip that had exploded. Her pale blond hair was arranged in fluffy curls and feathery waves, and her rose pink dress was made of a diaphanous material with rows of ruffles around the neck, sleeves, and hem. Even her eyeglasses had loops and curlicues on the frames.

Jackie and the grade school principal were the last to arrive. Jackie's hand was on Caroline's arm, and she was whispering in her ear.

The principal, a tiny woman with a puff of white hair, patted Jackie's cheek and said, "Thank you, my dear. You are just the sweetest thing to volunteer for recess duty. Our 'specials' usually claim they're too busy." Turning her attention to the assembled group, Caroline smiled, took a seat, and plucked gold-rimmed reading glasses from the pocket of her blazer. "Shall we start?" She peered at the list she had put on the table. "Our most pressing concern this morning is a new student. Vassily Warner is five years old and recently adopted from Russia."

"Do we have records on him?" Abby asked.

"None."

"Has he ever attended school?" Yvonne asked.

"All his adoptive parents know is that he's been in an orphanage since birth," Caroline reported. "They were assured he is healthy, but that's it."

Dang. From what Skye had read about Russian orphanages, she knew that in many, the preschool-age children spent most of their days alone in cagelike cribs. "Will the parents bring him in for an assessment?"

"Yes." Caroline handed Skye a Post-it note. "Here's their number. They'd like him to start school as soon as possible."

Skye hastily looked through her appointment book. "I'll call them this morning and try to set something up for tomorrow afternoon."

"I'd like to see him then, too, if that's okay?" Belle looked up from her own appointment book.

"Great." Skye's pencil hovered. "Is Friday at one good for you?"

"It's fine." Belle made a note in her calendar.

Abby said, "I'll stop by, too, and see if the parents have any health records."

"Uh . . ." Caroline cleared her throat. "There's only one problem."

"Only one." Skye chuckled. "That's a switch."

"Vassily doesn't speak English."

"That *is* a major problem." Skye tapped the pencil eraser on her lip. "I have no idea where we'd get a psychologist, or an interpreter, who speaks Russian."

"Me." Jackie smiled like a woman who had gotten the last pair of Prada sandals at a year-end sale. "I speak Russian. I can interpret for you."

Caroline beamed at Jackie, and Belle asked, "For me, as well?"

"Sure, no problem."

Skye smiled and thanked Jackie, but inside she was frowning. It was mighty convenient that their new social worker just happened to speak the one foreign language they needed. But she wouldn't lie about that, would she?

Then a thought popped into Skye's mind. If Jackie were lying, who would ever know?

CHAPTER 19

Walk This Way

Should she keep her appointment with Dr. Paine or not? Skye vacillated as she unlocked the Bel Air and slid behind the wheel. On the one hand, Wally *had* said not to do anything that would make Quirk think that she was still investigating, and if Annette was not the intended victim, there was no reason to talk to her husband.

Then again, maybe Quirk was innocent, and Dr. Paine had set up his wife's "accidental" death. If that were the case, he might let something slip to Skye—they usually carried on a friendly banter during her appointments. Now that she thought about it, he *was* rather flirtatious.

Besides, Dr. Paine was her regular dentist. Even if he or Roy Quirk was the killer, neither man would have cause to think she was going to the dentist for any reason other than a toothache. Having justified the visit to herself, Skye turned right on Basin Street, and a few minutes later pulled into the dentist's parking lot.

As she walked across the blacktop, she noticed the vehicle parked in the spot marked RESERVED FOR DR. PAINE. The older sedan looked very much like the car that had nearly run her down after church. It was the same color and general shape. Too bad she hadn't noticed the license last Sunday, because Dr. Paine's plates read 2THDOX.

Skye paused outside the front door. Was it foolish to put herself in the hands of a man who might have tried to run her over? No, it would look more suspicious if she didn't show up after making an appointment.

Once inside, Skye turned right and went through another door that led into a small waiting room. She stepped over to the window to check in with the receptionist, but there was no one at the desk, so she wrote her name on the sign-in sheet and took a seat.

Skye glanced at her watch. It was exactly four o'clock. Where was everyone? There was no bell or buzzer. After a few minutes she picked up a copy of *Good Housekeeping* and paged through it. When she checked the time again, fifteen minutes had passed.

Uncertain what to do, she stood, pushed open the inner door, and called, "Anybody here?"

No one answered, even after she repeated her question in a louder voice. Surely the staff wouldn't have left the office unlocked. Maybe, since she was the last appointment of the day, Dr. Paine had let the receptionist leave and Skye was supposed to go straight in. You would think, though, that someone would have left a note to that effect.

Annoyed, Skye eased through the door. The moment she was inside the hallway, anxiety spurted through her. It wasn't the pain that made her hate to go to the dentist; it was the noise and the smell. Today the office was as silent as a tomb; unfortunately, the odor of antiseptic and fear remained.

The first two alcoves on her right were empty, as was the small office to her left, but now that she had moved farther down the short corridor, she could hear groans coming from the treatment room at the end of the hall—the only one with a door.

Skye hesitated. It sounded as if Dr. Paine was working on a patient. Should she go back and sit in the waiting area? But with the receptionist gone, how would he know she was there? Maybe she should leave. No. She had come this far. She'd let the dentist know she had arrived.

"Dr. Paine." She knocked on the door, opened it a fraction, and said, "It's Skye Denison. I have a four-o'clock appointment."

No answer. She raised her voice, "Uh, Dr. Paine." She inched the door a little wider, stuck her head around the edge, and whispered, "Holy crap!"

Blond hair flowed over the headrest of the dental chair, and long pink nails clawed at a white butt going up and down like an oil derrick. The dentist wasn't filling a tooth; he was filling a much lower cavity.

Skye eased the door shut. Obviously Dylan Paine wouldn't be very cooperative if she interrupted him in the middle of his crowning achievement. But this, along with the incident at the grocery store, confirmed that Dr. Paine was indeed the Romeo of the rinse sink, and thus had a motive for doing away with his wife.

During her short ride home, Skye figured out who the dentist had been drilling that afternoon. The hair and nails had looked familiar, and she connected the dots. Dr. Paine's little afternoon delight was none other than Evie Harrison. *Hmm.* That gave Evie an even stronger motive for killing Annette.

Skye smirked. Clearly Evie had found some spare time in her busy schedule as Promfest chair. A talk with the blonde was way overdue, and now that Skye knew about Evie and Dr. Paine, no way could the woman get Skye fired or complain to Quirk about Skye harassing her.

Bingo met Skye as she stepped into the foyer, rubbing against her ankles and purring. She scooped him up and nuzzled his soft fur. "Were you a good boy today?" He bumped her hand with his head, demanding that she scratch under his chin. "Of course you were. Unlike some males in this town, you've been fixed."

Skye continued petting the cat until he tired of the attention, wiggled out of her arms, and herded her into the kitchen, where he stood looking meaningfully at his empty food bowl. She fetched the open can of Fancy Feast and gave him another third of the contents—he'd gotten the first third that morning.

She found herself smiling. Was she in a good mood because she was finally making some progress on the murder, or because she seemed to be over whatever bug had been causing her to feel sick the past few days? Or maybe her illness wasn't a virus. Come to think of it, because of her dentist appointment, she hadn't eaten her usual ration of cookies that afternoon.

Could she be allergic to Oreos? She shook her head, refusing to believe those delicious chocolate wafers with their luscious cream filling could be the culprit. It had been the flu, and that was that.

Grinning at her own silliness, she went to check her answering machine. The flashing light indicated four messages. The first was another one from her mother, which Skye erased. She felt a little guilty, but she knew Vince had talked to May that morning and assured her that Skye was fine, so there was no need for her to spend an hour—or more—reiterating the news.

The second was from Loretta again, short and to the point: "We need to talk about Vince. Call me."

Shoot. Skye's mood darkened. She should have known it wouldn't be possible to stay out of that mess. She only hoped she wouldn't lose Loretta's friendship over it.

The third call was from Hope Kennedy, saying she'd run into Quirk at the gas station and he'd threatened her again. Skye tried to call the teacher back, but no one answered.

The final message was from Wally. "Hi. I've got some bad news. Dad fired the original nurse I lined up—said he wanted a male RN. I've found one, but he can't start before Saturday, which means I can't come home until then. My new flight arrives at four thirty, so I should be in Scumble River by six thirty or seven, depending on traffic. I'll call

you when I get in." Skye thought he had hung up, but as she
started to press DELETE, he said, "Why don't you have your
cell phone on? I keep leaving messages on your voice mail,
but you never call me back."

Crap. She wasn't allowed to have her cell activated in the
school building, and she kept forgetting to turn it on once
she left. And she really needed to figure out how to access
her voice mail.

As she quickly dialed Wally's number, she wondered
were she had put the instruction booklet that came with her
cell. Of course, now Wally wasn't answering his phone, so
she left him a message about Quirk's latest threat to Hope
and hung up. Maybe tomorrow would be better.

Fridays were supposed to be good days, but Skye's sure
wasn't going that way. When she walked into the high
school, Homer dragged her into his office and began
screaming at her about some stupid traffic cones. "Do you
have any idea what a mess you caused this morning? Buses
were stacked up like the Tupperware bowls in my wife's
cupboard. We had to close off the whole damn parking lot!"

"I have no idea what you're talking about. I wasn't even
here this morning. I stopped at the grade school to speak to
a teacher." Skye had assured Hope Kennedy that Wally
would be back the next evening and would take care of the
Quirk situation. "I didn't get here until a few minutes ago."

"Fern didn't see you, and you didn't sign the attendance
log. I checked."

"I forgot to sign it because I didn't go into the office.
After I talked to the teacher, I spent an hour setting things up
for an evaluation this afternoon, then came over here," Skye
explained. "What happened?"

"You know darn well what happened." Homer loomed
over Skye, who was seated on a visitor's chair in his office.
"You put traffic cones funneling the buses away from the entrance and into the bus parking area in the back of the
school, which is a fricking dead end."

"I did not," Skye protested, her heart pounding. No one messed with the buses and got away with it. "Why would I do that?"

"How should I know? But you were seen." Homer crossed his arms and glared at her. "Mrs. Boswell, the old lady who lives across the street in the white house, was out walking her dog and saw you putting the cones out. She came to my office and told me all about it when she saw the traffic jam."

"That's impossible. I didn't do it." Skye ran her fingers through her hair. "What time was this?"

"Seven thirty-five. She remembers exactly because she waits until seven thirty to take Snowflake out. She said she knows all the teachers have to be here by that time, but the buses don't start to arrive until seven forty."

"But, but . . ." Skye trailed off.

"But nothing," Homer roared. "In my thirty-five years of experience, nothing like this has ever happened before."

Skye stopped herself from blurting out that in reality, Homer had had one year of experience thirty-five times, since he did the same thing over and over again.

Homer stared at Skye, and when she remained silent he demanded, "Why did you do it?"

"I keep telling you I didn't." Skye was getting frantic. "Did Mrs. Boswell identify me by name?"

"No," Homer admitted. "But she said she saw a female of your general build, with curly reddish brown hair."

"What do you mean, my 'general build'?"

Homer's eyes dropped. "Not thin."

"Fat?"

"That wasn't what Mrs. Boswell said." Homer didn't look up. "Not exactly."

Hmm. Homer was less of a jerk when he was embarrassed. Skye tucked that fact into her memory for future use, but quickly pressed on, not wanting to lose her slight advantage. "What exactly did she say?"

"She said she saw a big girl putting the traffic cones out."

"She used the word *girl*?"

"Now don't go all feminazi on me." Homer was already over his embarrassment. "Mrs. Boswell is in her nineties—anyone under sixty is a girl to her."

"I see. And she said curly hair?"

Homer nodded.

"My hair's straight today." Skye lifted a strand. "See? I had some extra time this morning, so I used my flatiron. It's only curly when I let it dry naturally."

"Do I look as if I care what you do with your freaking hair?" Homer's voice rose in anger. "Try to wiggle out of this any way you can—the description fits you." He jabbed her in the shoulder with his index finger.

Skye searched her mind. Had anyone at the grade school seen her at seven thirty? She'd talked to Hope quite a bit earlier than that. Yes. Thank goodness for Belle's talkativeness.

"I can prove it wasn't me. The speech pathologist stopped by my office at the grade school around that time to ask if I had been able to set up a testing appointment with the parents of the new student." Skye pushed Homer away from her, got up, and grabbed the phone. "Call and ask her if you don't believe me."

Once Homer verified her alibi, Skye fled the high school. Her schedule called for her to be there all morning, but she knew that if she stuck around, she'd end up telling the principal what she thought of him, which would result in tears—either on her part or on his, maybe both.

If she hadn't had the whole team set up to evaluate the little Russian boy, she would have given up and gone home. Instead, she spent the rest of the time until his appointment brooding in her office at the grade school.

Later she decided she should have taken the sick day. Nothing Skye said to the boy in English, or Jackie said to him in Russian, seemed to make any impression. Instead, Vassily spent the time tearing around the room and destroying anything that was not nailed down.

His parents said his behavior was similar at home, and

they were at their wits' end. Skye assured Mr. and Mrs. Warner that she would include a behavior plan when she wrote her report. Developmentally, he appeared to be less than two years old.

Vassily had cut a wide swath of destruction through Skye's office, and as she cleaned it up, she thought about the last few days. Chemical bombs at the high school, wannabe mommies at the junior high, and now a wild child at the elementary school—not to mention Annette's death and Hope's revelation about Quirk. What was next? An invasion by spacemen?

Why was she doing this? Yes, she wanted to talk to Evie about her affair with Dylan Paine, and also find out why the new Promfest chair had run away screaming the night of Annette's death. Yes, she was still afraid that she would look bad in comparison to Jackie. And yes, she had given her word, but in her heart, Skye knew it was a mistake to return to the haunted house.

She hadn't been in the bathroom for ten minutes when her instincts were proven right. As she took off her street clothes and prepared to slip her costume over her leotard, she heard a siren. Was that the police? What had happened now?

Before Skye could decide whether to put her regular clothes back on or go ahead with the witch's outfit, the building's fire alarms started to blare. Instantly the other women, who were also changing into their costumes in the bathroom, made a mad dash for the exit, each trying to be the first one out.

Skye stood undecided—there had been so many false alarms at school that she distrusted the system—but a nanosecond later common sense prevailed. Even the possibility of being charbroiled was enough to make her skedaddle.

Snatching her tote bag, which contained her jeans and sweater, and wiggling into the long black witch's dress as she ran, Skye followed the others. Regrettably, the women had halted only a few steps from the bathroom door, and Skye, unable to stop her forward momentum, plowed into them, mowing them down like a broom hitting a nest of dust bunnies.

It took her a few minutes to free herself from the tangle of arms and legs, and when she did she wished she could crawl back under the pile. Standing in the hallway, dressed like a cross between a cartoon astronaut and the Tin Man from *The Wizard of Oz*, was Earl Doozier. In his hand he held a toilet plunger. On his head was a portable siren duct-taped to a baseball cap, a stringy ponytail dangling out the opening in back. At his feet sat an industrial-size Shop-Vac. Glued to its canister was a hand-lettered sign that read GHOSTFLUSHERS.

Skye closed her eyes and prayed for a twister to transport her to the Emerald City. An instant later someone screamed.

CHAPTER 20

A Midsummer Night's Dream, aka A Midautumn's Nightmare

Skye watched in appalled fascination as Earl shouted something about evil spooks and bloodthirsty bogeymen while thrusting his plunger into the growing crowd. Drawn by his hollering and the women's screams, people from all over the haunted house poured into the hallway. Most of the group wore bemused expressions, but a few actually seemed frightened, and at least two folks were enraged.

Frankenstein, aka Dr. Paine, appeared furious enough to start busting heads, as did the woman next to him, Zinnia Idell. Skye shuddered. She knew from personal experience that Mrs. Idell could turn violent faster than a Weedwacker could decapitate a flower not perfectly aligned with its peers, and for as little reason.

Skye had forgotten that Mrs. Idell was involved in A Ghoul's Night Out. Her presence tonight meant she had been at the hall last Friday as well. Maybe she *was* angry enough with Skye to have strung up the rope that killed Annette. Come to think of it, Zinnia had been at Mass last Sunday, too. Skye wondered what kind of car she drove.

Mrs. Idell was fingering something in her jacket pocket, and Skye winced when Earl whirled on her and yelled,

"Y'all stand aside now. I'm here to save you from the spooks," and shoved his plunger in Zinnia's face.

When the woman whipped out a pistol and aimed it at Earl's heart, Skye took an involuntary step backward and shrieked, "Don't shoot!"

Despite the fact that Earl had traded his customary fall ensemble of sweatpants and flannel shirt for a Michelin Man jacket with the lid of a garbage can duct-taped to its front, Skye was pretty sure he was still in trouble. The new outfit might be the latest thing in fighting ghosts, but it wasn't bulletproof.

Skye's fellow haunted-house workers surged forward to get a better view of the show, crowding Mrs. Idell, Dr. Paine, and Earl closer together. The proximity caused Earl's thrusts with the plunger to become jerkier, and Mrs. Idell's hand to move back and forth. Dr. Paine stood absolutely still, staring at the gun as it swung from side to side.

Someone had turned off the alarm, but that shouldn't stop the firefighters from arriving to check things out. Where were they? Maybe, unlike the schools, this building's system wasn't directly connected to the fire station.

Whatever the reason, help didn't seem to be arriving. Now what? Skye briefly considered battling her way to the edge of the crowd and hightailing it out of there, but curiosity and her instinctive desire to help won out. She needed a plan.

Spotting Evie hovering near the exit with a cell phone pressed to her ear, Skye elbowed her way toward her, shouting above the noise, "Any thoughts on what to do about this?"

"As soon as I get a signal," Evie continued, pressing buttons, "I'm calling the cops to come arrest the freak."

Skye flinched. "You do know that arresting a Doozier usually takes the National Guard, and I have a feeling it might require the Special Forces to bring in Zinnia Idell."

"Don't be silly." Evie edged around Skye. "Situations

like this are why we pay taxes." Pushing open the exit, she stepped outside and closed the door emphatically in Skye's face.

Skye raised an eyebrow. If the chairwoman had that kind of confidence in the government, she must be a lot happier writing her check to the Internal Revenue Service on April fifteenth than most people were.

Cell phone reception on the sidewalk didn't seem to be any better than it was inside the building. As Skye watched, Evie furiously pirouetted in different directions like a ballerina dancing *Swan Lake*, all the while thrusting her cell phone in the air.

After a few moments of enjoying the performance, Skye realized this was her opportunity to get things under control before Quirk arrived and made a bad situation worse. Her adrenaline pumping, she zigzagged back toward the front of the crowd.

Following her belief that effective communication could solve most problems, Skye pushed through the crowd until she was only a couple of feet from Zinnia, and called in a loud voice, "Mrs. Idell. Mrs. Idell."

"You!" Zinnia kept the gun leveled at Earl, but turned her head toward Skye. "Why are you always around when there's a problem? What does it take to make you mind your own business, a grenade up your butt?"

"Uh . . . I'm just trying to help." Skye realized that putting herself within bullet range of an armed parent who hated her guts had not been a wise move, and she scrambled for something calming to say. "I know everyone's a little nervous, with the murder and all, but Earl, here, is completely harmless."

"No, I'm not." Earl grabbed the hose of the Shop-Vac and shook it. "I'm the Ghostflusher. I'm the only one here who can tell the fake ghouls and goblins from the real ones. Without me, you're all in danger." Earl made a loud woo-wooing sound.

Skye hissed at Earl, "Shut up." Then she turned to

Zinnia and said, "You know Earl, Mrs. Idell. His reality check bounced long ago."

"You ain't got no call to be talking about me that way." Earl gave Skye a hurt look. "I ain't never bounced a check. I ain't even got a checking account."

Zinnia's expression hardened. "That doesn't give him the right to come in here and scare everyone half to death." Her voice was querulous. "I ought to tie that long ponytail of his to the short hair on his ass."

Skye made a placating gesture at Zinnia. "Earl doesn't mean any harm. He's just a prong short of a plug."

Mrs. Idell scratched her head with her gun hand, and everyone around them ducked. "Then what's he doing here?"

Relieved that Zinnia was talking instead of shooting, Skye switched her attention back to the Doozier. "What *are* you doing here, Earl?"

"I heard that some ghosts were bothering you last Friday, Miz Skye, and I came to take care of them."

"That's very sweet of you, Earl, but I'm fine." Skye made a shooing motion with her hands. "Why don't you go to the Brown Bag and have a nice cold beer?" She dug in her tote bag and came out with a five-dollar bill. "My treat."

"Nosirreebob." Earl licked his lips, but shook his head. "I heard you were so scared they found you curled up in the fecal position. And that ain't right."

He was correct on that point. It wasn't right. Skye's brow furrowed. She fixed him with a hard stare and demanded in her best teacher voice, "Who told you that?"

"I can't rightly say, Miz Skye."

Earl's expression had gone from stubborn to mulish, and Skye knew she had to rethink her approach. The Dooziers were not your run-of-the-mill Scumble River family, and her usual methods didn't work with them.

The Doozier family was legendary—*colorful* and *bois-terous* didn't begin to describe them. They were a bit like

Bigfoot, but a lot more visible. Members of an extended clan of misfits called the Red Raggers, they seemed to be around whenever there was a troublesome situation, and Earl was their king.

The Red Raggers didn't usually make the first move, but they never missed an opportunity to make the second, especially if it involved a chance to fight or to make a profit.

Red Raggers didn't have stock portfolios—they had lottery tickets. They didn't have retirement plans—they had money buried in mason jars in their backyard. They didn't order personalized license plates—their kin made them in the local prison.

Earl regarded Skye as an honorary Doozier because of all she'd done for his children, sisters, brothers, nieces, and nephews in her job as a school psychologist. And in return, Skye had developed a certain respect for Earl and his relatives. Not to mention they had managed to save her butt on more than a few occasions. Unhappily, this meant they now treated her like their pet hound dog—with affectionate indifference, unless someone bothered her; then it was all-out war.

While Skye had been mentally reviewing the Red Raggers' résumé, Earl had stuck his hand into his pants pocket, and Zinnia had jerked her gun back toward him while ordering him to freeze.

Earl ignored the irate woman. He thrust a fistful of white rectangles in the air and said, "Here's my business card. I hear a lot of you good folks will be having trouble with spooks in your houses, and my rates are real reasonable." Zinnia fired a shot into the Shop-Vac at the Ghostflusher's feet. At the resounding boom, Earl leapt behind Skye and bawled, "Save me! Save me!"

"Hold your fire." Skye stepped as far away from the gunwoman as she could. "Remember, this is Earl Doozier. He's not all there." She pointed to the side of her forehead and twirled her finger.

Earl bleated, "That ain't a nice thing to say about a friend who's jist trying to help you and the community out, Miz Skye."

"Shut up, Earl." Skye looked nervously at Zinnia, who was a few bullets short of a clip herself. "Mrs. Idell, how about you escort everyone into the lobby and let me sort this out with Earl."

Zinnia didn't budge.

"Really, he doesn't mean any harm," Skye pleaded. "It's just that his antenna doesn't pick up all the channels."

"Miz Skye!" Earl fussed. "You know we got cable."

She ignored him. "Look, give us some room. You still have the gun. If he tries anything, you can shoot him."

"Hush, Miz Skye! You're gonna get me kilt!"

Zinnia shrugged, then, along with Dr. Paine, moved the crowd out of the hall and into the lobby, leaving Skye alone with Earl. She opened her mouth, but before she could speak, the outside door slammed open, and the queen of the Red Raggers burst into the passageway.

Skye whimpered. Just what she needed. Earl's wife, Glenda, had hair like a skunk's fur, breasts like a porn star's, and the personality of a Tasmanian devil.

Ignoring Skye, Glenda glared at her husband. "Earl Doozier," she screamed, "you get your ass home right this minute."

Earl backed up, keeping Skye between him and his bride. "But, sweetie, I told you I was startin' a new business."

"Why do I always find you doin' somethin' stupid with her around watchin'?"

Glenda jerked her thumb at Skye, whose gaze was drawn to the woman's bright red fingernails. They were long and curved, and Skye was fairly certain they could pry open tin cans.

"Now, honey pie, Miz Skye needs me—"

"Yeah. Like a dog needs a bra."

"You ain't got no call to talk to me that way." Earl took his life in his hands when he sassed his wife.

"I'm countin' to three." Glenda crushed out her cigarette under a scarlet stiletto–shod foot. "And you better have your skinny butt out the door and in the car, or you're in for the ass-whuppin' of your life."

Skye decided she needed to intervene if she was ever going to find out who had told Earl she needed saving. "Could I talk to him a minute first?" She took hold of his arm.

Tugging at the crotch of her pleather jeans, her skintight sweater riding up and exposing her chalk white muffin top, Glenda glared at Skye. "Whatta you want with my man?"

Skye kept a firm grip on Earl's arm, but said soothingly, "I promise I'll send him home as soon as he answers one question."

Earl looked from his wife to Skye, and backed away. "Both of you leave me alone."

Glenda narrowed her eyes and swung her gaze to Skye. "What's in it for me?"

Skye thought fast. "A free haircut, color, and style at Vince's salon." She would owe her brother big-time for this.

Not quite as thick as her husband, Glenda bartered, "And a new outfit from Wal-Mart."

Skye countered, "No more than twenty-five dollars."

"Deal." Glenda turned to Earl. "Okay, mister. You stay here." Earl started to protest, but Glenda shook her finger at him. "Shut your yap, and answer her questions."

Skye wrinkled her forehead, wondering if Earl had ventriloquist skills she knew nothing about.

After Glenda stomped away, Earl meekly followed Skye into the parking lot, where she deposited him in her Bel Air, away from prying ears, and demanded, "Who told you I needed your help?"

He immediately started to whine, "I don't rightly remember, Miz Skye. I jist heard it around."

"What exactly did you hear, Earl?"

"That the haunted house was truly haunted and the spooks were after you."

"Why would someone say that?" Skye stared out the car's window. "Nothing happened to me. Annette Paine was the one who was murdered."

"They're sayin' it was a ghost that killed Missus Paine, and the spook's coming after you next."

"Who said that?"

"I'm not sure who I heard it from." Earl screwed up his face. "I think one of the kids might've mentioned it."

"One of the little kids or one of the older ones?"

"It might have been Elvira."

Elvira was Earl's sister, who lived with him and his family. She was a senior in high school, and Skye vowed to talk to her first thing on Monday. "Okay, at least now I sort of understand why you're here, but how did you think you were going to catch this ghost?"

"I studied up all week and learnt how to get rid of spooks. I got me a degree in ghostology from Falconia University, and I'm starting a business. I figure there must be lots of bad spirits and evil around here. And once people hear how I saved you all, they'll be lining up to hire the Ghostflushers."

"How did you study? Are there books on ghost hunting?" She knew she shouldn't ask, but couldn't resist.

"I didn't need no stinkin' books. I got all I need to know from watching movies." Earl grinned, revealing several missing teeth.

"What movies taught you how to get rid of ghosts?" Skye couldn't believe someone was offering a course on the subject.

"Let's see now." Earl scratched his chin with the plunger. "*Ghostbusters*—that's the one I got my company's name from—and *The Ghost and Mr. Chicken*, and—"

Skye cut him off. "And you got a degree for watching these movies?"

"Yep. Right there on the Internet. Junior helped me print out the diploma. You want to see it?"

"No." Skye shook her head. "I believe you." She couldn't decide whether to laugh or cry; even the Dooziers were more computer-savvy than she was.

Earl handed her a stack of business cards. "You give these here cards to everyone and tell 'em that if they need their houses despookified, just call the Ghostflushers. Only twenty dollars a ghoul."

"I don't know if people will pay for something like that," Skye cautioned.

"You jist tell all those folks in the haunted house that a bunch of real ghosts is fixin' to plague Scumble River, and I'm the only one that can save them." He fumbled in his pocket and brought out a crumpled piece of notebook paper. "These here are the first ones to be infested."

"Earl." Skye's mouth pursed. "You aren't planning on having your relatives sneak into people's houses and pretend to be ghosts, are you?"

He shook his head, but refused to meet her gaze. "Just remind folks not to be penny-wise and dollar-dumb."

"I'll make sure to do that, but you keep in mind that breaking and entering is a felony." Skye knew there was no reasoning with a Doozier in denial, but had to give it her best shot. "You'd better get home before Glenda comes back looking for you."

"Yes, ma'am. I need to skedaddle." Earl slid out of the car. "I'll come back later to get rid of the spooks for you."

As Skye walked Earl to his car, she noticed that the driver's-side window had a spiderweb crack. She pointed to the broken glass. "What happened here?"

"I thought my window was rolled down, but I found out it was up when I put my head through it."

"I see." Skye was surprised the glass had been clean enough for Earl to make that mistake.

She waited until the Ghostflusher got into his Buick and drove away; then she headed back toward the old American Legion hall. As she stepped inside, she heard a police siren approaching. Evie must have gotten a signal on her cell phone. Skye blew out a long breath. There was a riddle for you: How many times did the police have to be called to the Promfest haunted house before they caught the one who put the lights out?

CHAPTER 21

Save the Last
Dance for Me

Once the police took Zinnia Idell away for unlawful possession of a firearm, the haunted-house rehearsal went smoothly, and A Ghoul's Night Out opened for business. It was a rip-roaring success, with a continuous stream of customers from the moment they opened the doors until they shut them at ten thirty.

At ten thirty-five, Skye was already out of her costume, into her street clothes, and looking for Evie. She found the chairwoman counting the night's receipts.

Positioning herself between Evie and the ticket booth's only exit, Skye said, "We need to talk."

"I told you I'd talk to you when I have time. Didn't you get my note? Do I need to call Officer Quirk?"

Skye pulled over a chair and sat, continuing to block the doorway. "This won't take long." She had no intention of letting Evie leave until the blonde had answered her questions. "And after you hear what I have to say, I doubt you'll want Quirk involved."

"What are you talking about?" Evie had shed the gracious demeanor she generally showed the public.

Skye ignored the question, and asked one of her own. "When you and I bumped heads last Friday at the haunted house, why did you run away screaming?"

"Duh." Evie looked at Skye as if she was an idiot. "I had just seen someone who looked exactly like you lying dead on the ground. I thought you were a ghost."

"How did you know the woman was dead?"

"I put my compact mirror to her lips." Evie shuddered. "She wasn't breathing."

That made sense—well, as much sense as anything was making in this case. Skye had nearly had a meltdown herself when she'd seen her own spitting image sprawled lifeless on the floor. "Why were you there to begin with?"

"Countess Dracula comes on right in the beginning, so my bit was over. I was using that passageway as a shortcut to get outside to my car."

"Why were you going to your car?"

"It's none of your business," Evie snapped. "You'd better leave me alone, or I'll have my husband talk the school board into firing you. I'm exhausted and I'd like to finish here and go to bed."

"Your own or Dr. Paine's?" Skye had decided a little shock treatment might make Evie more cooperative.

"What are you talking about?" Evie carefully rubber banded a bundle of bills, avoiding Skye's stare.

"I saw you Thursday afternoon." Skye raised an eyebrow. "It seemed like quite a thorough checkup."

"I don't know what you mean."

"Of course you do." Skye noted that Evie was no longer threatening to call the police or have her fired. "You, Dylan Paine, and the dental chair of love. I took a picture with my cell." Not that Skye had any idea if her phone even had a camera, but Evie didn't know that.

Evie wilted. "Are you going to tell my husband?"

Skye's voice was firm. "Not if you answer my questions."

"What do you want to know?"

"How long have you been having an affair with Dr. Paine?"

Evie counted on her fingers. "About a month."

"Why would you risk your marriage and everything

you've worked for on Promfest to have an affair with a man who screws anyone in a skirt?"

"What do you mean? I was the first time he strayed." Evie's tone was earnest. "The chemistry is too much for us. Dylan and I both feel bad about cheating on our spouses, but we don't seem able to stop."

"I see." Skye eyed the blonde thoughtfully. Was Evie really that naive? "There has to be another reason."

"Well." Evie gave a nervous little laugh. "He did promise to force Annette to give me the chairmanship of Promfest."

Skye smiled to herself. Now she was getting somewhere. "How was he going to do that?"

"He never said," Evie answered. "I thought maybe he would threaten to divorce her. Her position in the community was dependent on being married to a successful and wealthy man. She never worked or had a career of her own. Heck, she didn't even finish her first semester at Joliet Junior College."

"That's interesting, because I heard that Annette was threatening to divorce him." Skye tried to make sense of the conflicting information. "Of course, Dr. Paine could have been just feeding you a line to get into your pants."

"That's not how he is."

"Then maybe his plan to get you the chairmanship required killing Annette. With her out of the way, you'd get the job; in fact, you did get the job when she died." Skye leaned back in her chair. "It is surprising to see Dr. Paine here tonight. His wife's only been dead a week. You'd think if he cared for her at all, he'd still be grieving."

"Linnea insisted he remain active in the Promfest committee." Evie made a face. "She's sure that between the sympathy vote and Dylan's presence, she's got prom queen in the bag." Evie stared straight into Skye's eyes. "Which is why I would never have killed Annette. It would have given Linnea too much of an advantage over Cheyenne."

Skye raised a shoulder in a half shrug, but silently agreed. She had explained that same fact to Kurt a couple of days ago regarding Nina Miles. "One last question. What did Annette have on you that made you give up the chairmanship?"

"Nothing." Evie's pupils dilated.

"Look, I promise, unless it has to do with Annette's death, I won't tell anyone your secret."

"I don't know what you mean." Evie crossed her arms and refused to meet Skye's stare. "I don't have any secrets."

"Okay. Let me guess. Does it have something to do with your drinking problem?"

"How did you . . . I mean, I don't have a drinking problem."

"I'm truly sorry, Evie, but I know that you do." Skye went into counselor mode. "Did Annette threaten to tell everyone?"

Evie shook her head.

"It's nothing to be ashamed of, and once you admit it, you can get some help." Skye kept her voice gentle.

"Going for help is what got me into trouble." A tear slipped down Evie's cheek.

"How?" Skye dug a packet of tissues out of her tote bag and handed one to Evie.

"Annette found out I had been in rehab. She said she'd tell everyone if I didn't let her be the Promfest chair."

"Would that have been so bad?" Skye asked. "All the celebrities go to rehab, and everyone says they're wonderful and brave for admitting they have a problem."

"Their husbands are not ministers. You Catholics think you can just say you're sorry and be forgiven. Our religion isn't like that. We believe alcoholism's a sin, and that liquor is a tool of the devil. My husband told me to pray my way to sobriety, and that's exactly what he thinks I did."

"You mean, your husband doesn't know you were in rehab?"

"No. I told him I was visiting my parents in Florida— they retired to Naples a few years ago." Evie inserted the money into a pouch and zipped it shut. "But it was worth it. I haven't had a drink in four months."

"Okay. Say I believe you. Then how could you have been drunk and passed out the night Annette died?"

"After seeing you and thinking you were a ghost, I ran out to my car." Evie shoved her chair back and got to her feet. "Dylan found me there and was comforting me. When the police showed up, Dylan hid on the floor of the backseat, then sneaked back into the hall through the window in the men's room."

"By *comforting,* I assume you mean boinking your brains out?" Skye stood, not wanting Evie to loom over her. "So you were only pretending to be drunk? You'd rather your husband think you fell off the wagon than that you were riding Dr. Paine's chassis."

"You know"—Evie pushed her way past Skye to the door—"someday you'll go too far, and instead of investigating a murder, you'll be the victim of one."

Skye sped into her driveway, nearly rear-ending the black Land Rover parked in front of her house. Once she got the Bel Air under control, she hopped out of the car and dashed up the front steps. It was nearly midnight. What was Kurt doing here?

Kurt met her at the top of the stairs. His usual good humor was absent, and he stood blocking her access to the porch. "Why didn't you tell me Annette Paine's death was declared accidental?"

"What?" She pretended surprise.

"Don't try that innocent act with me," Kurt said sharply, biting off his words. "That's what Simon was here yesterday to tell you, wasn't it?"

"Go away. It's late and I'm tired." Skye shoved him back, walked past him, and unlocked the door. "We'll discuss it tomorrow."

He ignored her words and followed her inside. "You don't believe it's an accident, do you?"

"No, I don't." Skye went into the kitchen and took a two-liter bottle of Diet Coke from the fridge. "And I said we'll talk tomorrow."

Kurt reached around her and snagged a beer. "I promise to leave as soon as I finish this." He waved the bottle of Beck's at her.

"Fine." Skye narrowed her eyes. "But I don't know why it has to be this minute."

"Let's just say, so I can sleep better." Kurt joined her at the table.

Skye gave in. It was easier to go along with him than fight him. After all, she had agreed to work with Kurt on solving the murder. "Either Annette's asthma attack was brought on deliberately, or the rope strung across the passageway was meant for someone else."

"Like you?"

She nodded. Since Skye had heard from Simon about the location of the rope, it had seemed less likely that Quirk had tried to kill Hope. If he'd been after her, the rope would have been suspended in her assigned area, not Skye's.

"So who wants you dead?" Kurt made wet rings on the tabletop with his bottle.

"There is a parent who might be crazy enough to want to kill me, and no I can't tell you who. Or Quirk might have been right all along and Annette *was* the intended victim."

"So Quirk is wrong in calling Annette's death accidental."

Skye's jaw was set. "That's my current theory."

"I agree that her death wasn't accidental, but I don't think she was the one the murderer was after." Kurt's expression was dark and unfathomable. After a few seconds, he seemed to come to a conclusion and said, "Everything points to you—the rope being where it was, Annette looking like you, someone nearly running you over last Sunday."

"Maybe the driver was Annette's killer, and thinks I saw something incriminating the night of the murder."

"More likely it's that parent who's mad at you, and by the way, I know it has to be Zinnia Idell." Kurt stared at Skye, but she kept her expression blank. "Either that, or maybe it's an ex, or an ex's ex."

"No." Skye shook her head. "I dated Simon before Wally, my ex-fiancé lives in New Orleans, and Wally's ex-wife moved to Alaska."

"Are you blackmailing anyone? Do you owe money to anyone?"

"No to both."

"Murder is usually about love, money, or power. Do you have power over someone? Or do you have something someone wants?"

"Not that I know of."

"How about at school?" he asked.

"Not really. The principal or superintendant can overrule anything I do. Which is why the crazy-parent theory doesn't make sense to me."

"There's something we're missing." There was concern in Kurt's eyes as he fingered a loose tendril of hair on her cheek. "You need to be careful."

Skye felt a twinge in the pit of her stomach. Was it fear or attraction? "I'll be fine." Her voice sounded breathy to her own ears.

Kurt cupped her chin tenderly in his warm hand. "How can you be sure?" His gaze caught and held hers.

The rational side of Skye was frantically yelling, *You need to stop this right now*, but the wild part of her personality was murmuring seductively, *He's so hot, one little kiss won't hurt anyone.*

"I don't want anything to happen to you." Kurt leaned closer; less than a whisper of space separated their lips.

Before Skye could decide whether to lean forward or backward, a voice from the kitchen doorway said, "Nothing is going to happen to Skye. She's my number one priority."

Skye jerked away from Kurt and scrambled to her feet. "Wally!"

He strode across the kitchen, tossed a bouquet of pale pink roses on the counter, and thunked a bottle of champagne down beside it, then put an arm around Skye's shoulders. If looks could kill, Kurt would be vaporized, and Skye's life would be hanging by a thread.

Kurt certainly did not seem intimidated by the older man. He casually got up and sauntered over to where Wally and Skye stood, stuck out his hand, and said, "Chief Boyd, I don't know if you remember me. I'm Kurt Michaels from the paper."

Wally ignored the reporter's hand. "I remember you." He stared into Kurt's eyes. "I believe you were just leaving."

Skye stepped away from Wally, her emotions teetering between guilt and anger. Wally certainly was entitled to be upset after catching her in a fairly compromising position. But, they weren't engaged, and he had no right to order people out of *her* house.

Kurt turned his back on the chief and said to Skye, "Do you want me to go?"

"Please." She took his arm and guided him toward the foyer. "I'll talk to you tomorrow."

"Promise?"

"Yes." As soon as he cleared the threshold, she closed the door. One down. One to go.

When Skye returned to the kitchen, Wally was sitting in the chair Kurt had vacated. The champagne had disappeared and the flowers were in the trash can. He twisted off the top of a bottle of beer, took a long swallow, and raised his eyebrows. "So?"

An unwelcome blush crept into Skye's cheeks. "It wasn't the way it looked."

"It looked as if he was about to kiss you."

"Yeah, well, I wouldn't have let that happen." As with any good Catholic girl, guilt was winning, but she fought the emotion.

"You weren't putting up much of a fight when I walked in."

Attempting to deflect the focus from herself, she said, "Speaking of that, why didn't you ring the doorbell? You never just walk in."

"I did ring it." Wally stared at her. "Several times." His brown eyes were as hard and opaque as volcanic rock. "When you didn't answer I got worried. Your car was in the driveway along with a strange vehicle, and there's a murderer on the loose. So when I noticed that the door wasn't completely shut, I wanted to make sure you were okay."

"Oh." Skye's guilt ballooned. "I wonder why the doorbell didn't work." She tried to lighten the situation by joking, "Maybe my ghost is playing tricks on us again."

Wally didn't smile.

She tried distracting him. "I thought you wouldn't be able to get away until tomorrow."

"I offered the nurse a bonus and was able to arrange for an earlier flight. You weren't here when I got into town, so I dropped my luggage at my place, checked in at the PD, and came back to see if you were home yet." He took another swig of beer. "I missed you, and couldn't wait another day to see you. Guess the feeling wasn't mutual."

"No. It is. Truly." Her flush deepened to crimson. "I'm sorry. I don't know what possessed me. It was nothing." Kurt had a certain sexual magnetism, but she had wanted Wally for years. "I lo—" She cut herself off. Why couldn't she tell him that she loved him? Was it because love had never worked for her before, and she still didn't trust Wally not to leave her? "It's just that I'm tired and I haven't been feeling well and I . . ." She trailed off.

"I need to know that I can trust you." Wally's voice was ragged. "I can't take another betrayal." His ex-wife had left him without any warning, leaving a note and not much else behind.

"I promise I'll never do that." Skye flung herself into his lap, hoping Mrs. Griggs's ghost wouldn't blow up the house because she and Wally were touching. "Forgive me?"

For an instant Wally held himself rigid; then he wrapped his arms around her and whispered against her lips, "Always."

His kiss was hard and searching, and in returning it, Skye tried to show him the love she was afraid to express in words. She pressed closer, tunneling her fingers through his thick black hair.

His hands moved to her hips, lifting and rearranging her so that she straddled him. She could feel his arousal through the wool of his trousers and the denim of her jeans, and it increased her hunger for him.

Lifting his mouth from hers, he stripped off her sweater and unhooked her bra. As he trailed kisses from her neck to her breasts, she heard music.

Unfortunately, it wasn't celestial; "Hail to the Chief" blared from Wally's pocket. Skye let out a tiny cry of frustration. Apparently his new cell phone worked inside her house. His old one hadn't, and she'd never realized what a boon that had been.

She got off his lap and reclaimed her bra and sweater. As a little joke, she'd had Justin program "Hail to the Chief "as the ring tone for someone calling Wally from the police emergency line. She knew they wouldn't be getting back to their lovemaking anytime soon.

While she got dressed, she heard Wally's side of the conversation. "If she had a heart condition, why are you calling me about her death?" He listened intently, then stood. "Fine. I'll be right there." When he closed his phone, he said to Skye, "The high school's night custodian was found dead by her son in your office. She had a heart condition, so it's probably natural causes, but Reid is insisting it be treated as a suspicious death."

"That's horrible. I know—I mean, knew—Gloria, and I know her son, Cameron. He's a custodian at the grade school." Skye's voice cracked. She had liked Gloria, a woman who had worked hard all her life. "They're both really nice, sweet people."

Wally murmured something soothing, then headed toward the door.

"Can I come with you?" Skye followed him. "Simon isn't prone to flights of fancy, so if he thinks something more than a heart attack is involved, it probably is."

Wally hesitated a fraction of a second, then agreed. "Sure."

She wrinkled her brow. "Maybe it has something to do with Annette Paine's death."

"The connection being you?"

Skye nodded.

"I heard Quirk declared Annette's death an accident. I take it you don't agree."

"I'll fill you in on what's been happening on that front on the way over."

Once they were settled in Wally's car, Skye turned in her seat and said, "The good news is, I don't think Quirk had anything to do with Annette's death. Even though he threatened Hope again, it's probably a case of his bark being worse than his bite. The bad news is, there's a better than fifty percent chance that the intended victim was me."

"Why?" Wally shot her a concerned look before returning his gaze to the road.

Skye explained what she, Kurt, and Simon had figured out about the rope's location, finishing with, "So, either the killer somehow knew that Annette would be dressed as a witch, would run down the hallway in my assigned position, and was prone to asthma attacks, or the trap was set for me instead."

"But whoever strung the rope would also have had to make you run down the hall." Wally turned into the high school parking lot.

"That was part of my act. When the audience stepped into the passageway, I was supposed to jump out from behind a panel, scare them, and then run away and disappear behind another panel at the opposite end of the hall."

"That's not a very efficient way to kill someone." Wally got out of the car, went around to the other side, and opened Skye's door. "Maybe it was meant to be a joke."

"Maybe, but someone tried to run me over Sunday after church, too."

He stopped and swung her around to face him. "Why didn't you ever tell me that?"

"Quirk sort of convinced me it was an elderly driver who mistook the gas pedal for the brake, and at that time we still thought Annette or one of the other witches was the intended victim."

"But now you wonder."

"Yes." Skye took a deep breath. "I think either the crazy parent who slashed my tires tried to kill me, or Dylan Paine murdered his wife, thinks I saw something that will incriminate him, and is now trying to silence me before I realize what I saw."

"What makes you think that?"

Skye explained about Zinnia Idell's presence at the haunted house and Dr. Paine's affairs. Wally nodded and spoke briefly to Anthony, the officer at the door; then they walked silently to Skye's office. When they crossed the threshold, Skye was glad that poor Gloria had been taken away—she'd seen enough dead bodies to last her a lifetime.

Reid stood waiting for them, then without preamble said, "Cameron Unger arrived at midnight to pick up his mother, Gloria, who worked the four-to-twelve shift as the high school custodian. When she didn't come out by twelve fifteen, he went in looking for her. He had a key, since he works as a custodian at the elementary school and sometimes subs for his mother at the high school. He found her sitting at Skye's desk. She was unresponsive and he called for an ambulance. The EMTs summoned me as soon as they verified she was dead."

"But Cameron reported she had a heart condition?" Wally asked. "So why involve the police?"

Simon looked at Skye. "Have you filled him in on events since he's been gone?" She nodded and he continued. "At first, I was ready to believe it was natural causes, but then I looked at the scene and saw this." He led them around the desk and pointed to the bottom drawer. It was pulled out, and an open package of Oreos was propped up against the side. "I take it those are yours?"

"Yes." Skye felt her face grow hot. *Great.* Now both Simon and Wally knew she gobbled down cookies while she worked.

"I also take it you didn't leave your desktop like this?" Simon directed their attention to a scattering of chocolate crumbs.

"No, of course not." Skye shook her head for emphasis. "My mother raised me better than that."

"I figured as much," Simon murmured, half to himself.

"I always clean up before I leave," Skye continued. "I don't want to attract ants."

"Which means Gloria was having a snack," Wally concluded. "Have you noticed cookies missing before?"

"No." Skye closed her eyes, thinking. "But I have noticed the level in my candy jar seemed to be going down faster than it should. I give treats to the kids I test, and Trixie has a few pieces whenever she stops by, but they should be the only ones eating from the jar. I keep it filled with candy I don't like so I'm not tempted." All three of them looked at the jar in question, which was empty. "In fact, before I left today I noticed it was out of candy, and made a note to myself to bring in a bag on Monday to replenish it."

"So it's reasonable to assume that Gloria was in the habit of eating some candy when she cleaned your office." Simon pursed his lips. "And when there was none in the jar, she looked to see if you had any in the drawer, found your stash of Oreos, and helped herself."

"That all makes sense." Wally nodded. "But what does it have to do with her death? Unless you're saying you think Skye poisoned her."

"I'm sure it wasn't Skye, but *someone* definitely tampered with those Oreos."

CHAPTER 22

Destiny Awaits

"You think someone put poison in my cookies?" Skye squeaked. That was just plain wrong—Oreos were sacred, the food of the gods. People should respect that.

"Your imagination has run away with you, Reid," Wally said, his voice edged with impatience.

"Not at all." Simon's tone was unruffled. "As Skye will tell you, I don't have an imagination. I only deal in cold, hard facts."

"And they are?"

"When I saw Skye on Wednesday, she mentioned she'd been feeling sick on and off for the past few days. Her symptoms, together with Gloria's death and some further evidence, made me consider the possibility of poisoning."

Wally turned his scowl on Skye. "You never told me you weren't feeling well."

Skye felt like an escaped prisoner caught in a searchlight. "The flu is going around. I thought I was getting it."

"But you told Reid you were sick."

"When he stopped by to discuss the case, he noticed I was under the weather."

Wally's face was expressionless, but his hands were

clenched by his sides. "Sounds like you two have been spending quite a bit of time together while I've been gone."

Skye opened her mouth, but Simon answered first. "With Quirk refusing to consider any other scenario for Annette Paine's death, we've been sharing information." He met Wally's stare. "But that's all. Skye has made it clear it's strictly business."

"But you wished she hadn't." Wally didn't blink.

"Can't blame a guy for trying." Simon crossed his arms.

The two men reminded Skye of a pair of male lions preparing to fight for the right to lead the pride. First Kurt, now Simon; Wally's jealousy was getting out of hand. It was time to step in and get the discussion back on target.

She raised her voice. "If you are both through discussing me as if I weren't here, I'd like to know what other evidence Simon found that suggests my cookies were poisoned."

Simon refocused his attention on Skye. "When I examined the cookies' packaging with a magnifying glass, I noticed evidence of tampering. Skye had torn the cellophane down the middle, but prior to that, someone had teased it open at the crimped end and glued it back together. And when I looked at the cookies themselves, I detected tiny holes in the edges of the cream centers—as if they had been injected with something."

"You know"—Skye replayed the past week in her head—"I don't think this was the first package of cookies that was dosed. I remember eating a cookie on Tuesday from a previous package that tasted funny."

"Did you throw the rest away?" Simon asked.

"No." It was embarrassing to admit it, but she didn't want to lie. "There were only a couple left, and the flavor was okay if I ate them whole, rather than licking off the cream center from the chocolate wafer."

"Hmm." Simon stroked his chin. "When did you start this package?"

"Wednesday. And I had some again on Friday, as well,

and those were the days I felt sick. I didn't eat any on Thursday, and I felt fine that day."

Simon nodded. "I've asked the ME to do a tox screen on the victim, and I'll ask the county lab to test the remaining cookies. I have a book on poisons and, comparing your symptoms, I should be able to narrow it down for them."

"That's a good plan," Wally agreed. "But why did Gloria die when Skye only got sick?"

Simon rocked back on his heels. "Gloria may have had an allergy or preexisting condition that made her more susceptible."

"That sounds logical," Wally said. "I'll have the cellophane from the cookies fingerprinted, as well as Skye's desk." He turned to her. "Who has access to this office?"

"Anyone who's in the school building," Skye answered. "As long as the confidential material is locked away in the file cabinet, I don't lock the door every time I leave for a minute. Then there are the master keys, which the main office and all the custodians have."

Simon pointed out, "It doesn't really matter. The locks on these doors are fairly easy to pick." He added, "Since Skye is in danger, I'm asking that this case be considered urgent, and I hope to have the results by Monday."

"Good." Wally put his hand on Skye's waist and guided her toward the door, saying over his shoulder, "Keep me informed."

On Saturday, while Wally spent his time catching up on police matters, Skye tried to figure out who was trying to kill her. Even if Simon was right, and her cookies had been poisoned, that didn't tell her whether she had been the intended victim from the beginning, or had become a target because Annette's killer thought she had seen something.

Skye shivered, then straightened her spine. She wasn't going to let the killer scare her. She wasn't going to give him that much power. Besides, Mrs. Idell was being held until Monday's bail hearing on the concealed-weapon charge from Friday night's haunted-house incident, which meant that she, for one, wouldn't be coming after Skye for the next two days.

Wally had found out that both Mr. and Mrs. Idell drove BMWs, vehicles that didn't look at all like the car that had tried to run down Skye last Sunday, but he still wanted to question Zinnia, so he was going over to the Laurel County Jail to interrogate her at ten a.m.

Which left Annette's enemies for Skye to consider. Skye evaluated the suspects. She'd already talked to Nina and Evie, and she was convinced that neither of them would risk giving Linnea an advantage in the race for prom queen by killing her mother.

Which was exactly what the two mothers of the other queen candidates said when Skye stopped by their houses Saturday afternoon. Kurt hadn't been able to find anyone else with a grudge against Annette, and Skye was running out of people to interrogate.

She considered going to see Elvira Doozier. Earl's statement had raised some important questions that only she could answer, but with a Doozier, often the direct approach wasn't the way to go. Especially since Elvira's sister-in-law would probably refuse to let Skye talk to the girl without extorting another Wal-Mart outfit from her. Glenda had already blackmailed Skye once that weekend, dangling Earl's information over her head for bait, and it wasn't going to happen again.

After careful consideration, Skye decided to concentrate on Dr. Paine. Knowing that he saw patients from eight a.m. to four p.m. on Saturdays, she decided to chat with him at the haunted house that evening. Wally wasn't thrilled when she called him and told him her plan, but he agreed, as long as she took Anthony with her for backup.

Skye and the young officer arrived at the old American Legion hall early. Anthony stationed himself within earshot, but out of sight, and Skye approached Dylan Paine, who was playing a handheld video game as he reclined on the operating table in the Frankenstein scene.

"Hi, Dr. Paine."

"Hello, Skye." He sat up, appearing sheepish. Even though he hadn't seen Skye when she'd opened the door on him and Evie, he'd probably noticed afterward that she'd signed in at the exact same time he'd been "thoroughly occupied."

Skye felt no obligation to spare his feelings. "I stopped by for my Thursday appointment, but you were busy with Evie."

"Oh. Yeah. The receptionist forgot to tell me you were coming in. Sorry." Dylan gave her a "boys will be boys" smile. "Did you reschedule?"

"No. I didn't really have a toothache; I just wanted to talk to you."

"About what?"

"Your wife's murder."

Dylan frowned. "She wasn't murdered. The police said it was an accident."

"I think they were wrong."

"Really? Why?"

He sure didn't seem upset by her questions or the idea that his wife might have been a murder victim. Skye decided to try to shake him up. "It just seems too convenient. She was going to divorce you and take half your assets. You couldn't let that happen. And as a dentist, you knew all about how to trigger a fatal asthma attack."

Dylan threw back his head and laughed. "You've been listening to the gossips, haven't you?"

"I saw your infidelity with my own eyes."

"Annette knew all about my affairs, and she didn't give a damn. All she cared about was my money and being Mrs. *Dr.* Paine. I found out early in our marriage that she never loved me. She was happy that I got my itch scratched elsewhere and didn't bother her." For a second his expression saddened. "She would never have divorced me. In a weird way, we were made for each other."

"I see." Skye wasn't sure why, but she sensed he was telling the truth. "Still, a car that looked a lot like yours almost ran me down last Sunday after church."

"I went to the Feed Bag as soon as Mass ended." The lights flashed indicating that the haunted house would be opening in five minutes, and Dylan jumped off the operating table. "I heard it was fifteen or twenty minutes later that you were nearly hit." He stuck his video game in his pocket. "Feel free to check out my alibi with Nina and Burt Miles. They had breakfast with me."

"Thanks, I will," Skye muttered as she walked away.

After checking with Anthony, who was staying at the American Legion hall for the rest of the evening to keep an eye on the event, Skye hurried to her spot and got ready to scare the patrons.

Saturday's A Ghoul's Night Out went as smoothly as Friday's had, and when the haunted house closed for the night, Skye drove to Wally's place. He met her at the door and handed her a glass of wine.

Wally had redecorated a year ago, replacing the shag carpeting with hardwood floors. The walls were now painted a deep taupe, and a mushroom, cream, and rust–colored area rug occupied the center of the room. Arts and Crafts–style bookcases and tables took the place of the fake Early American ones that Skye had hated when she first saw his living room.

After they settled on the new cream leather sofa, Skye filled Wally in on her chat with Dylan Paine, concluding with, "I believe him about his and Annette's relationship, and I don't think he was involved in his wife's death. I checked with Nina during one of my breaks, and she confirmed that Dr. Paine was with her and her husband at the restaurant at the time that the car nearly ran me down."

"And, considering Gloria's death last night, I believe Quirk." Wally peeled the wrapper off his beer bottle. "I talked with him today, and he denies any involvement in Annette Paine's death. He swears he just loses his temper whenever he sees Hope, but would never really hurt her. He was afraid you'd think less of him if you found out about his brother, which is why he didn't want you on the case."

"What did Zinnia Idell have to say?" Skye asked. "It would have been easy for her to sneak into my office and poison the cookies. She's been around the school a lot the past month."

"Well . . ." Wally's brow furrowed. "She does hate you, and she admits she's hired an attorney to sue you and the school district, but my impression is that if she wanted you dead, she would have shot you, not messed around with ropes and poison."

"Great." Skye's heart skipped a beat. She was more afraid of lawsuits than she was of a murderer. "Did you get any prints from the Oreo package?"

"There were three sets of prints on it. We were able to manually match yours and Gloria's, since we had yours on file and could fingerprint the body, but the unknown set will have to be put through AFIS as soon as the PD's computers are up and running again." Wally anticipated Skye's next question. "And no, Zinnia Idell's prints didn't match the unknown set."

Skye sighed. "What happened to the computers?"

"McCabe somehow managed to screw up the system."

"Anything on the tox screen results yet?"

Wally shook his head. "Reid said not until Monday at the earliest, remember?"

"So if someone is trying to kill me, he has the rest of the weekend to do it."

Wally wrapped her in his arms. "Guess you'll have to stay close so I can protect you."

"Hmmm." Skye drew his face to hers. "If I do, will you show me your pistol?"

"I think that can be arranged." He claimed her lips, crushing her to him.

Wally's kiss sent her senses into a wild swirl, and she forgot about everything in the world except him.

Skye and Wally slept late; then, while she attended noon Mass, Wally went in to the PD. After church, since there was no one else Skye needed to question regarding the murder investigation—having decided to wait until she could chat with Elvira at school, where she wouldn't have to pay a Wal-Mart fee—Skye went home.

Once she'd changed into sweatpants and a T-shirt, she checked her answering machine and found two messages.

The first one was from Homer. "Some jerk started a rumor that school is going to be closed on Monday because of Gloria's dying in your office, but it isn't, so you'd better be there." There was a pause; then he said, "Hey, I told those county crime scene guys not to bother returning your chair when they finish with it. I figured you wouldn't want it, since Gloria was sitting in it when she kicked the bucket. You can order a new one tomorrow."

Skye grinned. Just when she thought there was no hope for him, Homer did something nice.

The other message was from Loretta. Skye tried to think of a reason not to, but finally forced herself to return her sorority sister's call. As she waited for Loretta to answer, she prayed her friend wouldn't ask her to take sides. No matter what Vince's faults were, he was still her brother, and she could never turn her back on him.

"Hello." Loretta's voice was lifeless.

"Hi. It's Skye."

"I wondered if you would call or not. Are you mad at me?"

"Of course not. There's just been a lot happening around here, and Wally was out of town for most of it, which made everything worse." Skye finished telling Loretta about the two murders, then said, "So, that's what's been going on with me. How about you?"

"Let's put it this way. Being the possible target of a deranged killer would be the high point of *my* week." There was a hysterical giggle, then a sob. "I think I made the biggest mistake of my life."

"Breaking up with Vince?"

"Yes. I never should have done it. I'm so miserable."

"Why exactly did you break up with him?" Skye was confused. "Vince said you told him you two have different goals and dreams. Is that what you said?"

"Yes." Loretta hiccuped. "But that wasn't the real reason."

"What was?"

"I knew he wasn't the settling-down type, and time is running out. I want to have children while my parents are still young enough to take care of them."

Skye giggled. Even when Loretta was upset, her dry humor was a hoot. "But you didn't tell him that?"

"No."

"Why?"

"I didn't want to sound needy." Loretta's tone was stubborn. "Besides, I said we had different goals and dreams. He should have known I meant I wanted to get serious and he didn't."

Skye blew out an exasperated breath. "What he thought you meant was that you're an important attorney and he's a hairdresser. He figures your family is rich and powerful and ours is poor, and the only place we have any influence is in a town of three thousand people."

"I hope you told him that was stupid." Loretta was starting to sound like her old, confident self. "Do you think Vince could get serious? Settle down?"

"I think that's something you two should discuss."

"But he probably hates me now."

"Talk to him and find out," Skye prodded. "You're a tough criminal lawyer; surely you're not afraid of my brother."

"He might not even want to speak to me."

"You'll never know until you try," Skye encouraged.

"So you think I should call him?"

"I think you should get naked, put on your fur coat, and show up on his doorstep." Skye smirked. "It's hard for a man to stay angry when he's hard."

Loretta giggled. "That's not a bad idea." Her voice was hopeful. "I'll let you know what happens."

"Not the play-by-play." Skye so did not want to know the details of her brother's sex life. "Just the final outcome."

She and Loretta said good-bye, and Skye put the phone in its cradle, but before she could walk away, it rang again. Thinking it might be Loretta needing another pep talk, Skye scooped up the receiver and heard, "We're home. How come you never returned any of my calls? What in the world have you gotten yourself into this time?"

She cringed. May was back, and there would be hell to pay.

Skye dreaded entering her office on Monday. The body had been removed Friday night before Skye had arrived, so at least she didn't have a picture in her mind of poor Gloria dead. But the guilt of knowing that the woman had died from poison that was probably meant for Skye was hard for her to shake. Still, it wasn't as if Homer would give her another space to use. She was pleasantly surprised he was springing for a new chair.

She checked the schedule on the office door; Jackie was at the junior high, so Skye had the office to herself. That reminded her—however much Homer and the other principals sang Jackie's praises, Skye had yet to see her produce much in the way of results. The woman did a lot of talking, but hadn't written one social history or Individual Educational Plan goal. It seemed to Skye that when all was said and done concerning Jackie, far more was said than done.

Skye shrugged, then dragged a folding chair from the closet to sit on. Jackie wasn't her problem. Figuring out who wanted her dead was what she needed to focus on. But, when Simon called at ten, she still hadn't made any progress toward that goal.

He said, "I got the results from the lab. Your cookies were dosed with atropine."

"What's that?"

"The scientific name is dl-hyoscyamine. It's from the belladonna plant. The type that was put in your cookies is a medication found in prescription eyedrops."

"Oh." Skye tried to remember if she had seen anyone using eyedrops lately.

"The funny thing is that an atropine overdose is not considered life threatening."

"Then why did Gloria die?"

"The ME concluded that because she was taking digoxin for her heart condition, the atropine intensified the effect of that drug to a fatal level."

"So her death was an accident," Skye speculated. "Whoever injected my Oreos wanted me sick, not dead."

"Or they didn't know an atropine overdose isn't usually fatal."

Skye thanked Simon and hung up, then called Wally. Simon had already reported his findings to him, and Wally told Skye there hadn't been any hits on the fingerprints yet. Disappointed, Skye closed her office and left for the elementary school. She and the team were meeting with Vassily's parents at eleven to draw up an IEP for the little boy.

Although Skye was distracted, the conference went well. Mr. and Mrs. Warner agreed to the proposed IEP, and Vassily was set to start school on Wednesday. They were finished before noon, and Skye decided to return to the high school to talk to Elvira Doozier.

Normally Skye avoided taking students out of gym, since most of the kids enjoyed the class, or at least hated it less than the academic subjects, but Elvira was a different story. When Elvira arrived in the psych office, she said, "Thanks for getting me away from those Twinkies."

"Twinkies?" Skye hadn't heard that expression before.

"Overly processed, too sweet to be real, and leave a bad

aftertaste." When Skye still look puzzled, Elvira explained, "Most of the Pops are in my class."

"You meant the popular girls?" Skye studied the adolescent, who nodded, then flung herself into a chair and began examining her belly-button ring. She was dressed in low-riding wide-legged denims and a hooded crop top. Her dyed black hair fell to the middle of her back, and her face was eerily pale.

Elvira hung out with the Rebels. Of Scumble River High's cliques, it was by far the roughest. And unlike the teacher-pleasing groups, they did not volunteer information to adults. Skye was counting on the fact that over the past four years she had built a relationship with Elvira and her family, odd as that bond might be.

Skye started to offer Elvira a piece of candy before she remembered that Wally had suggested she not keep any food in her office for the time being. Without a bribe, how could she loosen up the teen?

Hmm, giving her an opportunity to show how smart she is might work. "Hey, do you know anything about cell phones?"

"If someone said I had one at school, they were lying." Elvira peered suspiciously out from under her hair. "Mine's out of minutes and I have to wait until I get my Social Security check the first of the month before I can pay the bill."

"No one said anything. I was just wondering if you could help with mine." Skye dug in her tote bag and handed the small silver device to the girl. "I can't figure out how to get into my voice mail."

"You're supposed to be so smart, and you can't figure out how to use your own cell phone." Disdain dripped from Elvira's words.

Skye stopped herself from rolling her eyes and leaned back in her chair. "No one can be good at everything." Teenagers had attitudes rivaled only by French waiters, and required similar treatment: Never let them see that they got under your skin. "So, can *you* figure it out?"

"I'll take a look." Elvira flipped open the phone and pressed the ON button.

While the girl studied the keypad, Skye said as casually as she could, "Hey, I saw your brother Friday night. Interesting business he's starting."

Elvira snorted, but didn't shift her attention from the phone.

"He mentioned he decided to become a Ghostflusher when you told him how badly I'd been frightened during the first haunted-house dress rehearsal."

Elvira's fingers were flying over the tiny buttons, but she paused to smirk. "Yeah. She said you were practically peeing your pants."

"Really? Who said that?" Skye watched the girl closely, but she still seemed engrossed in the electronic device. "I thought I was alone when I was that panicked."

"The social worker. Last Monday I stopped by the *Scoop* office to talk to Xenia, and Ms. Jennings was telling all the kids there the story about how you kicked in the doors of the bathroom stalls and were afraid of a toy ax and screamed when you ran into a rubber hand in the hall." Elvira passed Skye the phone. "Anyway, you press this little triangle on the left, scroll down to voice mail, and type in your PIN number."

"Thanks." Skye wondered what her PIN number was. "I figured you could help."

"Yeah." Elvira got up and sauntered toward the door. "And you figured if you gave me something to do, I'd tell you what you wanted to know."

"Uh. I didn't . . ." Skye's cheeks flushed. "Well, I mean—"

"I can read you like a comic book." Elvira shook her head. "Just ask next time. I really hate it when adults try to manipulate me."

"Sorry," Skye called as the girl walked out of the office,

slamming the door behind her. *Shoot.* She'd have to make things up to her somehow, but right now she had to consider what Elvira had said.

Why would Jackie ridicule Skye to the students? What did she gain? Skye had had a bad feeling about Jackie from the beginning, but she'd written it off as jealousy. Except now that she thought about it, it seemed that all the trouble had started when the social worker was hired.

Since Jackie's arrival, both Skye and the school had been having nothing but problems. The social worker had been the one to find the chemical bombs, insist on talking to the wannabe mommies at the junior high, and magically speak Russian—not that Vassily had responded to one word of it.

Jackie had also changed the office locks and failed to give Skye the new key, which resulted in her being late for an important meeting. Skye had a slashed tire, a rope strung at her height in her assigned spot at A Ghoul's Night Out, almost been run over, and had poison added to her cookies.

Not to mention the tricks that had been played on her in the haunted-house bathroom. Come to think of it, Jackie had been acting the part of Lizzie Borden, so it was probably her ax that had been strategically staged in the handicapped stall.

Could Jackie be behind all of it? And if so, why? Skye needed proof. A good place to start was Jackie's background. And in order to look into her history, all Skye had to do was persuade her godfather, Charlie, aka the school board president, to get her Jackie's personnel file. Piece of cake. Or not.

CHAPTER 23

Worlds Collide

"Please, please, please, Uncle Charlie," Skye pleaded into the phone.

"No. I can't let you see Jackie's personnel file." Charlie's voice was firm.

"It's a matter of life and death."

"Now, Skye, you don't really think that nice lady is trying to kill you."

"Yes, I do!" Skye yelled, her patience wearing thin. "I told you, Simon found evidence my cookies were poisoned."

"But not that she poisoned them. You admitted that anyone could have gotten into your office."

"Please, Uncle Charlie, you're the only one who can help me."

"Well . . ."

"You'd do it for Vince," Skye whined.

"No . . ."

"What do you think Mom will say when I'm murdered, and she finds out you could have saved me?" Skye played her trump card—Charlie thought of May as the daughter he'd never had, and he would do anything for her.

"What exactly in the file do you want to see?"

Skye thought fast. Charlie was weakening. She wanted to

see the whole thing, but if she couldn't, what was the most important part? "Did anyone check her references?"

"No."

"You're kidding." Skye knew that the Scumble River School District didn't set high standards, but still . . . "How could the board not check her references?"

"You have no idea what hiring is like nowadays." Charlie's voice bristled. "Say we do call the people she's listed as references; no one will say anything negative because they're all too afraid of being sued. The only thing we can find out is if she was fired or if she quit. And look at you; you were fired for doing your job—not because you did anything wrong. So calling is just a big waste of time. Jackie had a graduate school diploma and a school social worker certificate from the state of Illinois. That was enough."

"I can see your point, but I still want to try to talk to the people she listed as references."

There was a long pause before Charlie caved. "Okay. Give me half an hour. I've got to go over and get the file from Wraige's secretary. Any suggestion as to why I might want it?"

"You're the board president; order her to hand it over."

After hanging up, Skye straightened her desk, packed her tote bag, and told Opal she wasn't feeling well, so she was taking half a sick day.

When Skye arrived at the Up A Lazy River Motor Court office, Charlie handed her the list. "Here. I hope you're happy," he complained. "I had to agree to take Karolyn to the lodge dinner in order to get this without an explanation."

"Thank you, Uncle Charlie." Skye smiled to herself. So Karolyn wanted to go out with Charlie. That was extremely interesting, considering it was common knowledge that she was already boffing her boss. Maybe Dr. Wraige and his secretary had had a tiff.

Charlie shook his head. "I'm leaving for a doctor's appointment. Lock up when you're finished."

"No problem." Skye waved Charlie out the door.

"Remember, don't draw to an inside straight." She knew his appointment was really a poker game.

Skye checked the clock. It was past two. Not bothering to take off her coat, she quickly took a seat at Charlie's desk and pulled the phone toward her. Taking into account the time difference between Illinois and the East Coast, she was worried about catching people before they left for the day.

As she dialed the first number, a school district in New York, she crossed her fingers, hoping the personnel manager would be available. Luck was with her, but the person Skye spoke to stated that no one named Jacqueline Jennings had ever taught for them.

The next person Skye tried was Jackie's internship supervisor. That woman said that Jackie had been a promising young social worker. When Skye questioned the use of the word *young*—after all, Jackie had been eight years older than most interns, the woman claimed that Jacqueline Jennings was in her mid-twenties.

The last name on the list was that of a professor at the university from which Jackie's graduate degree had been issued. He said that the Jacqueline Jennings he'd had as a student had been killed in a hit-and-run accident last December, a few months into her first year as a school social worker.

Stunned, Skye let the receiver drop into the cradle. The real Jacqueline Jennings had never worked for the school district listed on her résumé, was ten years younger than the one in Scumble River, and was actually deceased. Something was definitely not adding up. It was time to call the police.

Wally listened to all Skye had found out, then said, "Interesting, but there's no hard evidence, so about all I can do is drop around school tomorrow and talk to her. I haven't met her yet, so I can use that as an excuse."

"But she's pretending to be a dead person. Stealing their identity."

"Maybe. Or maybe there's some kind of mix-up. We need more evidence before the police can get involved."

Skye bit back a scream of frustration. "I'll bet the fingerprints on my cookie package are hers."

"Unfortunately, if she isn't in the system, we can't compel her to let us fingerprint her."

"But she had to be fingerprinted in order for the school to employ her."

"Yes, but those prints are only compared to the criminal database. They aren't actually entered *into* a database," Wally explained.

Skye felt as if her head were going to explode. "How about if I get her prints on something and bring them in?"

"Even if they match, we can't arrest her. Since you share an office with her, any halfway competent attorney would claim Jackie had merely helped herself to one of your cookies."

"Crap!"

"Look," Wally soothed. "I think you're on the right track, but the question comes back to motive. Why is she doing this? If we could figure that out, it would help us build a case. Do you have any theory?"

"I have no idea."

"Maybe when the school board looks into her background, something will give us a lead." Wally paused. "If it turns out she really has stolen someone's identity, we can charge her with that, and she might confess or let something slip during the interrogation."

" 'Maybe.' 'Might.' " Skye's voice had a sarcastic edge. "What am I supposed to do in the meantime? Wait for her to try to kill me again?"

"You're right," Wally agreed. "It's probably not a good idea for you to be alone until we figure this out. I should have thought of that Friday night after we found out about Gloria. How about if you move in with me?"

She froze. This was not the way she wanted the next step in their relationship to come about. Besides, her mother would kill her before Jackie could. Years ago, Skye had lived with her fiancé in New Orleans and gotten away with it, but Scumble River was a small town, and both she and Wally were public figures.

Wally broke into her thoughts. "You don't have to decide right now. We'll talk about it tonight. Are you still at school?"

"No. I'm at Charlie's."

"Good. Stay there. I'll finish what I'm working on, swing by the motor court, and follow you out to your house so you can drop off your car; then we'll go to Laurel. We both need a nice dinner away from town."

"Fine." Skye fought to calm down. None of this was Wally's fault. "How long will you be?"

"Fifteen, twenty minutes, max."

"Okay. See you then." Skye hung up, not satisfied with Wally's wait-and-see attitude. She wasn't letting Jackie get away with Annette's and Gloria's deaths. And she wasn't prepared to allow her own life to continue to be destroyed either.

Wait a second. Could that be Jackie's motive? It sure seemed as if she wanted to ruin Skye's life, not kill her. What would doing that accomplish? Revenge was the only reason she could think of. But revenge for what? Skye had never met the woman before—at least, not that she knew of.

Okay, if not payback, then what? Well, if Skye were fired, Jackie would have the office all to herself. *Hmm.* Was she onto something? Could Jackie not only want Skye gone from school, but gone from Scumble River as well? Did she think she could scare her away? But again, why would Jackie want that?

Skye took a deep breath. Speculation wasn't getting her anywhere. She needed facts. Maybe Wally couldn't do anything to obtain information, but she could.

It was only three thirty. Jackie had said that she was meeting with a parent at quarter to four, which meant she couldn't possibly leave school for another forty-five minutes. Certainly that was enough time for Skye to have a look around her cabin, especially since Jackie was staying right there at the Up A Lazy River Motor Court. Skye wished she had her Taser with her, but she needed to seize the opportunity.

Recalling that Charlie had mentioned that Jackie was in the cabin directly across from the office, Skye grabbed the master key from the desk drawer and stepped outside. The parking lot was empty and the motor court appeared deserted. Most people who checked in arrived late in the evening, leaving the interstate only to grab some sleep before getting back on the road.

Skye took a pair of rubber gloves from the first-aid kit in her car, then made her way across the asphalt. She knocked on Jackie's door, waited, and knocked again. When no one answered, she used the master key and slipped inside. The drapes were drawn, so she flicked on the overhead light.

Once her eyes adjusted, Skye blinked, not sure that what she was looking at was real. Several moments later she still couldn't comprehend what she was seeing, but as her brain began to process it, she gasped.

Covering the walls were hundreds of pictures, and every one of them had Jackie's face Photoshopped onto Skye's body. Jackie must have been following her around for months and months, maybe as long as a year, snapping photographs with a telephoto lens. There were images of Skye at the grocery store, at school, at her parents', out with Wally, driving the Bel Air.

Feeling violated and defiled, Skye turned to leave. Why would anyone do this? A shiver ran up her spine. How sick did someone have to be to try to become another person? How mentally ill did someone have to be to try to erase the essence of themselves?

Her hand on the doorknob, Skye paused. She couldn't run away. This might be her only chance to prove Jackie had set the trap that killed Annette and poisoned the cookies that killed Gloria. Skye had to stay cool and not freak out. Taking a calming breath, she moved over to the dresser and snapped on the latex gloves.

In the bottom drawer, concealed inside a tampon box, she found IDs of every description. There were driver's licenses in a half dozen names, all from different states, credit cards, Social Security cards, and an Illinois State Police identification card in the name Veronica Vail.

Veronica Vail. Why did that name seem familiar? Wait, wasn't that the special agent who had turned up to help with the spa murder? The one who had mysteriously disappeared, leaving a wig and a theatrical makeup kit behind?

Skye flipped through the rest of the IDs and found one for Imogene Ingersoll. Skye remembered her, too, a contestant in the cooking contest Skye had participated in last spring. She'd bribed her way into the finalist position and been asking questions about Skye and her family.

Now that Skye knew that Jackie was both Veronica and Imogene, she could see the resemblance. The nose was the same, as was the size of the eyes, and the small mole on her right cheek. These features were hard to alter without plastic surgery.

But apart from those details, Jackie's disguises had been amazing. She had changed her hair and eye color each time, as Imogene she'd worn glasses, and she'd even changed her build, going from a slim Veronica to an average Imogene and then to a curvy Jackie.

Skye shoved everything back in the box and forced herself to continue searching. So far all she could prove was that Jackie had pretended to be three different people.

The night table contained a three-ring binder with notes on Skye—her history, her habits, and her family. *Ick!* This was beyond creepy. There was nothing remarkable in the tiny closet, under the bed, or in the rest of the room. The only place left to investigate was the bathroom.

Skye flipped the light switch and stood in the doorway looking around. Her search would be easier if she knew what she was trying to find. The counter contained various toiletries, but nothing suspicious. Where would Jackie hide something incriminating?

She checked the toilet tank, behind the shower curtain, and in back of the door. She stood tapping her finger on the sink, letting her gaze wander from floor to ceiling. *Ooh, wait a minute.* What was that dark spot in the light fixture?

Dragging a chair from the bedroom into the bathroom, Skye positioned it under the light and climbed up. She carefully unscrewed the globe and shook a small bottle into her palm. Turning it, she read the label—it was prescription eyedrops, and Skye would bet the farm they contained atropine. She had the smoking gun—so to speak.

She was screwing the fixture back in place when she heard the outer door open. Scrambling off the chair, she tucked the eyedrops in her pants pocket and looked for a place to hide.

Before she found one, a familiar voice demanded, "What the hell are you doing in my room?"

It was a reasonable question. Skye tried to come up with an answer that wouldn't get her killed, but her mind refused to cooperate, as did her mouth, which hung open, producing only incoherent sounds.

On another level Skye noticed that Jackie, or whatever her name was, looked pale and that her skin was stretched tight, making her face resemble a skull. It was as if she were morphing into yet another persona, and Skye automatically knew that this one was even less sane than Jackie's previous self.

"I'm really sorry." Skye stripped off the plastic gloves and concealed them in her palm, all the while struggling to come up with an excuse. "I know you said you didn't want housekeeping services because you didn't like strangers messing with your things, but Uncle Charlie asked me to drop off fresh towels because he had to lock up the office early today." Skye gathered the soiled towels from the floor, shoving the discarded gloves into the pile, and took a step toward the door.

Jackie's gaze flicked to the empty rack and back to Skye. "You must really think I'm stupid." Her mouth flattened and her face turned red. "Or maybe you think that because you've always had it so easy you can get away with anything."

"No." Skye's voice cracked. "Of course not. I . . . uh . . . forgot the fresh towels. You know what a scatterbrain I can be. I'll go get them right now." Jackie blocked Skye's attempt to edge around her by producing a switchblade from her pocket.

Jackie flicked the knife open. "You've ruined everything."

Skye leapt back until she was pressed against the bathroom wall, clutching the towels to her chest like a shield.

"Why couldn't you just leave Scumble River?" Jackie waved the blade in the air. "You left once before."

Skye forced herself to remain composed. Which personality disorder did Jackie's behavior indicate? She narrowed it down to three—borderline, histrionic, or narcissistic. Jackie wasn't charming enough to be sociopathic. Skye needed to make the correct diagnosis in order to know the best way to deal with her assailant. Stalling for time, she asked, "Why do you want me to go?"

Jackie snapped, "Because you stole my life."

Okay, that was a clue. "What do you mean?" She needed to keep the other woman talking. Soon Wally would arrive, and, seeing her car in the parking lot, he'd know she had to be somewhere on the premises. Surely he'd figure out she was in Jackie's cabin.

"We were born on the same day, at the same time, in the same hospital."

"How do you know that?" Skye glanced at the counter to her left. Was there anything she could use as a weapon?

"A little over a year ago I went to the county courthouse in Laurel to request a certified copy of my birth certificate so I could get a passport. They gave me yours by mistake. Our surnames are similar."

"What *is* your real last name?" There was nothing Skye could use to defend herself near the sink.

"Dennison, same as yours, only with two Ns. And my first name is Stacy, close enough to Skye to confuse the stupid clerk."

"Oh. What a weird coincidence." Skye noticed that this line of questioning seemed to have a calming effect on Jackie, and she struggled to think of a way to continue it. "So we were both born in Laurel Hospital."

"Yes. But you got to go home with a loving family, and I was stuck with a mother who didn't want me," Jackie rasped in an ugly tone. "And when I started to follow you around last Thanksgiving, it finally all made sense. The hospital had made the same mistake the courthouse did—only they had switched babies—and I knew I had found my real life."

Holy crap! Jackie's brief visit to the land of sanity was over. "Why do you think that?"

"Because I deserve your life and you don't. You never wanted to live in Scumble River and be near your family. You wanted to live in a big city and marry some rich guy. You're only here because he dumped you and you were fired. You *had* to come back, but I *want* to be here."

"Sometimes we don't get what we deserve, but that doesn't mean we aren't who we are," Skye pointed out.

"Wow. You're so perceptive." Sarcasm dripped from Jackie's words. "That must be why those idiots at the schools think you're such a hotshot psychologist. I can't believe they don't see that even without a college degree, I'm a thousand times better than you."

"But they do. I've heard Homer and Neva both say how wonderful you are," Skye assured her, playing to Jackie's grandiose sense of self-importance.

"Then why did Homer yell at me for not getting that Idell bitch to back down on her plan to sue the district?" Jackie's voice held an unreasonable rage.

"That's just his way," Skye soothed, trying to both calm and stall the woman. "He's like that with everyone."

"But. I. Am. Not. Everyone." Jackie seemed to lose the thread of what she was saying. Suddenly she lunged at Skye. "Why didn't you leave town when you were supposed to? I heard about your haunted-house phobia and I got Justin to tell you about the real ghosts. I was sure running into that rope would be enough to make you go away, but that idiot Annette ruined everything."

"Pretending to cry and then locking me in the bathroom was a brilliant touch." Skye was not above kissing up if it would keep her alive.

"I didn't pretend to cry. That must have been the real ghost, because I heard it, too, and there was no one else around."

"But it was you who tried to run me over, right?"

"Yeah, Dylan hung his jacket on the rack near the door of the restaurant, and I borrowed the car keys from the pocket. The hardest part was slipping them back before he left. Good thing he and his friends stayed there so long—they must have drunk two whole pots of coffee." Jackie appeared to refocus. "But since I couldn't scare you into leaving town on your own, and you saw my little art gallery here, I'm going to have to get rid of you myself."

"No, you don't need to do that." Skye scrambled to find the right thing to say. "We know Annette's and Gloria's deaths were accidents. You won't be charged with their murders. You can disappear and assume another identity."

"You'd like that, wouldn't you?" Jackie's tone was remorseless. "But you're the one who is going to disappear. And I'll be here to take over for you at school, to comfort your friends and family, and to fill the emptiness in poor Chief Boyd's broken heart." Jackie waved the switchblade in Skye's face. "In a few months no one will remember you. I'll be Skye Denison. I've always been good at taking on a new identity. The woman who claimed to be my mother used to call me her little chameleon. That is, until the hair dryer *accidently* slipped from my hand and fell into her bathtub. That closed her yap."

Skye's blood was roaring in her ears, as loud as the noon coal train. "Okay." She made one last-ditch effort, ignoring the fact that Jackie had confessed to killing her own mother. "I'll be the one to leave. I'll write a letter saying I'm sick of everyone, and bored with Scumble River, and that I'm never coming back."

"Shut up!" Jackie backhanded Skye across the mouth. "Why do you persist in treating me as if I'm stupid? You must know by now that I'm way smarter than you."

Skye felt her rapidly swelling lip, then stared at the blood staining her fingertips. She was too stunned to respond. She could see that the other woman was getting more and more mentally disorganized, her thoughts zipping from idea to idea like a Ping-Pong ball. She was starting to unravel at the edges. It showed in the way her mood changed so fast, and in her uncontrolled jittery movements.

Jackie nodded to herself. "And after I get through with you, I'm going to kill Simon. Everyone will think you two ran away together, and that will teach him to reject me."

"He rejected you?" Skye blurted out, then bit her tongue. That had been stupid.

Jackie ignored Skye and continued to babble to herself. "I was so happy when I asked him out and he said yes. And it was perfect, because on one of my secret visits to your house, I overheard you talking on the phone, telling Vince that you and Wally were going to a movie in Joliet, then out to dinner at Merichka's. So when Simon picked me up, I told him that's where I wanted to go. We had such a wonderful time, but when he dropped me off after our date, he said he couldn't see me anymore. He wasn't ready to start dating someone new yet." Jackie refocused on Skye and pointed the knife at her. "He wanted you, not me."

Skye tensed, ready for Jackie's attack, but instead she stepped out of the bathroom, saying, "Be right back. I need something from my purse."

Before Skye could take a breath, Jackie returned. She dragged Skye away from the wall, put an arm around her throat, and pressed a gun to her temple. Pushing Skye in front of her, Jackie passed through the bedroom, opened the outside door, and walked over the threshold. Her car was parked in front of the cabin, and she thrust Skye toward the trunk. Skye knew she had only moments to save herself.

As Jackie fumbled in her pocket for the key, someone leapt out from behind a clump of bushes and yelled, "Freeze."

Kurt Michaels stood in the classic shooter's stance, aiming a huge silver gun at Jackie's head. A nanosecond later Simon, unarmed, emerged from between the two cottages, and Wally burst out of the motor court's office door with his weapon drawn.

The three men, clearly surprised by the others' presence, all started shouting, but Skye only heard the click of a trigger being pulled back near her ear, followed by a gun discharging into the air.

The gunshot abruptly focused the men's attention back on the women, and shut them up. In the stunned silence, Jackie said, "If you all don't leave before I count to three, the next round will go into her head."

Kurt took a step forward, and Jackie hit Skye across the face with the pistol, as she yelled, "One."

He stopped as if he'd been tagged in a game of Statues.

Seizing the opportunity that Kurt's distraction had provided, Simon tried to come at Jackie and Skye from the side, but Jackie spun around and hit Skye again, and screamed, "Two." Simon halted.

Pain consumed all Skye's thoughts, and she cringed when Wally said, "Okay. You win. You don't have to hit her anymore. We're all leaving. Right, guys?"

Kurt and Simon hesitated, and Wally ordered, "Move it. Both of you get into the squad car."

They walked slowly toward the car and got into the backseat. Wally followed, slipped behind the wheel, started the engine, and drove away. Skye couldn't believe he had left her. He hadn't even tried to save her! He'd had his gun out.

Why hadn't he shot Jackie? His desertion hurt more than the pistol-whipping.

Once the men were gone, Jackie stuck her free hand into her pocket and pulled out the car key. But when she tried to fit it into the trunk's lock, she dropped the key ring and it bounced under the car's bumper. Forcing Skye to her knees, Jackie knelt beside her, reached under the car, and swept the ground with her hand.

Jackie wasn't having any luck with her search, and Skye felt a ray of hope until Jackie's hand emerged clutching the key ring. As they got to their feet, Skye made a decision: If she let Jackie get her into the car, she was as good as dead. She had to make a break for it.

Waiting until Jackie was distracted with opening the trunk, Skye wrenched out of her grip and whirled around, prepared to run for the office. But before she could take a single step, the world exploded, and Jackie crumpled onto Skye. Blood oozed out of the hole in Jackie's chest, and Skye shoved her away. Jackie fell, sounding like a sack of something heavy and wet thumping down on the asphalt.

When Jackie's body hit the ground, Wally dashed out from behind the adjacent cottage. Beads of sweat stood out on the skin above his top lip, and the expression on his face was a combination of anger, agitation, and terror.

As Wally handcuffed Jackie and called for an ambulance, Simon and Kurt ran out from where Wally had emerged. Then, as if on cue, all three men turned on Skye and started yelling at her for putting herself in danger.

Your Wildest Dreams

"I knew I'd find you here." May stood in the open doorway of Skye's office with her hands on her hips. "You promised you'd stay home today and rest."

"I said I'd think about it." Skye wasn't surprised to see her mother at the high school. Although she had spent two hours on the phone the night before reassuring May that despite the bruises on her face she was fine, Skye knew her mom wouldn't be convinced until she saw for herself that her daughter was unharmed.

"It's a shame Wally isn't a better shot." May marched across the room to Skye's desk.

"What do you mean?" Skye glared up at her mother. "Wally's a great shot. He saved my life."

"Maybe." May's expression was rigid and hard. "But if his aim were better, she'd be dead, instead of just wounded."

"I thought you liked her."

"I had her to dinner once." A faint flush rose in May's cheeks. "It's not like I adopted her."

"Only because you couldn't get a court date."

May ignored Skye's snide comments and asked, "You

said her real name was Stacy Dennison, with two Ns, right?"

"Uh-huh." Skye wasn't surprised by the change of subject. It was a tactic her mother often employed when she didn't want to admit she was wrong.

"You know, now that I think about it, I must have met her mother when I was in the hospital giving birth to you. The woman's name was Mary Dennison. Our rooms were next to each other, and the nurses kept getting us mixed up. She even got flowers that were sent to me." May tapped her lips. "At the time I wondered if she was related to your father's side of the family, but when I looked into it, she didn't seem to be."

"Thank goodness." The last thing Skye wanted was to find out she and Jackie were cousins.

May nodded, then gestured at the cluttered room. "Why is this place such a mess?"

"Jackie kept starting projects, but never finished them." Skye decided it was easier to refer to the fake social worker by that name, rather than try to get everyone to use her real one. "And I've been too busy to clean up after her."

"I'll help you straighten up." May opened her purse and pulled out a dust cloth and a can of Pledge. "You'll feel better once everything is spick-and-span."

"Knock yourself out, Mom." Skye didn't bother to point out that she was fine with the way things were. A busy May was a happy May, and a happy May didn't ask as many probing questions.

"The first thing we need to do is get someone to haul this stuff away." May pointed to the knee-high piles of folders and the old file cabinets Jackie had placed next to the door, but never arranged to have removed.

"I can do that." Kurt sauntered in. "I'm Kurt Michaels." He held his hand out to May. "I don't think we've met, but I've heard a lot about you. I understand you're the best cook in Stanley County."

"I've heard a lot about you, too." May looked him up and

down. "You've managed to charm a good portion of the female population here in town."

"Thank you, ma'am."

"That wasn't a compliment." May's lips twisted. "A charming man is like a dog with his tail wagging—you're never quite sure if he's going to fetch your slippers or bite the hand that feeds him."

"On that note"—Kurt looked chagrined—"how about I get rid of those files you mentioned?"

May nodded regally, and he began loading the folders on the wheeled chair behind Jackie's desk—the one Jackie had managed to charm the custodian into finding for her.

Skye told him where the incinerator was located, and added, "Go ahead and leave the chair in the boiler room, too." She wanted it, and all things that reminded her of the pseudo social worker, out of her sight.

Once he disappeared down the corridor, May made a clucking noise, and said, "He sure is a handsome devil, but I wonder about him. Everyone says he doesn't talk much about himself."

Skye picked up her pen, intent on going back to work on the report she'd been writing. "That's for sure." She had some questions for Kurt as well. He had disappeared while Jackie was being loaded into the ambulance. It was as if he didn't want to be around once Wally wasn't distracted by more pressing matters.

"I'm surprised you're at school today." Simon's smooth tenor drew Skye's gaze to the doorway. He greeted May, then said to Skye, "I stopped by your house thinking you'd take a sick day."

Skye quelled her impatience. "I wasn't sick." Why did everyone think she should have stayed home?

"Any word on Jackie, or whatever her name really is?" Simon took a seat in a visitor's chair.

"Wally called before I left for work and said she was going to be okay."

"That's good." Simon straightened the crease in his

pants. "At least Boyd won't have her death on his conscience."

"Yes. Mom was just saying that." Skye shot her mother
a pointed look, but May had found a couple of flattened
cardboard boxes and was busily assembling them.

Before Skye could continue, Kurt returned, trailed by
Trixie, who said, "Look who I found wandering the halls."

"Guess I can't get away with anything around here."
Kurt flashed Skye a mischievous grin and leaned against
the old file cabinets.

"I bet you've gotten away with plenty," Skye challenged
him.

Trixie, refusing to be sidetracked, demanded, "So, fill
me in." She dropped into Skye's second visitor's chair.
"Everyone is buzzing about Jackie being a fake, but I have
a feeling that's only the half of it."

"Okay." Skye leaned forward, placing her elbows on the
desktop and folding her hands. "First of all, Jackie has been
in Scumble River before—twice. She was here about a year
ago during the spa murder. She called herself Veronica Vail,
and claimed to be a state police officer. Then, in the spring,
she pretended to be Imogene Ingersoll, a contestant in the
cooking contest."

"Why, Ms. D?" Justin edged his way into the room and
settled cross-legged on top of the testing table—the one
Skye had retrieved after Jackie had thrown it out.

"She was studying me and my life. Those previous times
she was just an observer, trying to figure out the best way
to get rid of me and take my place. Once she decided on a
plan, it took her a while to steal her social worker identity.
She had to get the real Jacqueline Jennings's birth certificate, then use it to get her graduate school diploma, which
she then parlayed into the school social worker certificate."

Before anyone could respond, Homer pushed his way in.
"What in the hell is going on around here?"

"I have no idea." Skye wondered how many more people
would try to crowd into her tiny office.

Homer claimed one of Jackie's visitors' chairs and turned it to face Skye. "Boyd called me at midnight and gave me some half-assed story about Jackie's not being a real social worker and trying to kill you. I thought he was drunk, but I guess it must be true, because the superintendent is running around like a chicken with its head cut off, trying to find someone else to blame for hiring her."

"Yeah." A baritone voice boomed from the doorway. "And guess who he's got his beady little eyes on?" Charlie stomped in and took the last chair.

Skye looked around the room. "It's really no one's fault, or maybe it's everyone's fault." Her office was beginning to look like the inside of a subway car during rush hour. She half expected people to start popping out of the desk drawers. "Dr. Wraige should have checked Jackie's references and credentials. Homer and the other principals should have been more suspicious that she was always Johnny-on-the-spot, and I should have trusted my instincts that there was something off about her."

"I didn't hear everything you said to Boyd after we went back to the police station yesterday," Simon said. "But I gather Jackie was responsible for all of the unfortunate events that have happened to you and the schools during the past couple of months?"

"Yes. She confessed everything to Wally before she went into surgery last night at the hospital. He said she thought she was dying."

"What did she own up to?" May finished filling one carton with things from Jackie's desk and started on another.

"Let's see." Skye closed her eyes and tried to put Jackie's actions in order. "The first thing was slashing my tire and leaving me that note to make me think Mrs. Idell had done it. Maybe she was retaliating because I yelled at her for changing the locks on our office and taking my chair."

"How about what happened to you at the haunted house?" Justin asked.

"Yes. She tried to scare me into quitting A Ghoul's Night Out by leaving the bloody ax for me to find and blocking the bathroom door so I couldn't escape. She also strung up the rope, hoping I'd injure myself and have to drop out, maybe even leave town."

"She used me to try to scare you, too. Didn't she?" Justin said, his expression guilty. "By having me tell you the story about the American Legion hall being haunted."

"Yes, but there was no way for you to know that," Skye reassured him. "The weird thing is, she said she wasn't the one I heard crying. No one else was in the bathroom, so maybe I just imagined that part."

"Or it was the ghost." Justin grinned.

Everyone ignored him.

May said, "So Annette's death was an accident."

"Yes." Skye's expression was grim. "A series of unfortunate coincidences." She sighed heavily. "Jackie was also the one who tried to run me over using Dr. Paine's car—she claimed she was only trying to scare me into leaving town. But when those attempts didn't work, she started poisoning my cookies, trying to make me so sick that I'd have to go on disability and be stuck at home." Skye's voice quavered, and she blinked back tears. "Gloria's death was another accident."

"I bet she planted the chemical bombs here at the high school, too," Trixie exclaimed.

"Right you are. She wanted the principals to love her. She needed to be seen as the hero," Skye clarified. "She was the one who steered the girls at the junior high to the Internet site that said getting pregnant would be cool, as well. My guess is she's the one who changed the meeting time in order to get me into trouble. And I doubt she speaks Russian. We'll have to reevaluate that poor boy."

"What I don't understand is why." Simon wrinkled his brow. "Why did she do all that? It doesn't make any sense."

"I'm sorry to say, in a twisted way, her actions do make sense." Skye gave an uncomfortable laugh. "She thought she was entitled to my life, that it had been stolen from her." After explaining what Jackie had told her about her background and her thought processes, Skye concluded with, "She is a classic case of narcissistic personality disorder."

"You mean someone who is charming, but has no conscience?" Charlie asked.

"No. That's a sociopath. A narcissist can win people over only in the short term. He or she can't maintain the illusion of friendliness and caring for very long." Skye struggled to explain, finally quoting the definition of narcissistic personality disorder from the *Diagnostic and Statistical Manual of Mental Disorders:* "'Someone with grandiose fantasies, a total lack of empathy, and a hypersensitivity to the evaluation of others.'"

"In other words"—Homer snorted—"she can't take criticism, takes advantage of the people around her, and thinks her shit doesn't stink."

"In a nutshell, yes," Skye agreed. Trust Homer to cut to the chase. Then she muttered under her breath, "And since you usually believe only what you want to believe, you ate it right up."

"But why?" Justin drew his brows together. "What caused her to be that way?"

Skye felt a twinge of concern. Maybe she shouldn't have allowed the teenager to stay and hear all this. But since she had, she needed to try to help him understand.

"The closest I can figure is that all her life, Jackie felt like a nonentity—a blank slate—which is why she was so good at assuming other people's identities. Then when the county clerk made the error with our birth certificates, she saw it as a sign. There had been a mistake. She wasn't a nobody. She was Skye Denison. Which meant I had to disappear, so she could become the person she was meant to be."

*   *   *

After what seemed like a thousand questions later, everyone left, and Skye breathed a sigh of relief. She was returning to her desk, hoping to get some work done, when Kurt slipped back into her office.

She turned toward him with a questioning look. "Forget something?"

He closed the door. "I need to tell you something before you hear it from Chief Boyd."

"What?" Skye mentally raced through the possibilities.

"I'm not who you think I am."

"You don't say." She was taken aback for a second, but recovered quickly and added, "You didn't fool me for a minute with that small-town-reporter bit." Okay, he had fooled her for way more than a minute, but he didn't need to know that.

Kurt raised an eyebrow. "What gave me away?"

"For someone who supposedly wrote for a weekly newspaper, you were much too interested in hard news. Small-town reporters are more interested in the high school football team or who was drunk Saturday night than real crime." Skye summed up her suspicions: "And then, there's that honking big gun you were aiming at Jackie at the motor court yesterday afternoon."

"Guess I'm not as good at being undercover as I thought I was." Kurt's smile was tentative.

Skye wasn't distracted by his charisma. "So you were using me."

"I'm sorry about that, but I had no choice." All humor was gone from his handsome face, lines etching themselves around his mouth and eyes.

"I knew all that flirting was only an act." Skye told herself she had no right to be upset about that. She was in love with Wally and didn't want Kurt's attentions. Still, she couldn't help but add, "It's not a big surprise that you weren't really attracted to me."

"That isn't true." Kurt cupped her chin in his palm. "I think you're smart and fun and incredibly sexy."

"Right. *Playboy* is always calling me up to model for them."

"Just because most men like stick women who wouldn't jiggle if you tied them to a paint mixer"—Kurt caressed her cheek with his thumb—"doesn't mean that I do. I'm not most men."

His blue eyes were mesmerizing, sending a ripple of awareness through her, but Skye forced herself to step away from him. "Yeah, well, we know who you aren't. The question is, who are you?"

"I'm a private detective." His fingers threaded through hers and stopped her from backing any farther away from him. "I was hired six months ago by the family of Veronica Vail to look into her death."

"The woman Jackie impersonated last fall." Skye jerked her hand from his. "You knew Jackie was a fake all along, and you didn't warn me."

"I didn't know. That was the problem." He scratched his chin. "I found a story about the spa murder that mentioned State Special Agent Veronica Vail. And considering that the real Veronica was already dead by that time, I came to Scumble River to investigate. It wasn't much of a lead, but it was all I had."

"Oh?"

"Yes. I was here during the cooking contest, and when I checked out all the contestants, I found out that the real Imogene Ingersoll was dead, too. Unfortunately, the fake Imogene disappeared before I could talk to her." Frustration deepened Kurt's voice. "Which made me think that there must be something about this town that was attracting Veronica's killer."

"But how did you get a job at the *Star*?" Skye asked.

"Pure luck. When I was here during the contest I grabbed a newspaper, saw the ad for a reporter, and since my undergrad degree is in journalism, I applied for the position."

"I'm surprised you were hired so easily."

"I did work as a reporter for several years after college, so I had references and a portfolio." Red crept up his neck. "I may have flirted with the owner a little, too."

Skye didn't comment on his admission. Instead she asked, "What made you suspect Jackie?"

"I narrowed my search to anyone who was new in town since April, but it took me until a couple of days ago to nail down everyone's background information."

"And when you did, you didn't think to warn me?" Skye's stare bore into him.

"Well, I had no proof of anything, and at first it seemed as if the impostor was after Annette's identity. But that didn't make sense, since she hadn't left town once Annette had been killed. Everything suggested you were her intended target, but I couldn't be sure."

"Right." Skye stepped around him and opened the door. "What you really mean is that you didn't want to tip your hand and let her get away."

"I was watching to make sure nothing happened to you." Kurt followed her and took her by the shoulders. "I thought I could protect you *and* solve my case."

"But your case came first."

He struggled to respond, then shrugged, bent his head, and kissed her.

The touch of his mouth on hers produced a delicious sensation, and for a long moment Skye responded. Finally she pushed him away. "No. I can't do this. I can't betray Wally."

"That's good to hear."

They both turned toward the door, where Wally stood with his hands in his pockets.

Kurt looked from Skye to the chief. "I had to try."

Wally dipped his head in silent acknowledgment.

After stroking Skye's cheek with one finger, Kurt saluted Wally and walked away.

Skye hesitated for a heartbeat, then threw herself into Wally's arms. "You're not jealous?"

"Should I be?"

She shook her head. "Never."

Crushing her to him, he whispered against her lips, "Will you marry me?"

Before Skye could respond, Wally pressed his mouth to hers, kissing her until she could no longer think. Which was a good thing, because she had no idea what her answer would be.

Here's a sneak peek at
Skye Denison's next exciting adventure
in the Scumble River Mystery series,
coming from Obsidian in April 2010.

November

Skye Denison twisted her left hand from side to side, admiring the glitter of the diamond engagement ring on her finger. The sunshine streaming through the windshield of her aqua 1957 Bel Air made the two-karat gemstone blaze like a Fourth of July sparkler. Reluctantly she slid the ring off her finger, tucked it into its blue Tiffany box, and zipped it into the inner pocket of her purse. The last thing she wanted was her mother getting the wrong idea.

Wally Boyd, Scumble River Police Chief and secret heir to a Texas oil fortune, had asked Skye to marry him a couple of months ago. Although she hadn't said yes, he'd insisted that she hold on to the ring until she decided. It wasn't that she didn't love him; it was more that she didn't trust her judgment where men were concerned. Her history included a series of bad choices, making her leery of commitment.

Skye knew she had to decide about marrying Wally soon, but not today. Today was all about Skye's cousin Bailey Erickson. Skye was in the peace corps when Bailey left their hometown of Scumble River ten years ago to attend college in California, and she had later decided to stay there. Now

Bailey was finally back, and Skye didn't want to be late for her party.

After checking her lipstick in the rearview mirror, Skye picked up the strawberry pretzel salad she'd made and got out of the Chevy. The Denisons didn't have get-togethers as often as her mother's extended Italian clan, the Leofantis, so Skye looked forward to catching up with her dad's side of the family.

As she put her hand on the knob of the kitchen's screen door, the excited chatter echoing through the aluminum mesh brought her up short. For a nanosecond she wasn't sure she was at the right house. The Denisons came from stoic Swedish farm stock. They never got worked up. Heck, they seldom raised their voices, and certainly they didn't squeal like a gaggle of schoolgirls.

What in the world could cause her unflappable relatives to make sounds like a whooping crane on crack? There was only one way to find out.

Skye pushed open the door and walked into pandemonium. Her great-aunt Dora was crying. *Yikes!* Had someone died? No. The focus of the uproar was a silver-blond beauty in the center of a flock of women who were all fluttering around her like birds at a feeder, talking a mile a minute, and patting her as if she were a prize parrot.

Although it had been nearly seventeen years since Skye had seen her cousin and she wouldn't even have recognized her in a crowd, she figured the blonde must be Bailey.

No doubt the men were in the living room, probably watching a football game or whatever sporting event was on TV in late November, but Skye was surprised that there was no food on the table, and no one at the stove cooking. One thing the Denison and Leofanti females had in common was their prowess in the kitchen.

Skye spotted her mother on the fringe of the group, and joined her. Come August, May would be turning sixty, but she looked at least fifteen years younger. With a petite build and short salt-and-pepper hair, she had the liveliness of the high school cheerleader she'd once been.

Before Skye could speak, her mother grabbed her arm. "Isn't it thrilling?"

"What?" Skye set the salad bowl she'd been carrying on the kitchen counter before May accidentally knocked it out of her hands.

"Bailey's getting married right here in Scumble River on June twenty-fifth!" May trilled. "And she wants you to be her maid of honor."

"Why me?" The question slipped out before Skye could stop it.

"*Shh!* Do you want Bailey to hear you?" May dragged Skye through the dining room into the nearest bedroom and whispered, "She'll think you aren't tickled pink that she asked you."

"Well, technically, she hasn't asked me." Skye stalled for time, knowing that her mother would not be happy with Skye's decision to refuse her cousin's request.

But sometime after Skye had hit thirty, being in weddings had lost its appeal. She'd stood up for several of her sorority sisters right after college, a couple of friends while she'd been in the peace corps, and her graduate school roommate the year before she'd moved back home. Being a bridesmaid was a lot of work, not to mention a huge expense, and seven hideous dresses she could never wear again were her limit.

May narrowed her emerald eyes and stared into her daughter's matching ones. "But once she asks you, you are going to say yes, right?"

"My question stands. Why would Bailey want me to be her maid of honor?" Skye held firm. "She was only twelve when I left for college, by the time I moved back to Scumble River she'd left, and we haven't seen each other in all those years."

"Blood is blood no matter how long it is between visits," May countered. "She idolized you. She followed you around at family gatherings and begged her mother to hire you as her babysitter."

Skye refused to be swayed. "But we haven't kept in touch. Not to mention, I'm not even entirely sure how we're related."

"Your grandma Denison, and Bailey's grandmother Dora, are sisters. That makes your father, and Bailey's mother Rose, first cousins," May explained to Skye. "And since both Rose and Bailey are only children, close or not, you are Bailey's only female relative young enough to be in her wedding."

"How about Bailey's father's people?" Skye knew Rose was a widow, but couldn't remember the details.

"He wasn't from around here, and Rose lost touch with them after he died."

"Oh." Skye paused, then shook her head. "Anyway, I just don't have the money."

"That's the best part. Bailey's fiancé is filthy rich—it's a shame he couldn't come with her so the family could meet him—and he's paying for everything. They've even hired a wedding planner from California who's going to be in Scumble River for the entire month before the wedding."

"Impressive." Skye understood her mother's awe. May had never had a lot of money, so being able to spend it on frivolous nonessentials seemed like a fairy tale to her. "But I'm sorry. The answer's still no."

"I wish you'd reconsider, Skye," an elderly, quavering voice said from the bed.

Skye whirled in that direction. She and May had been so intent in their conversation, she hadn't realized anyone else was in the room.

Cora Denison, Skye's grandmother, swung her legs over the side of the mattress and struggled to get up. At eighty-five, she had buried a husband, two stillborn babies, and a grandson. Up until Halloween, she'd made a batch of her famous Parker House rolls nearly every Sunday, but she hadn't been feeling well for the past few weeks.

Skye rushed to her side and helped Cora to her feet, then handed her the cane that had been leaning against the wall. Skye felt her heart sink. Having lost both her grandfathers and her grandma Leofanti, she wasn't ready for her last remaining grandparent to die, but it was clear that Cora was failing.

Once she was steady, Cora said, "I'd really like you to be in Bailey's wedding."

Skye opened her mouth to explain why she couldn't, but a movement near the door drew her attention. Standing on the threshold was Skye's father, Jed, his faded brown eyes pleading with Skye to agree with her grandmother's request.

What could she do? Skye knew a lot of people thought she needed to grow a spine where her family was concerned, but there was no way she could disappoint her grandmother or her father, neither of whom often asked her for anything.

Smiling, she said, "If *you* want me to, Grandma, I'd be happy to be Bailey's maid of honor."

As she gave Cora a hug, Skye mentally shrugged. How bad could it be? All she'd have to do was buy a few gifts, throw a bridal shower, and attend the rehearsal dinner, the ceremony, and the reception. The wedding planner would do the rest.

Suddenly a shiver ran down Skye's spine. All the murders that had taken place in Scumble River during the past few years flashed through her mind. Most of them seemed to occur when some big event in town brought in a lot of outsiders. She sure hoped this wedding didn't prove to be equally deadly.

Signet

Denise Swanson
The Scumble River Mysteries

When Skye Denison left Scumble River years ago, she swore she'd never return. But after a fight with her boyfriend and credit card rejection, she's back to home-sweet-homicide.

MURDER OF A SMALL-TOWN HONEY

MURDER OF A SWEET OLD LADY

MURDER OF A SLEEPING BEAUTY

MURDER OF A SNAKE IN THE GRASS

MURDER OF A BARBIE AND KEN

MURDER OF A PINK ELEPHANT

MURDER OF A SMART COOKIE

MURDER OF A REAL BAD BOY

MURDER OF A BOTOXED BLONDE

MURDER OF A CHOCOLATE-COVERED CHERRY

MURDER OF A ROYAL PAIN

Available wherever books are sold or at
penguin.com